W9-CFK-891

FIFTEEN POINT NINE

HOLLY DOBBIE

GULF GATE LIBRARY
7112 CURTISS AVENUE
SARASOTA, FL. 34231

3 1969 02630 9590

Copyright © 2018 Holly Dobbie
This edition copyright © 2018 DCB, an imprint of Cormorant Books Inc.

No part of this publication may be reproduced, stored in a retrieval system or transmitted, in any form or by any means, without the prior written consent of the publisher or a licence from The Canadian Copyright Licensing Agency (Access Copyright). For an Access Copyright licence, visit www.accesscopyright.ca or call toll free 1.800.893.5777.

Canada Council for the Arts

Conseil des Arts du Canada

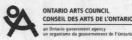

ONTARIO ARTS COUNCIL
CONSEIL DES ARTS DE L'ONTARIO
an Ontario government agency
un organisme du gouvernement de l'Ontario

Canadian Heritage   Patrimoine canadien   Canadá

The publisher gratefully acknowledges the support of the Canada Council for the Arts and the Ontario Arts Council for its publishing program. We acknowledge the financial support of the Government of Canada through the Canada Book Fund (CBF) for our publishing activities, and the Government of Ontario through the Ontario Media Development Corporation, an agency of the Ontario Ministry of Culture, and the Ontario Book Publishing Tax Credit Program.

LIBRARY AND ARCHIVES CANADA CATALOGUING IN PUBLICATION

Dobbie, Holly, author
Fifteen point nine / Holly Dobbie.

Issued in print and electronic formats.
ISBN 978-1-77086-523-5 (softcover). — ISBN 978-1-77086-524-2 (HTML)

1. Title.

PS8607.O215F54 2018   JC813'.6   C2018-900037-6
C2018-900038-4

United States Library of Congress Control Number: 2017964199

Cover design: angeljohnguerra.com
Interior text design: Tannice Goddard, bookstopress.com

Printed and bound in Canada
Manufactured by Friesens in Altona, Manitoba, Canada in May, 2018

DCB
AN IMPRINT OF CORMORANT BOOKS INC.
260 SPADINA AVENUE, SUITE 502, TORONTO, ONTARIO, M5T 2E4
www.dcbyoungreaders.com
www.cormorantbooks.com

For E, A, C, and L

1

❧

Even though there is no cure for high school, I've heard that with the right therapy it's still possible for people to lead a happy, normal life. Whatever that is.

Oh crap. It's them. Those Girls. I hide behind my locker door. Susan cowers behind her books.

"Good morning, Pork and Beans!" Chrissy Crop Top yells at us.

Susan's Pork, I'm Beans. Apparently, I smell bad.

"Today's your lucky day!" Bevy says. "It's time for your makeovers." Bevy grew to over six feet tall by the time we were in grade eight and now she's even taller than the teachers. She hands each of us a party mask. Susan's is a pig face and mine is a skunk. "Put these on and we'll let you live."

I drop my books in protest and unfortunately, that's the extent of my plan.

"What's your problem?" Chrissy Crop Top asks. "Bevy told you to put on your face, skunk. You should be happy. It's an improvement."

I stare at my reflection in the little window of my locker.

"You ignoring me?" She grabs my hoodie and yanks so hard that I choke. "Don't you know that's rude?" she yells. "We bought these especially for you, so everyone knows your new identities. You're now a Junk Skunk, and she's a Porky Pig." I place the mask over my head, and Susan puts on hers. "Okay, this one's for the yearbook!" Chrissy Crop Top holds up her phone and takes our picture.

"Nice," Bevy says. "And don't worry, we'll add your names so you'll be celebrities."

Brrrrring!

Time to learn about useful things like chemical compounds and alliteration. Susan walks past me. "Why?" she whispers.

I wish I had an answer for her, and even though we used to be Pork and Beans, and now we're Porky Pig and Junk Skunk, we don't know one another very well. I think we're both afraid of people, though. Especially people like Those Girls. Maybe if we became better friends we could work together and be Wonder Woman and Super Girl. I tuck my mask into my backpack, because maybe one day, a cele-brated and handsome Skunkologist will come to speak at The Torture Chamber and he'll ask if anyone in the auditorium would like to travel the world with him to help him further his research on the increasing rate of skunk populations. All the girls will raise their hand, but I'll put on my mask and he'll choose me because he'll know that I'm the most sincere. Oh, and also because if Those Girls ask me to wear it again and I don't have it with me, it'll give them another reason to hurt me.

My first class is French. I always sit in the first row, last seat, for three very important reasons: one, I'm right by the wall; two, I'm close to the escape door; and three, no one can sneak up behind me. And if someone's away, or if it's not a full class of thirty-five, the seats around me are vacant. But being aroma-challenged isn't my biggest problem. At least not anymore. My biggest problem was exposed on the day the front door of The Dump was opened.

"Bonjour class. Mademoiselle Agatha ..." (Teachers call me Agatha.) "*... comment était votre weekend*?" She's asking me about my weekend.

"*Je ne sais pas*," I say, as usual. *Je ne sais pas* means "I don't know."

I'm pretty sure I'll manage to make it through life single-lingual. The only French I need to be fluent in is french fries.

"*Stupide putain*," someone says• and everyone laughs because apparently I'm a stupid slut, which is totally inaccurate because I've never even kissed a guy. Or a girl, for that matter.

"*Chien* butt," someone else says. Cue more laughter.

"You're all idiots," Joanie says, and then looks at me. "*Je ne sais pas*, either." Joanie Charles is the only self-proclaimed "out" in the school, and the serial wrath of Those Girls in response to her courage has left her almost completely shattered. Her arms and legs are covered with the marks of her excruciating and fearless habit of self-stapling, and I think it must be the only way she keeps herself together. She spent the entire summer at Sunny Slope Wellness Centre, and now almost everyone stays away from her.

"Class, turn to page *cinquante-cinq*. Monsieur Alexander, read aloud, *s'il te plait*."

Another gripping story about French skiers lost in the Alps. No one cares.

I look out the *fenêtre*. It wasn't always this bad, but my whole life fell apart because we don't own a washing machine.

IT HAPPENED ON the day Jane (the woman who claims to be my mother) and I were at Lou's Laundry and Liquor, washing our tragically hideous clothes. A few of the Idiot Boys — boys who follow Those Girls around for the sole purpose of hooking up with, and then being immediately shunned by them, broke into The Dump (a.k.a., my house). Not the greatest accomplishment of all time, considering the stupid doorknob-thingy has been broken since the dark and happier times of Pangaea.

My guess is that the Idiot Boys were searching for any available weekend intoxicant they could get their hands on. Jane is the most notorious mother in the neighborhood. When all the other houses around us are carefully adorned with seasonal straw-hatted scare-crows and white lights reindeer, our all-season broken igloo stacks of empty wine boxes decorate the lawn.

Jane likes to drink.

At least I think she likes it. It's not the most beautiful thing in the world to watch, but it could be worse. We've all seen on TV how some moms mess with their kids' heads and tell them they're stupid and accidental, but when Jane drinks she tells me she loves me, which is totally awkward because I never say it back, and it makes me wonder if she loves me when she's sober. The next day, *after the fun*, if there's food in the house, I'm not allowed to use the toaster or eat cereal because the clink of the spoon hitting the side of the bowl is too loud. I wish someone would invent a quiet morning food for kids of bingers. Like an über-nutritious marshmallow. Bananas are quiet, but how many of them can a person eat for breakfast? One?

"Merci, Monsieur Alexander. Please answer *tous* les chapter questions. I will collect them at the end of class."

I'm going to write "*Je ne sais pas*" for every question.

So Jane and I finished our can't-afford-soap-just-wash-with-water laundry, and stuffed the garbage bags filled with dampish clothes into Turdle, our crap-tan van that was donated to us by the local church group — the one where the girls have to wear long denim skirts, even on snow days. Come to think of it, I'd like to own a long denim skirt. Maybe I should join a church group. I'm sure they'd take better care of me than my useless mother, and they drink wine only on Sundays, out of a thimble.

We got to The Dump and although the place was deserted, the front door was wide open, welcoming *everyone in the neighborhood* to peer into our spectacular house of grunge. Jane pretty much died. I actually heard her whimper, like the sound a balloon makes when you blow it up and then slowly let a little air leak out through its rubber lips. I still hear it sometimes when I'm trying to fall asleep, which sucks because the last thing you want to think about when you're trying to fall asleep is your sniveling mother.

SO THERE IT is. Jane and I are scavengers.

Like crows.

I guess there's a reason for it. I thought it was fun at first, like a game, but now I can't help myself. It's the one thing Jane and I excel at. The one thing we have in common. Not only do we keep things that we find on purpose, we actually make a point of collecting stuff that normal people have tossed. In fact, you can't get in The Dump through the front door. The Idiot Boys must have human-battering-rammed it open before they went around the back to climb in the broken window. To help illustrate our Dracula-worthy commitment to burying ourselves alive, I'm going to make a list, and I'll use roman numerals because it's more sophisticated:

  (i) Waxy boxes filled with putrefied mismatched shoes.
 (ii) Freaky one-eyed porcelain dolls with scissor-butchered hair.
(iii) Musty old-lady lace and pukey baby clothes rotting under alien mold.
 (iv) Food that is more compost than food (retch!).
  (v) Faded blue and yellow plastic playground equipment chunks.
 (vi) Gross pink velveteen chairs with kill-a-vampire-stake backs.
(vii) Photo albums of families we've never met (not *too* weird, right?).
(viii) A pile of discarded museum-worthy vacuums with no hoses.
 (ix) Stacks of dented baseball bats. (I find them at the park.)
  (x) A big green wheelbarrow that has no wheel, which I guess makes it just a barrow.

And all of this you can see just by looking in our front door.

Naturally, this fabulous mix of methane gas and bad karma generates a unique perfume that you won't find in any store. In the winter you can't smell it from the road, but in the barbecued heat of the summer the fumes simmer and The Dump morphs into a reeking dead beast that has washed up onto the shore of the cul-de-sac.

But no one on the outside knew any of this until the Idiot Boys came to steal Jane's booze.

So now they think it's okay to hurt me because I'm no longer a human, I'm a rodent. The very next day at school the Idiot Boys piled stacks of garbage outside my locker and told Those Girls that I was a garbage collector and that they should help me out. They left their used latte cups on my desk and Frisbeed their food-stained cafeteria plates at me when I walked down the hallways. Bevy went to the trouble of cutting holes in a garbage bag for me to wear. That's the day I started to pull out my eyelashes. And that's the day I could no longer look at myself in the mirror.

Brrrrring!

Time for gym. I'm still sore from yesterday's physical education because Chrissy Crop Top booted me in the kidney so hard that I have a massive purple bruise on my back. But the pain doesn't bother me. What bothers me is that I don't want to be me anymore because I hate who I am. And because my life is so pathetic, getting revenge on the people who are mean to me is really the only thing that I have to look forward to. Is it wrong for me to feel this way?

Nah.

2

"Can ... you ... feel ... the ... love tonight?" Jane shreds a medley of Broadway show tunes and it's musical barf.

But listen to this: last night when Jane was coma-drunk on her bedroom floor, I decided that it was up to me to purge The Dump of some of our worthless valuables. My most devious plan of awesomeness is to remove one thing from The Dump every day and put it in the ladybug backpack that I got for my ninth birthday, then leave it somewhere. Maybe I'll throw it in the big metal garbage bin at The Torture Chamber, or maybe in Swing Set Woods on the way to The Torture Chamber, or maybe just on the side of the road. And when The Dump transforms into a livable place instead of a science experiment, I will ceremoniously re-name it The Former Dump.

Now, as simple as this sounds, it took me four hours to decide what to take. It had to be something Jane wouldn't notice, because even though she's always half-wasted, she has a disturbing power that allows her to recognize the slightest shift in her personal inventory.

"What happened to the envelopes that have the birds of Capistrano on them?"

I guess those envelopes were more important than I thought when I found them stuffed inside a *Do not remove from store* plastic grocery basket. I needed them for another pitiful art project that is meant as a healing outlet for *troubled* teens.

I took the entire box, and before an hour had passed, Jane had a full-on breakdown. It took her three days to drink herself through that one. Fortunately, the tears dried up before the wine did.

But here's the best part of the story: I found *two* things to get rid of: a VHS recording of *A Muppet Family Christmas*, and a prehistoric camcorder that was hidden inside a box of men's polyester socks. I packed them up with my dried-sweat gym shirt, shorts, and socks, and my gross and clearly inedible lunch.

I am in control. For once.

I count the cracks in the sidewalk and look for a suitable place of distinction to ditch the video. Fifty-nine. Fifty-nine is a pretty good number, as long as it's not your age or your IQ. The best thing about numbers is that they can't be misinterpreted, the way words can. Even when someone assigns you a number, you know exactly what they're talking about: I'm a three. Fifty-nine cracks later, I arrive at the fringe of Swing Set Woods.

I remove the camcorder and the VHS from my backpack. There's a small tape inside the camera so I press *Power* and a green light flickers on. I rewind and press *Play* and watch an awkward hand-held angle of Jane singing and it's so impressive that I erase it. I press record and hold the camera in front of me, focused on what I'm about to do.

"Bye, Kermit." I catapult him into the waist-high horsetail weeds where he belongs, like any good frog. And now it's official. I've thrown something away and I have it documented. I replace the camera back into my pack.

"OBSTRUCTION!" BEVY YELLS. She holds her field hockey stick above her head and brings it down, full force onto my shin, and because of her unusual height, there's a lot of momentum behind it. I'm sitting on the floor in front of my locker, which is never a safe place to be sitting.

"Foul, you're a foul!" Chrissy Crop Top screams and hits me on the other leg with her stick. No matter what the weather, Chrissy wears a crop top to school. She even tucks her gym shirt up under her bra so that her stomach is exposed, and we all have to look at it. I think the reason the teachers ignore it is because she's from Denmark. She came here a few years ago and at first she was nice and kinda awkward-foreign, but then Bevy got hold of her and now she fits right in.

"C'mon, Chrissy, you know that's dangerous play. And besides, you didn't have the correct angle on your stick. You have to hold it higher, like this." And bam! Bevy hits me again, this time on my thigh. She bends down to my level. "Red card for not wearing your mask, Junk Skunk."

They walk away and shrink into tiny specs like a scene at the end of a movie: A story about The Torture Chamber, in which, obviously, I'm the heroine. A heroine without a leading man, a.k.a. boyfriend, or supporting characters, a.k.a. friends. And that's the beauty of being me: I've got nothing to lose.

The pain in my leg resonates down my calf. Two Idiot Boys approach and when they're in front of me, one grabs the other one's arm and says, "Dude, you need to take a shower."

"No, dude, I had a shower this morning," the second I. B. says.

"Well, someone needs to take a shower and it's not us, so it must be her." He stands close to me and announces, "Yup. It's her, all right." He reaches into his backpack, takes out his blue sports drink and Formula 1 winner champagne-sprays me. When the bottle is empty, he throws it at me and it bounces off my head.

"Direct hit!" The second Idiot Boy high-fives him. Another scene out of my Torture Chamber documentary.

And that's when my scheme direct-hits me.

It's time for me to risk my nothing and use that ancient camcorder as the secret weapon of my revenge. I'll document all the mean stuff that happens to me and the other prisoners in The Torture Chamber.

Prisoners like Susan. Maybe Susan has access to a camera and a computer and when we have enough footage (which won't take long), we'll show it to people, and then it will stop.

I get up and drag myself to science class. First row, last seat.

" … and if global warming continues at the rate it's going, we'll all be dead in a few hundred years."

Do teachers even hear what they're saying half the time? It doesn't even matter, anyway, because I can't concentrate. I'm trying to remember the storyline of *A Muppet Family Christmas*. I should have watched it one more time. The first time I watched it was years ago. With Jane. We sang along to the Christmas songs and it was fun, but that was before fun became a thing of the past. I attempt to distract myself by digging my dirt-caked saw-toothed fingernails into my hands hard enough to break the skin. It doesn't help.

I have to escape.

I have to exhume the Muppets from their weeded burial grounds and return them to The Dump. I should have taken something less valuable. Something that doesn't make me want to smile when I see it.

I grab my books and head for the door and accidentally bash my thigh on the desk where the girl Those Girls call Creepy Claribel sits. I think they're secretly freaked out by her because she belongs to the drama club. I give her my best *sorry* face. She frowns at me and Mr. Big Head Kraus just keeps on talking.

I run (ignoring the leg pain and the sidewalk cracks) the whole way back to Swing Set Woods, find the place where I threw the video, and bend down to retrieve it.

Nothing. It's gone. And that's weird.

I walk to the old metal swing set which is notorious because it's haunted by the ghosts of twin children who were apparently strangled *at the exact same time* by the heavy chains that support the seats.

I sit on one of the rust-worn swings and drift into one of my most reliable daydreams — you know the one: A lonely and independently wealthy vampire whisks me away to his Gothic castle where I have to wear a stunning and appropriately gauche red velvet dress that has a sweeping train and a plunging neckline and there's only candlelight with which to see our posh and elaborate meals, served by a mysterious butler named Godfrey.

So I'm smiling at one of Godfrey's little jokes and dipping a piece of lobster (even though I'd rather have mac and cheese) into a silver filigreed dish of melted butter when I hear the distinct foot on a dry twig *snap* behind me, which totally creeps me out. I jump off the swing and look toward the sound and there it is: Kermit's face. My video sits upright atop a large rock and because I have to have it, I run to the rock and tippy-toe reach for the video, awkwardly grab for it, and it teeters and falls into my hands.

"Nice catch!" a boy's voice calls from the trees. A *boy's* voice? What the heck? Maybe this place really is haunted. I need to get out of here *now*.

I stuff the video into my pack, turn and leave the woods, and look over my shoulder every fifteen steps. Ninety-nine fifteens later, I get to The Dump and fortunately, Jane is out. She must have sensed that something was missing, so she's gone hunting and gathering on the streets for more beautiful stuff. I sit on a massive stack of dead-spider-nested cardboard boxes and turn on the TV. I take the VHS cassette out of its box and a sticky note is jammed on the inside. I smooth out the note and read three small words: "*I like you.*"

Oh God. If I were a normal girl, finding a note that says *I like you* is probably pretty normal in the world of romance, probably like a five out of ten on their Official Romantic Scale, but because I'm disgusting and nothing romantic happens to me in real life, a note like this is one part romantic, and one part scary. It's nice, though, to have something happen that's at least one part romantic. Unless, of course, it's all a big hoax and I'm the total loser who thinks her entire life might change because of three words scribbled on one crumpled sticky note.

3

It's so small in here that I have to crouch.

My closet is my favorite place in the world and hiding in here is the only thing that gets me closer to the only thing I really truly want, and the only thing that I really truly want is to be invisible. To never again have anyone see me or speak to me or *accidentally* bash into me in the hallway at The Torture Chamber and say, "Watch it, freak!"

Today is the second-worst day of the year. The first worst day of the year is obviously Valentine's Day; the second-worst day of the year is Picture Day.

"Aggie, you're going to be late," Jane says to my closet door. Leaving only my shoes behind, I want to melt into vapor like the Wicked Witch of the East, whose hostility, by the way, was totally justified. The Good Witch got all the good stuff: iridescent bubbles and Munchkin groupies passing around heavy lollipops. Meanwhile the Wicked Witch was surrounded by a pack of stinky monkeys. So not fair. "C'mon, Aggie, don't do this to me."

I wonder what it is exactly that I'm doing to *her*. She opens the closet door, gives me the I'm-psychotic-death-stare, and stomps out of the room. The closet isn't safe with the door open, and if I don't go to The Torture Chamber today I'll be called out of class for retakes, which is worse than just getting it over with now.

"There's a comb in the bathroom."

Thanks, Jane. I thought we kept the combs in the fridge. Without combing my hair, I tie back my unintentional dreadlocks and leave.

"YOU LOOK NICE today, *Raggy*," Myhell offers. I call her Myhell because that's what she is: my hell. The teachers call her Michelle. She's pretty much the czar of Those Girls and her hair is an arsonist's playground. In elementary school, people called her names like Ginger Minge and Frotch, which I guess was pretty embarrassing at that age. So now *she* calls people names and beats them up. She and Bevy stand by my locker and they laugh so hard at the name Raggy that I actually think it's funny. I try to stop myself from smiling, but Only Boy sees me and grins, and it's so dazzling that I must avert my eyes. I call him Only Boy (I don't actually know his real name) because he's the only *cool* boy in the whole Torture Chamber who has ever said something nice to me.

Yes, I'm that lonely.

It was at the beginning of the year and I was trying to locate my locker. I must have looked freaked because he stood right beside me and said, "I had trouble finding mine too. The guy who designed this school must have been dyslexic."

Not only was it a nice thing to say, it was even a little joke. Not that I want to make fun of people who are *actually* dyslexic, but it wasn't said to be mean, it was said to make me feel better, and nothing is ever said to make me feel *better*. And because no one ever says anything nice or funny to me, my utter astonishment shaped my astounding and quick-witted reply,

"Yeah, really."

That's what I said. *Yeah, really*. And now he catches me almost smiling, and I catch him catching me and I look away like I'm witnessing a hacksaw fish-gutting. Nonetheless, this moment was so amazing that it gives me reason to regret not combing my hair. So today, on Picture Day, because Only Boy sort of maybe smiled at me, I am going to try to be more of a human being and less of a rodent, although it's obviously something that I'm not very good at.

Ptcheew

The flash goes off and my new goal is frozen in time, my fate unequivocally sealed.

DURING THE THREE hundred and twenty-one steps back to class, I pass a kid I don't even know and he pinches his nose when I walk by, and says in a weird nasally voice, "Oh, right, I forgot it was garbage day."

A folded fingerprint-smudged paper with my initials on it lies on my desk. Am I being *Punk'd*? I wait a moment for the cameras and public ridicule, but nothing happens, so I stealthily unfold the paper to find a clue for The Sticky Note Mystery, which I almost forgot about 'cause of the Super Romantic Incident with Only Boy.

It's not easy being green.

A Kermit the Frog quote. In my case though, a more appropriate quote would be, *It's not easy being clean*. With exaggerated nonchalance, I glance around the room. Okay, so no one has any sort of *it's me* expression on their face, and no one is laughing *at* me, so whoever it is must not be in my science class. Whoever it is must have come into the classroom when we were at pictures, and knows where I sit and, I must admit, this excites me. And now, because that *I like you* sticky note was obviously from a boy who is here at The Torture Chamber, it's no longer one part scary, it's a whole part romantic, which means that I can now place it on my Official Romantic Scale as an 8.9, making the second-worst day of the year now one of the best days of my fantastically enviable life. More likely, though, I'm being totally ridiculous and Those Girls have come up with a new and more almost believable plan, masterminded for the sole purpose of further breaking my heart.

BACK AT THE Dump, I lock myself in the bathroom, sit on the toilet, and begin the arduous task of combing the shocking mass of snarls and mysterious clumps that adorn my head. The comb, like an old-maid prairie school teacher, snaps and reprimands my hand. I return to my closet.

Maybe it's too hard to be a human being, and maybe Only Boy wasn't even smiling at me; he was probably looking at one of Those Girls.

I've got some birthday money hidden away that my Aunt Never-see-'er gave me before disappearing to Vegas. She suggested that I save it for something important, and right now I can't really think of anything more important than a trip to Nancy's Bohemian Beauty Boutique. Besides, it's only twenty bucks. There's not a lot of important stuff I could do with that sizeable a bankroll, except buy a Christmas tree for some *poor* family. I'd cut my own hair, but that's something someone really sad would do, and I'm not sad, I'm messy — although most days it's hard to tell the difference.

I reach for the video camera from under my bed and my hand shakes as I take it out of its case. I erase the footage of me throwing away the Muppet video. I doubt that Susan would want to be friends with me, anyway. It seems that everything I want to do to make my life better, frightens me. I place the camera back into its case and push it back under the bed, as far as it will go.

4

❋

"That's $22.49."

"I'm sorry," I say. "I only have twenty dollars."

"Oh."

The dark lip liner, heavily drawn around the hairdresser's mouth makes her look like she's just finished eating a licorice ice-cream cone.

"Yeah … umm … sorry."

"Oh. Well, I guess you can come back later with the rest. Including the gratuity. I know your mom, I seen her sometimes, at meetings. Oh crap-stick! That's supposed to be anonymous."

She's referring to the meetings Jane used to attend to try to make herself quit drinking for more than three consecutive days. She stopped going because, "the people at those meetings are only there to spy on me."

"It's okay, I know about that stuff. Thanks. I'm sorry … Nancy?"

"No, I'm Raynine. Nancy died years ago. Choked on a green jujube." She pulls out a pack of cigarettes from her plastic apron pocket and thumps it a couple of times on her left hand to release one. "You sure you like it? I can give you a hand mirror to see the back."

"No that's okay, I'm sure it's great. I gotta get home to clean out the garage. Donating a bunch of stuff to the less fortunate." I stared at the floor as much as politely possible while she was cutting my hair, but at the moment of unavoidable truth, I did see that it's army-boy short on one side and angled longer on the other side. Just edgy enough to make people think that I listen to indie music. I don't want to like it too much because I doubt I'll ever have enough money to get it done again.

"Oh, that's cool." She puts the cigarette in her mouth and lights it, takes a long drag and blows the smoke into the ceiling.

"Yeah, thanks."

Neither of us has anything else to say, so I get up and leave.

I don't look in the store windows on my way to the bus stop because store windows are like mirrors. Not that I deep-down care about how I look. Well, maybe I sort of care. At least I think this is what it feels like to care about something. Generally, I try to avoid caring because once you start caring about one thing, you start caring about another thing, and then there's no stopping it.

I actually gave up caring on the day of my eighth birthday when Jane told me that my dad was a one-night stand. I didn't get how my father could be a night-stand. She wanted me to pledge my allegiance to the plight of women and take her side, but I was too consumed by my celebrity crush on a purple dinosaur. Is it weird to be in love with something that doesn't exist? I've never told anyone about this, nor will I ever, except for my husband when we're having dinner in our vineyard in the South of France. We'll laugh and watch the sunset through the grapevines and he'll tell me how *très* beautiful I am and it'll be so romantic that I'll almost die from it. Official Romantic Scale Level: 9.7.

"Hey, are you getting on or what?"

It's the bus driver. I jump up out of the vineyard and onto the bus. The intolerable rolling of his eyes is undeniable evidence that he's never been to France. I take the only seat available and look out the window.

It's *him*. Only Boy.

Even his distorted reflection is breathtaking. He sits three rows ahead of me, and he's wearing headphones. I bet the songs on his playlist are so cool that I've never even heard of them. His salmon-colored golf shirt perfectly complements his white, fitted ski jacket, and because he's so daring, and I'm so boring, we'd make the perfect couple. Where's he going? Maybe I'll follow him. Maybe I love him. I should have brought snacks.

Hang on. He's getting up … ringing the bell. He must be getting off at the next stop. Oh, please don't look at me. I stoop down to pick up an imaginary dropped item and the bus stops, the door opens, closes. I look outside the window and scan the area for clues. There's only two places he could have disappeared into: Winston Churchill Smokes, or Birdie's Golf. He either works at the golf shop or, more likely, he's planning a passionate excursion for the two of us to an all-inclusive resort in Cuba and he's come here to do research. Official Romantic Scale Level: 8.2. I wish I had a bathing suit that fit.

"Hey, Aggie, nice hair."

Oh-my-God he's still on the bus.

"Oh, hi, ummm …"

"Well, bye.

"Yeah, bye." The bus door opens. He leaves. I break into a cold sweat.

"Excuse me, young man."

The old guy beside me attempts to adjust his old guy coat that I'm half sitting on. *Excuse me, young man?* It must be my personal flair for fashion that makes me look young-mannish: frayed grey sweats, stringless hoodie, thrift-store Converse hi-tops, black, of course. There's really nothing about me that indicates my gender. I could be Barbie's boyfriend. I'd go shopping, but there's a rumor going around that you need money to do that. I guess he knows my name, but I don't know his because everyone always knows the weird people's names. I wish I were normal.

Wait!

Susan (Porky Pig) just got on the bus. Too bad I don't have the guts to tell her about my documentary idea. Susan's actually really beautiful — probably the most beautiful girl at school, and if I looked like her I'd start looking in the mirror again. She steps sideways to squeeze past the rows of very annoyed regular-sized people. Every seat is occupied and her thighs alone block the entire aisle.

The bus driver talks into his over-sized rear-view mirror, "Hello? Miss? Find a seat." Susan looks around but no one offers her their seat. Riding the bus route North of Intolerance, everyone remains keenly focused on not acknowledging her massive presence. "We can't go until you sit down."

Obviously mortified, Susan's top teeth clamp into her lower lip. The irritated squeak of the chair cushion announces the driver's impatience as he gets up, "Look, if you don't sit down, I can't go, and all these people need to be somewhere." Desperately clinging to the steel rail as though she might lose all sense of equilibrium, she stands frozen, apparently unable to speak.

"Oops!" I stand. "This is my stop. Sorry. I was totally zoning out." I walk to the exit. "Can you open the door for me. *Please*? I need to *be* somewhere." He shakes his head disapprovingly, returns to his seat and opens the door. "See you at school, Susan." The door closes behind me and I feel amazing, better than just normal. What was I thinking? Why settle for normal?

I walk the remaining twenty-three blocks to The Dump. The Converse feel good, the sweats are comfy and the hoodie covers my head. I find a broken dog leash on the ground and stuff it into the pouch of my hoodie. And by the way, Only Boy went into the Island Tan salon, which would be a little unusual if it weren't for the fact that he's getting ready to take me to Cuba.

5

"Two hundred and ninety-seven. That's pretty good. Almost fifteen dollars."

Counting the empty plastic bottles and cans that sit in haphazard piles on our kitchen floor is one of Jane's favorite rituals. The magic number is five hundred. Reaching the five hundred mark is when we load up Turdle, return the bottles, and reward ourselves with Chinese takeout because it takes effort to watch something accumulate.

"Mom, so you don't have to count them again, why don't you put them in bags and mark the number on the outside?"

"Because that, Agatha, that would ruin the surprise." She picks up the broken dog leash that I found earlier. "This'll come in handy someday. Good find. I'll put it in the van." Even Turdle is filled to capacity with come-in-handy-some-day crap.

The doorbell rings and we both stop breathing. Our doorbell never rings. Even the delivery guys know to go around back.

"Tell them we're not home. Tell them we're housesitting. Tell them we're foreigners. From Alberta."

"Relax, Mom. I'll go see who it is." Jane + the unexpected = panic.

"Be careful Aggie. Good God, don't people know how to use a phone?"

I go out the back door and peer around the corner. No one. I walk to the front steps and on the stoop sits a small ordinary box.

Gasp.

There's a big red heart sticker over the cardboard flaps, bordered by a white lace doily. Inside the heart, hand-drawn with fancy flowing script, is my name. But it looks distorted — it looks like a *pretty* girl's name.

"Hello?" I look around. "Hello!" The neighborhood betrays me with silence. Thief-like, I continuously check over my shoulder as I walk the seventeen steps back to the kitchen. I hide the box in full view, on top of a pile of last year's supermarket flyers and innumerable off-gassing milk cartons.

"Who was it?" Dressed in her ratty used-to-be-pink-but-now-a-disgusting-shade-of-*eww* housecoat, Jane peers out the bathroom door, "Tell them I'm in the shower."

"It was no one, Mom."

"No one? That's not good. Do you think they're checking to see if we're home so that they can burglarize the place? Or worse?"

Worse, I suppose, would be to redecorate.

"No, Mom, it's just some stupid kids."

I want her to go to bed so that I can open the box. She usually falls asleep in front of the TV, watching shows about people with extreme addictions. It makes her feel better knowing that there are people out there who have *real* problems, like eating light bulbs or snorting cinnamon.

"Hmph. I'm going to bed. I have a job interview at Spendapenny Consignment tomorrow."

Just what we need: employee discounted dead people's junk.

"That's great, Mom. I hope you get it."

She shuts her bedroom door and turns on her *Tranquil Moments* cassette tape which drowns out the tormented noises that spew from our puke-green refrigerator, circa 1972.

And now, I wait. I can't risk her coming out and catching me opening the box, as too many questions and too much drama would ensue. Normally, I would hate waiting because it gives me an opportunity to look around and absorb the hopelessness of the situation, but tonight is different — tonight I think of the possibilities. But then again, maybe I *shouldn't* open the box. What if it's a piece of dried dog poop, or a dead rat, or something horrific like a sawed-off bloody thumb or a mangled crow's wing?

I gently shake the box and it rattles, just slightly. It could be a bird's petrified eyeball, waiting for me to shine light on its glassy cynical judgment of my abysmal existence.

I wish I'd brought home my homework.

I wish I had a crappy hobby like rock-polishing to keep me busy. Hang on … releasing my inner ninja, I run into my room and open my closet door.

It's packed full of garbage.

Sometimes I really hate Jane.

My stomach quickly reacts. Rare and previously unseen footage of the Mount Vesuvius eruption now playing at a toilet near you. I have to look away as the half-digested remnants of my macaroni-and-ketchup dinner swirl around the bowl.

I sit on my bed, tenderly hold the box and peel away the paper, careful not to tear the little heart. Opening the first flap of cardboard, I see a bit of crumpled Easter bunny tissue paper. It's October. I uncrumple the paper. It's the coolest and most amazing gift I have ever received in my entire life: a long white shoelace with two rainbow beads knotted at each end. It must be for my hoodie — Official Rating on the Romantic Scale Level: 9. I reach under my bed and find the camcorder. I take a shot of the rainbow beads and the box where my name is, because this is worth documenting. This I won't erase. I put down the box and something inside catches my eye. A ticket.

"What's that?"

It's her. I shove the camera under a pile of old Sears Christmas catalogues.

"Something for school. Homework. You can go back to bed."

"I heard noises."

"That was the TV. Some unrealistic reality show about kids whose mothers drink too much and fill their houses with things they don't need."

"Oh. Don't watch that trash. And don't stay up late."

Thanks for your concern, Jane, whoever you are. I know who you used to be, years ago, before the booze took over. You used to be Mom. Now you're Jane. I wonder how many more boxes of wine it'll take before you become a complete stranger.

"Good night," she says. I get up and shut my bedroom door.

"You don't have to do that, you know!" She yells from the hallway.

I take the ticket out of the box and examine it closely to make sure it's not a clever replica or a photocopy. It seems genuine. Someone has given me a ticket to the annual Winter Solstice Carnival dance that takes place every December twenty-first.

This is horrible.

I can't go to a dance by myself, and I certainly can't wear a hoodie, with or without rainbow beads. I've heard Those Girls talk about it; how amazing they all looked in their formal gowns. The whole idea is impossible, and it's probably just part of the bigger plan to kill me with my own dreams.

I remove the garbage from my closet and stack it outside Jane's bedroom door. I crawl inside and imagine a new ending to the story: Cinderella is squished beyond recognition by a giant pumpkin coach. Orange mush everywhere, shards of broken glass slippers, and the prince moves to Utah with both of the ugly stepsisters.

6

Aaggggh eeee.

What the? Muffled noises of distress jar me awake. Oh right. Jane is imprisoned in her bedroom. Fine. I'll go, but I'm going to walk the five steps to her door as slowly as humanly possible. Step 1: Stop. Check fingernails. Step 2: Stop. Look at ceiling. Step 3: Stop. Lean on wall. Step 4: Stop. Consider going backwards. And step 5: Stop.

"You okay in there?" I ask.

"Get me out of here, Aggie!"

Maybe I will, maybe I won't, Jane. Maybe you should've chosen me over your drinking. Maybe you should've bought me some new clothes for school, and provided a suitable place where I could bring a friend.

"Aggie, enough! I have my job interview. Are you there?" I say nothing. A small voice, not like Jane's voice at all, says, "Why are you torturing me?"

Crap. I'm acting just like her. And I'm doing it on purpose.

"Hang on."

I work fast. It takes only a few minutes to clear the door and open it. A faint yet distinct raunchy aroma surrounds us. She's peed herself.

"Sorry," I say. She walks past me into the bathroom.

I hover outside the locked door.

"I have my interview. I have my interview today," she chants.

"Sorry, Mom."

"Go away!"

"I hope you get the job." She doesn't answer.

I put water in the coffee pot (we re-use the same grounds two, sometimes three times), turn it on and shove a Sears Christmas catalogue into my backpack.

I walk around to the front of The Dump and she's standing at the window watching me.

I need to make some friends.

MY CLASS IS going on a field trip to Science World this morning and we are supposed to have money for lunch. I guess I should have had breakfast. Looks like I get to spend the entire day thinking about food rather than how to predict volcanic patterns.

Even though the bus is packed and some kids sit three to a bench, no one sits beside me. With concentrated intent, I pull out one, by one, by one, the eyelashes of my right eyelid. As they come out, I carefully balance each eyelash on the top of my left hand and make a wish: *please bring me something to eat* and blow it away: *phe*. Oh, and *world peace: phe*. I used to like science, but not anymore. The teacher is a first-rate chauvinist. It was our genetics unit that turned me off.

"Females are predisposed to nurturing," he said. He obviously hasn't met Jane.

THE CLASS MOVES around the exhibits, looking at all the fascinating displays and filling out the equally fascinating worksheet that must be turned in at the end of the day. I place the Sears Christmas catalogue on a table of ancient artifacts. There's at least three other schools here and some of the kids have bagged lunches. I will follow the lunch-bag kids around and wait until one of them throws out their apple, orange, fruit snack, juice box. So often survival is a matter of being in the right place at the right time.

Shoot. Where is everybody from my school?

KREETHUNK … KREE KRee Kree kree

Yes! A boy just threw his *entire lunch bag* into a pendulum-lidded garbage can.

The hallway empties and I reach into the garbage with one arm. I feel the bag and I grab on to it.

Chikee

"I found her!"

Mandy Kronk holds her phone out toward me. She's never been particularly mean to me, and she's not one of Those Girls, but this photo of me might guarantee her a rare spot in the inner circle.

"Mandy, did you take my picture? Can you delete it? Please?"

"No way. This is gold."

"I'll pay you to delete it. How much do you want?" Obviously, I'm bluffing.

"Sure, you will. Hey guys! Come look at this."

Help! What can I say or do that will get her to delete the picture? What do I own that someone else would want? Nothing! Nothing! Nothing! Wait! I have one thing.

"I'll give you my Winter Solstice Carnival dance ticket if you delete it."

She lowers the phone to her side. "You don't have a Winter Carnival ticket. There's no way."

"I do! I really do! I won it … in a radio contest. And it's yours if you delete the picture. I'll bring it to school tomorrow."

"Umm, no. How 'bout you bring the ticket to school tomorrow, and *then* I'll delete the picture."

"But you can't show it to anyone."

"Sure, whatever." A few kids from our class join Mandy.

"What up?" One of them asks.

"Nothing. Let's get out of here." She speaks over her shoulder to me, "Kraus is looking for you."

I open the lunch bag to find a mayonnaise-covered ball of sandwich wrap, a brown apple core, and an empty juice box. Grape.

7

"Trouble?"

"No."

"Life?"

"No."

"How about Scrabble?"

"Mom, I really don't want to play a board game right now."

"Can you believe these were only a dollar? They obviously have no idea what things are actually worth in that store."

She bought five crappy board games, a broken-tailed ceramic horse lamp that has a bile-green beaded shade, and a cloudy plastic bag of bacteria-infested Lego. Why the Lego? *Because this stuff is going to be worth something someday.* Jane getting a job at a thrift store is like a goat working at a Krispy Kreme. Not a good idea. A *good* idea is for me to go through our bags and take our *own* stuff to that store and have them sell it. I'll go in on her day off and open an account.

"Oh, I almost forgot. I got you something really special."

Oh joy. My very first Easy-Bake oven.

"Look at these. Aren't they super cute!" She holds up a pair of camo military pants.

"You could sew sequins on them, girl them up a bit."

Besides the fact that they're obviously men's, I kinda like them. Maybe it's the new haircut. I take the pants to my room. They're only five sizes too big, which would be perfect except that I have to hold on to the waist with one hand to keep them from falling to the floor.

"Did you happen to buy me a belt?" Jane stares at her own eyebrows. "Maybe you could make me one out of Lego."

"You know ... I'll be right back." She leaves the room for 2.1 seconds and returns with the mangy tie from her housecoat. "You can use this."

Now admittedly, I'm no fashion expert, but I do know that nasty old housecoat belts are not currently in vogue.

"Mom. Seriously? Just forget it, okay?"

Back in my room I thread the long white shoestring with the two rainbow beads through the pant loops and pull on it as hard as I can to cinch the waist. I finally have it tight enough and *snap*, it breaks. It's now too short to use it for my hoodie. Typical. I mess everything up. I'm a stupid idiot who does stupid idiot stuff all the time and I hate me. I hate me so much that I wish I could find a place where I don't exist. Maybe I'll knock myself on the head and get amnesia and then I could be whoever I want to be. I'll call myself Monique and take a bus to Absolutely Nowhere and get a job at the Absolutely Nowhere Diner and the boy who drives the old yellow convertible will pick me up after my shift. I'll wear his football jacket to the movies and because it's too big for me and the sleeves are too long we'll find it really funny because I have trouble getting my hand into the bag of double-buttered popcorn. Official Romantic Scale Level: 7.5.

"Aggie, I have a belt!"

Great. She's probably excavated a beautifully preserved prehistoric macramé plant hanger.

"It's a good thing I didn't give any of these clothes away." She holds up a worn leather belt with a rectangular brass buckle and it's almost kind of cool. "This is definitely an antique. I'm sure it's very valuable." She examines it carefully, calculating its exaggerated worth.

"It's only valuable if it holds up my pants, Mom." And surprisingly, it does.

"You look great. Like a real soldier. At boot camp."

"Sir, yes, sir!" I salute, teetering ever so slightly on the tentative verge of fun.

"Aggie, don't make jokes about the military. You have no idea what those people go through." What *those people* go through? Are you *kidding* me? Tomorrow I will give up my ticket to the only awesome thing that I may or may not have been "invited" to because I was hungry.

"I'm going to bed," I say.

"Why? What's the matter with you?"

"I'm just tired, Mom."

"What about Boggle?" She displays the box as though it were a game-show prize.

Back in my room I reach for the video camera that is stashed under my bed. Tomorrow I have to be brave. Like a real soldier.

Torture Chamber documentary list of cast members in order of appearance: Mandy.

8

"Hey *Garburator*, where is it?"

Inside my locker, the camera is focused and the power is on. I've covered the red *record* indicator light with an old gum wrapper, and, allowing for personal space and other complicated mathematical formulae (a lucky guess), Mandy stands on the exact spot that I have secretly plotted for her. Shout out to the school district for the seismic upgrades, and the installation of retrofitted locker doors that have coated polycarbonate windows above the ventilation slats to *defer the concealment of weapons and drug paraphernalia*. Money well spent, considering the bottom three-quarters of the locker is still solid sheet metal.

"Where's what?" I say.

"The dance ticket, obviously."

I raise my voice, "Why should I give you my Winter Solstice Carnival dance ticket?" I could be an FBI agent.

"Because if you don't, I'll show everyone the picture of you groping garbage." She holds up her phone and displays my picture.

"So, this is blackmail?"

"Whatever."

I take the ticket out of my pocket.

"You can have it when you delete the picture." She pauses.

C'mon, fall for my tough-guy act.

"Fine." She presses a button and my picture disappears. "Okay, now give me my ticket."

"Yeah, sure, here's *your* ticket."

She grabs it out of my hand like it's a ticket off the *Titanic* and walks away.

"Watch out for the iceberg!" I say.

She stops, turns around, and says, "Not to be rude, but why are you so weird?"

Not knowing the answer to that question, I say, "Not to be weird, but why are you so rude?"

"Don't even talk to me."

Bye, Mandy Kronk, have a perfect life.

"Hey, stink-factory."

Oh my gosh, this is great! It's two of Those Girls and I actually *want* them to be mean to me. I love my new hobby. Kicks the crap out of rock polishing.

"Listen, Skunk, our mothers are organizing the Christmas Hamper Drive this year and we're supposed to ask if you and your weirdo mother want to be put on the list," Bevy says.

"I guess they don't think you have enough stuff already," Myhell says, and flips her fantastically red hair.

"Oh. No, we don't need a Christmas hamper. Give it to someone who could use it," I say.

"You know Skunk-butt, you should really reconsider. Maybe someone will donate a toothbrush for you and a box of whiskey chocolates for your mother."

"Oh," I say, "that would be nice, wouldn't it?"

"Oh, that would be nice wouldn't it!" They mimic me, cracking up. "Oh, that would be nice, wouldn't it!" Myhell stops mid-laugh, stands oddly close to me and says, "You know what would be even nicer?"

She pushes my shoulder. "You off the face of the earth, that'd be nicer."

"Yeah, then we wouldn't have to smell your dog-shit smell anymore," Bevy adds. She takes a bottle out of her purse and sprays me in the face. Vanilla maybe. Mango? Whatever it is, it burns my eyes and, too late, I cover my face with my hands.

"Have a gross day, Douche."

They laugh, walk away. And, cut! End of scene two. I open my locker and the bell rings. I want to bring the camera with me, but I haven't figured out a way to properly conceal it, which is too bad because I have gym today, a.k.a. semi-supervised physical activities that provide ample opportunity for peer persecution. There's a girl in the class, Tanette, who Those Girls are mean to because she has 38 Double Ws, or whatever they are, and she won't change in front of anyone.

I open my locker to shut off the camera and an idea hits me. Best idea ever. What if I leave the camera *on* for the next couple of hours? Just call me Nancy Drew in Sweats.

"Aggie?"

Carson Turndale, looks up at me. Carson Turndale has a hormone growth disorder and he's unusually small. He looks about six, even though he's in my grade. About a month ago some of the Idiot Boys duct-taped a diaper on him and shoved him on top of some lockers. Carson told Miss Strand, the Chamber's counselor, and she said that she would *look into the incident*. The Idiot Boys denied everything and went unpunished, as usual. Maybe there's a role for Carson in my Torture Chamber documentary.

"Hey, Carson. What's going on?"

"Can I talk to you?"

"Yeah, for sure, umm, when?" Is it him? Is *he* my mystery person? If he is, then that's good news and bad news: he's not exactly my type, but at least he's real.

"Maybe after school? Can you come over to my house? Do you know where I live? The blue house by the park?"

Everyone knows where Carson lives; his family are gazillionaires. And why does he want me to come over to his house? No one ever invites me over to their house. The only time I've seen the inside of someone else's house is on Halloween night when they briefly open the door.

"We can't talk here?"

"Nah, I hate it here."

"Okay. I guess. Carson, how do you feel about the Muppets?

"What? Why?"

"Never mind. See you after school."

"Great. And I hate the Muppets. They're about as low-tech as it gets." Carson runs away.

I doubt it's him. I mean, he's nice, but nice isn't romantic. Nice isn't something that you ride off into the sunset with. Nice isn't something that makes you unable to sleep at night because you're remembering every word it ever said to you. I mean, Carson and I are allies because we belong to the same designated freak association, but I've never been to his house and obviously he's never been to The Dump. No one has. Not ever. Maybe that's one of the reasons why I'm so lonely. I might even be the loneliest person on the planet. I've heard about how celebrities are lonely. Maybe that's it. I'm far too famous to have any *real* friends. Maybe at next year's red carpet event I'll put more effort into nurturing my relationships with the Hollywood crowd.

The rest of the day is a total bore factory. I'm excited to watch the footage the camera has accumulated; maybe my knight in shining tinfoil came by my locker just to feel close to me. Maybe he spent two hours trying to figure out my locker combination so he could leave the outrageous stack of love poems that he's written to me, along with a meatball sub sandwich. Official Romantic Scale Level: 8.2.

On my way to Carson's house, I place the 2009 Sears Christmas catalogue inside a random mailbox. Every November, Jane and I would sit under a cozy blanket together and flip through that year's catalogue and I'd make a long list of the toys that I wanted, which was a pretty dumb thing to do because I never once got any of them.

I've known Carson since first grade, when he was the same size as the rest of us. I can't imagine what it might be like to find out that you're never going to grow. Maybe it's like finding out that no one will ever think you're beautiful.

I press the buzzer outside his gated driveway.

"Hello?"

"Hi, I'm Carson's ... friend."

The heavy iron gate crawls open. I wait for the vicious dogs with saber-toothed-tiger fangs to leap out and take a chunk out of the meaty part of my calf. The driveway is lined with shrubberies so perfectly manicured into the shape of giant candy-flosses that Disneyland groundskeepers would be unhappiest-place-on-earth-envious. A thick glass door adorned with an intricately etched flying crane opens and Carson's hand, covered in candy sprinkles, reaches out towards me.

"Here. My mom made them."

It's the prettiest, most magazine-cover-looking cupcake I've ever seen. Man-in-control-like, he takes my backpack and places it behind him onto a dark wood bench.

"Is it your birthday, Carson?"

"Why would it be my birthday?"

"Because your mom made cupcakes."

"Nah, she does that all the time." Wow. A mom who makes cupcakes, *all the time*, instead of a Jane who drinks, *all the time*.

"So, come on in."

I step into Carson's house and immediately panic. It is so breathtaking in its beautifulness that I shouldn't be here; the walls are white, the floor is clean. On a circular table, a blue orchid slouches, heavily weighted by its own gracefulness. An Old Hollywood black-and-white movie staircase spirals into what must be heaven. I take off my shoes. A gilded floor-to-ceiling mirror catches my reflection and I see myself in all my spectacular wretchedness, a rhinoceros in a swan pond.

"I have to go," I say.

"What?"

Shoes on, I back away.

"Sorry!" I'm a spooked horse running, I run and run and run. I stop when I reach my street. I'm not sure what I did with the cupcake, it's probably lying dead, icing-side-down, on Carson's posh, polished floor, an unintentional insult, a casualty of my awkwardness.

Relief rushes over me as I breathe in the stale air of The Dump and the familiar mess comforts me. I head for my closet. Finally safe, I close my eyes and hide inside my sweetly putrid sanctuary of solitary confinement. I'm too sad to think, so I'm going to count.

When I get to exactly ten thousand, I feel calm enough to come out. Jane's in the kitchen, pretending to cook. Her forehead wrinkles like one of those weird Chinese dogs as she reads the instructions from the side of the box of One Pan Tuna. She doesn't look at me when she speaks. "You finished your homework?"

Oh. No. My backpack is at Carson's.

"Ah, what?"

"One cup of milk. Shoot. We don't have any milk. I'll use water. Fish like water. I was asking about your homework, pay attention."

"Um, yeah, actually, I have to meet a friend at the library. We're doing a school project together."

"On what?"

"Oh, umm. Orchids. It's a research assignment on tropical vegetation."

"What class is that for?"

"Humanities. You know, greenhouse gases and stuff. I dunno."

"That's too complicated for grade nine." Grade ten, Jane, I'm in grade ten. "I'll make an appointment with that teacher. You're always so crabby and aloof. All this work is obviously elevating your stress level."

Thanks, Jane, world-renowned psychotherapist, for once again offering your expert opinion.

"No, Mom. You don't have to meet with the teacher."

"What friend?"

Right. What friend. I don't have any friends.

"Umm. Susan."

"Oh. The obese girl."

"Mom. She's actually really nice.

"Yes, well, she sort of *has* to be nice."

I eat three bites of the Tuna Belcher, struggling to keep it down; it's runny and cold and the noodles look like snot. Jane sorts through a recently exhumed stack of *Reader's Digest*s — not the ones in our bathtub. She attempts to organize them chronologically, stopping every 3.5 minutes with a, "I remember 1986," or a, "Laughter really *is* the best medicine."

"Okay, I'm going," I say. I tuck a Sears Christmas catalogue inside my shirt.

She peers over her magazine trench.

"Listen, Aggie ..." She points at me and beats one finger on an imaginary tiny floating drum to emphasize her statement. "... I don't want you talking to any of those creepy men who are always on the computers."

"Sure, Mom."

I leave the house, pull out an eyelash, and wish for something that I will never own as long as I live: a cellphone. Randomly showing up at Carson's is gauche; people in their tax bracket prefer to be warned — it gives them time to polish the silver. Tonight, after Jane goes to bed, I'll go through some bags to find stuff for the consignment store. I walk past the park and my teeth clack against each other like a wind-up toy. Next eyelash is a winter coat.

The gate is open. What's the etiquette here? I push the button.

"Hello?"

"Hi, umm, is Carson here?"

I wait.

"Carson isn't available."

"Oh. Well, I, umm, I left my homework in your foyer this afternoon. In my backpack." I love that word: *foyer*, I learned it from one of the 750 or so issues of *Reader's Digest* that we *do* store in the bathtub.

Carson looks at me through an upstairs window. He looks at me and I look at him and we're both just looking at one another when the etched glass crane barely takes flight and the front door opens just a crack. A disembodied arm places my backpack on the stoop and closes the door. I leisurely walk to the door, pick it up, and slowly turn away, allowing time for Carson to come down and talk to me, but when I look back up to the window, he's vanished. Maybe he's in trouble. Maybe he's being held hostage by evil rebels pretending to be his parents who have taken his real parents to Albania where there are no cupcakes. Or maybe he just hates me. I wait another minute, but the door remains closed.

I GET TO the public library and look for an outlet to plug in my camera. I should come here more often. It's my kind of beautiful: peaceful, orderly, Janeless. I could totally be a librarian. And then, when my branch hosts a Meet the Author night, a brooding and remarkably famous writer will observe how skillfully I sort books and he'll be so mesmerized by my unprecedented ability to recall the alphabet (even the more difficult letter combinations like *l-m-n-o-p*), that he'll try to convince me to fall in love with him by writing a scandalous romance about the two of us. I'll have to break his heart, of course, because I will already be betrothed to a *creepy* man who is *always on the computer*.

I place the Sears catalogue on the magazine shelf and plug in the camera and rewind to the start. I watch the part where I am extorted into giving Mandy my dance ticket. It's not a whole picture because the camera needs to be tilted slightly downward, but the audio is perfect. I fast-forward and find nothing, but then the screen changes and I'm looking at a wall that I don't recognize. From the side of the screen, Carson appears.

"Hi, Aggie. I'm sorry you had to leave today. Well, actually, I'm kind of glad you left."

I knew it. He hates me.

"I'm glad you left because it's easier to ask you this not in person. You see, today you asked me if it was my birthday, and that's so weird because it actually is my birthday. I'm sixteen today. Yeah, I know. I seem younger."

Carson looks away from the camera, breathes deeply a few times and continues, "So the thing is, I'm sixteen, and well, I've never … I've never … I've never … I've never kissed a girl. So, I was hoping that you might be able to come over again someday when you don't have to rush off, and maybe you might let me kiss you? I know this could get really awkward at school, but the thing is, school already is really awkward, so I figured, what have I got to lose?"

"Carson, it's time for your nap!"

And that's where the video ends. Kiss me? He wants to kiss me? No one wants to kiss *me*.

"Hi."

I look up from the camera and Susan is standing beside me with a pile of books.

"Hi!" I say, surprised.

"I was walking past your house, your mom was outside rummaging through your neighbor's recycle box. She called me over and told me that it was disrespectful of me to be late because you were already at the library waiting for me to work on our project. So, I decided I'd better come over and find out what I've signed up for."

9

"So, tell me, what have you been working on?" Susan asks.

"Umm, orchids?"

"I like orchids." She sits down at the table. "That's an old video camera. What is it? Nineteen nineties? I'm pretty sure my parents had one of those."

"Yeah, I'm ... I'm trying an experiment at school."

"Cool. Can I help?" She pulls out a bag of mini licorice allsorts and tosses a handful into her mouth. (I like the blue and pink ones that have the beaded candies stuck on the outside.) Clearly, now is the time to let Susan in on the Master Plan.

"What I'm going to tell you is ..." I look over my shoulder and whisper "... completely confidential."

"No problem. I got no one to tell. Except maybe my friend, Little Debbie Cakes and her cousin, Twinkie."

I explain everything to Susan and she is so enthusiastic that we are shushed by the librarian. I didn't know they actually did that, but I guess it's in the *Librarian Code of Behavior Handbook*.

"We'll call it *The Pig Mask Chronicles*," Susan says, "And tomorrow, we'll meet early, before school, and set up your camera in my locker — you'll be amazed at the daily level of harassment that comes with being fat."

I should say, "You're not fat," but I don't. I want to say something encouraging, but because I'm not very good at getting personal, I say, "Yeah?"

"Are you kidding me? Just when I think it can't get any worse, they somehow manage to hate on me even more. It's so bad that some days I think I'd rather just be dead."

"No, no, no, no, no. You dying won't change anything. But exposing them for what they are, *that's* what matters. That's when everything will change."

"You know what's weird?"

"What?"

"I'm sort of looking forward to being bullied tomorrow."

"Yeah. I know exactly what you mean."

I'M UP SO early that I'll be halfway to the Torture Chamber before Jane even crawls out of bed. I change the tape in the camera, and check that the battery is fully charged. I place the tape with the kiss proposition inside the box that the dance ticket came in and hide it under my bed. I don't know what I'm going to say to Carson. It's not that I don't want to kiss him, it's just that it never crossed my mind until now. And he's so much shorter than me. Am I supposed to lean down, or is he supposed to stand on a chair? None of it sounds particularly romantic. And what if he wants to *really* kiss? You know, like we're in *love* or something. I guess that would be a bit romantic. Maybe like a Level 6.4. But even that's generous.

When I get to school, Susan is waiting for me beside her locker. She is not happy.

"What's wrong?" I ask.

"I'm having second thoughts."

"Why?"

"What if we record all this stuff and they just get meaner? What if they gang up on us and they actually *hurt* us?"

"They already are hurting us, Susan. And no problem. We'll keep the *The Pig Mask Chronicles* to ourselves, until you're ready."

"Really?"

"Really. Believe me, I don't want to be hurt anymore, either." And then something happens that has never happened to me before: Susan and I share a hug, the way two friends would hug and the truth in it shocks me so much that my eyes water with something that isn't sadness. I don't recognize this feeling, and I don't want to because I'm afraid that if I do, it'll be gone and I won't have it anymore. "Okay," I say quickly, "let's set up."

We position the camera. Carson walks toward us. Oh, snap. I'm not ready for him — *it*, the decisively clumsy encounter when our lips attempt to make contact. When I accidently kiss his forehead and he accidentally kisses the place where my boobs are attempting to be.

"Hi, Aggie, hi, Susan." He walks by casually, as though we *don't* share a giant secret. He turns back and, like the most confident person on the planet, he brings an exaggerated arm to his mouth and swoops it into the air and blows me a kiss.

"Does he *like* you or something?" Susan asks me, a huge smile crossing her face.

"What?"

"Carson, does he like you?"

"I don't think so. Why?" Maybe she didn't notice that flying gesture of complete unabashed flirtatiousness.

"Oh, gee, let's see, maybe the fact that *he just sent you a massive kiss!* I know it wasn't intended for me."

"Oh, that. He's just joking around."

Susan looks down. Her voice is quiet, "I wish someone would joke around with me like that."

I should change the subject, but I'm caught up in how euphorically astonishing it is to have a boy pay boy-likes-girl-type of attention to me, even from a boy who has always just been a friend.

"What's your favorite flavor of popsicle?" I ask. Brilliant segue. Just brilliant.

"Huh?"

"You know, cherry, grape, orange."

"Definitely orange," she says.

"Really? Mine, too!"

"Most people like cherry, but they taste too artificial to me."

That seals it. It's obvious that Susan and I are meant to be best friends.

"Okay. The camera's recording. Now all we have to do is get on with our day and wait for someone to be mean to you." I close the door to Susan's locker.

"That won't take long. As a matter of fact ..."

I turn and see a group. Two of Those Girls and two Idiot Boys with their tongues hanging out. They walk toward us and Bevy puts her hand over her mouth. "Save yourselves and hold your breath! Human feces ahead!"

And Grant Mikorski, the most proudly idiotic of the Idiot Boys says,

"Hey fat-girl, you wanna squash me?"

Susan turns a deep purple. Chrissy Crop Top moves trash-talk-close to Susan's face, "You're not going to explode, are you? 'Cause that would just be totally foul."

"Yeah, there'd be guts and blubber everywhere!" shrieks an Idiot Boy apprentice.

"And curly fries!" Bevy offers.

And then, empowered by the video camera, I say, "You suck."

"What'd you say?" Bevy towers over me.

I have to ask, "What's *your* favorite flavor of popsicle?"

"My favorite flavor of *popsicle*?" She pushes me and I stumble backwards and almost fall. "Do you even *know* how strange you are?" The bell rings and, because she's so cool, Bevy picks up my ladybug backpack, drop-kicks it across the hall, and the four of them leave, completely caught up in the supposedly random topic of popsicle flavors.

Susan's mouth hangs open, "You're the bravest person I know."

"No, not the bravest. Maybe the stupidest."

"I think this belongs to you?" It's him. Only Boy, the reddish-hued beginnings of a tan cover his face and neck. He offers me my backpack.

"Ah, thanks."

"I saw what happened. They can be so annoying. The best thing to do is ignore them," he says. It occurs to me that he could have said something to intervene while they were here, which would have totally counted as a Level 7.9 on the Official Romantic Scale. Nonetheless, I want to keep him talking.

"Oh, yeah. Um, so, have you ridden the bus lately?" Wow. I'm so witty and alluring. No wonder so many boys are infatuated with me.

"Ah, not really. Why?"

Oh great, the most monumental moment of my entire life, seeing Only Boy on the bus, and he doesn't remember it.

"Oh. No reason," I say.

"Right. See you later." He smoothes back his hair and shakes his head, sprinkling the area with a light dusting of *gorgeous*. Susan looks at me like I'm more than I am. Like I'm actually not some freak show whose mother is the president of the Mentally-Unstable-Moms Club.

"You *know* him?"

"No, not really. I mean, I see him around … I mean, he's …"

"Tasty." Susan's voice carries down the secluded hall.

"Yeah, he's not bad." Hey, you wouldn't happen to know his name, would you?"

"You don't even know his name, and he *talks* to you? *Seriously?*"

"Seriously."

"Yale," she says.

"What about it?"

"That's his name."

"Actually?"

"Yup. His parents named him after their alma mater. It's probably where they fell in love. It's unusually beautiful." Susan sighs. "So tonight. We'll meet at library headquarters, review the *Pig Mask* plan, and eat candy."

"Ladies! May I ask why you're not in class?"

It's the vice-principal, a.k.a., the Prince of Vice. Last summer I saw him in the grocery store with his frowny-faced wife. She was reprimanding him for squeeze-testing *every single bag* of freshly baked bread. I had to look away.

"Ah, we were just …"

"Skipping class! I want to see both of you after school, *in-my-office*!" He loudly claps his hands together in between the words. "Now get to where it is our government funding is paying for you to be. Such a waste, loitering. Such a waste! I will phone your parents immediately. Immediately!" He claps again.

"But we're not skipping." Susan's voice warbles. "We're just a little late."

He speaks harshly. "No excuses!"

"Aren't we supposed to be innocent before proven guilty?" I say this with such conviction that even I'm convinced that I'm saying something significant.

"I know you." He points a nubby finger at me. "You're the one whose father works at that downtown law firm. Don't try to outsmart me, Miss Smarty Smarts. Your father needs to know this is a school, not a courtroom. I will contact him, first."

And so obviously, because I doubt that even Jane knows who my father is, I say, "That's a great idea."

"Of course, it's a great idea! Now get to class, and I'll see you at 3:10!"

He doesn't move. I look at Susan and she is also trying to keep a straight face. We turn to go in opposite directions.

I clap my hands between the words,

"See-you-after-school-Susan! 3:10!"

"Absolutely, Miss Smarty Smarts!" she replies. We both crack up.

10

I open the door to the main office and there sits Jane, dressed in a fringed Mexican poncho, an acid-washed denim miniskirt, and a pair of yellow rubber boots, and, despite the festiveness of her outfit, she is furious.

"Well!"

"Hi, Mom."

"Don't *Hi, Mom* me. Skipping class? Who do you think you are? Einstein?"

"Yeah, Mom, E equals MC squared. Susan and I were just late."

"I knew that roly-poly was trouble."

Susan arrives with her parents. They're an odd match. Her mom's skin is kinda oily and it shimmers against her magenta yoga ensemble, and her dad's sleepy eyes appear underlined with linebacker grease. The Prince of Vice's door opens and he walks out like they've just announced his name at the Academy Awards. "Hello! And welcome, parents!" He claps his hands, applauding himself. "Please, come in."

There are two available chairs. Susan's dad slumps into one, and, like someone just told her that when the music stops they're going to take a chair away, Jane races to the other. Susan's mother does on-the-spot calf-raises. Susan and I attempt to camouflage ourselves behind the dust-gusting silk ferns in the corner.

"Let me start by saying that I'm impressed by your commitment to your children's education. So often parents do not *find the time* to come into my office when there's been an infraction of the school rules. A very serious infraction."

Clueless. Torture Chamber administrators are all clueless. Susan and I are not the problem and this is a total waste of time.

"I maintain a zero-tolerance policy when it comes to truancy." He smiles, like a wolf does, right before it eats your head. "Now, when I was contemplating the punishment for Miss Susan and Miss Agatha, I took into consideration that this was a first violation for both young ladies. I have decided —" He reaches into his desk and brings out two pairs of metal tongs. He picks up one pair in each hand, lobster-like, and holds them up. "— that both girls must pick up garbage around the school grounds after school. For a month." He *snap-snaps* the tongs twice to emphasize his point. Startled, Susan's dozy dad springs up in his chair. "I have a sign-in sheet prepared for each girl and ..."

"No." Jane stands, her boots release an embarrassing fart.

"Excuse me?" says the Prince of Vice.

"My *young lady* has never skipped a class in her life. Your punishment is preposterous." (Word courtesy of *Reader's Digest*.) "Miss *Agatha* will *not* be here after school picking up garbage, but she won't be late again. You got that?"

Susan's now fully awake dad, undoes the top button of his pristine white shirt, and her mom freezes mid calf-raise.

"Now, Mrs. ..."

"Forget it! That's all I have to say. Except the next time you drag parents into the school to listen to your ball shoot, you should offer them a cup of coffee. You're lucky I'm not charging you for the cost of my gas to get here." Jane storms out the door, the fake foliage teeters in her wake. I follow. When we pass the office counter she takes a pen out of the secretary's pencil holder, looks at me and says, "It's the least they can do."

On the walk home (no, she didn't actually bring Turdle), Jane is in the best mood I've seen her in since I don't even remember.

"You know, Aggie, I think it's time to take you out of that school and home-school you myself."

"Mom, remember, I'm in grade ten. I doubt there's a lot of home-schooling that you can give me."

"Oh, come on, it's just a matter of reading a fancy-pants old book, and learning what ten percent of a hundred is. I know *all* that stuff. And I could teach you new words — the ones from *Reader's Digest*. I *knew* I kept those for a reason."

I have to think fast.

"Yeah, that would be awesome, Mom, but the sad thing is, we do most stuff on the computers now. Even math. Everything's online." Saying "online" to Jane is like saying "microwave" to a caveman.

"That's not possible. We don't own a computer."

"That's what I'm saying. And I have to go to the library right after dinner to do my homework on one of *their* computers."

"No. Tomorrow's my day off, so I've planned our night. I got a paint-by-numbers kit from the shop. It's a jungle scene with wild animals and I think some of them are even *endangered*. It'll be a really fun thing for us to do together."

"Well, I'm not gonna be late. You can start it, and I'll be home before you can … paint to ten."

"I guess. But we have to eat dinner together."

"I know, Mom."

I quickly finish my lavish dinner — a boiled wiener rolled up in a piece of untoasted Wonder bread, something Jane thinks sounds more palatable by calling it indoor camping food. I'm almost out the door when the phone rings.

"No, she's at the library."

"No, I'm not!" I race to the phone, but she's already hung it up. It's one of those old phones (big surprise) that doesn't have call display.

"Who was that?"

"I didn't get a name."

Not wanting to ask if it was a boy or girl, I continue, "Who did it sound like?"

"No one I know."

"Could it have been Susan?"

"Hmmm, I doubt it."

"Could it have been my um, lab partner, Carson?"

"Look, Aggie, I don't have time to chat. My art awaits and you'd better get going so you're home in time to enjoy this. Besides, he'll phone back. That's the second time he's called today. I find it annoying."

"*He's* already called? Why didn't you tell me?"

"Well I guess I've been busy. Busy bailing you out of detention. Busy making your dinner. I'm not your personal secretary, Mrs. Trump."

She stares at the picture on the front of the box. The conversation is over. Jane has faded into that cracked and thorny cavern inaccessible to humans.

I leave The Dump and make a mental list of the things I need: a job, a cellphone, and some decent food. Maybe I could volunteer at a soup kitchen just so that I could get a bowl for myself. I doubt anyone has made a steady income painting-by-numbers and I'm down to my last three eyelashes. The consignment store might be my only hope because I don't really have any skills, except maybe walking. Maybe I could get a job as a dog-walker and one rainy Saturday afternoon at the park, all my dogs get tangled up in their leashes, and a handsome boy who goes there to write love songs hands me his umbrella and I stay dry while he separates the dogs. And then, every Saturday after that when I'm walking the dogs, he brings me a peach — for no particular reason — and he brings little biscuits for the dogs. We walk the dogs together and talk about all our favorite things, and, after about twelve peaches, we realize that our favorite things are each other. Official Romantic Scale Level: 9.8.

I get to the library, and along with a couple of Those Girls, who are looking through sex techniques/anti-aging tips magazines (I guess they don't realize there's a Sears catalogue on the rack somewhere) Susan is also here, flipping through a do-it-yourself costume book. I forgot that the school Halloween dance is this weekend.

"You going to the dance?" I ask.

"As what? Big Bo Peep? Big Red Riding Hood? Maybe Big Miss Muffet. Think about it, there is no such thing as a flattering plus-size costume. People think it's *so* funny to stuff their shirts with a pillow and put on a pair of suspenders, when in actuality, they look just like me." She glances at me curiously. "Are *you* going to the dance?"

A tiny part of me wants to, but that tiny part doesn't have a say in the real world.

"Seriously not happening," I say.

"Hey! That was awesome — the way your mom handled that."

"Yeah, I guess."

"So, did you look at the video?"

"What? No, I can't do that stuff at home. There's no privacy."

"Yeah, same. My mom is always hovering, trying to get me to do a YouTube workout with her and drink her homemade Skinny Girl tea. Plug it in!"

I set up the camera and we lean toward it. The sound is clear and we can see that it's the two guys who have their lockers directly across from Susan's. One of them is Idiot Boy Grant Mikorski and the other one is Travis Tarkington, the brainiest boy in The Torture Chamber. And naturally, intelligence doesn't go unrewarded in The Torture Chamber. Back in grade four our teacher let us take turns cleaning out the cage of what she thought was a gerbil. Travis, unfortunately, informed the teacher that her crepuscular Cricetinae was not a gerbil, but was, indeed, a hamster. And that was that. It began with people calling him "Indeeda Hamster," but that was too complicated, so now they just call him "Hamster."

"Hey, Hamster droppings, you wanna move?" (Pause.) "I said move it, jerk!" Grant slams Travis hard into his locker and leaves. The next thing we hear is a kind of sniffling. Travis is crying, which is really awkward. The tape continues on with a long redundant shot of the wall across from Susan's locker.

"Fast-forward it." We stare at the continued nothingness when suddenly Susan sees something.

"There! Go back!" We sit and watch in total shock. Travis lights matches and tries to maneuver them into the slats of Grant's locker before they snuff out. He is unsuccessful. "This could get dangerous."

"Yeah. We have to be really careful to not hurt our own people with this stuff."

"We'll ask Travis to join our club. And Carson. And that girl Nicole — the one who is tormented by Bevy and Chrissy because of her *affliction*."

"Nicole has an affliction?" I ask.

"Yeah, it's kinda unusual. She sweats from only one armpit, like there's a garden hose up there. You never noticed? It's pretty obvious when it's badminton day in gym. We'll conceal the camera in my lunch bag." Susan's lunch bag is covered with yellow happy faces. "People are used to seeing me with my lunch bag. I can video at any moment. I see this all day, and I'm totally sick of it! Aren't you sick of it?"

"Yeah, for sure I'm sick of it."

"So, let's make this happen, okay? For real."

"For real," I say.

"Great," she says. "Tomorrow night. We'll call a meeting and talk strategy. I'll ask Nicole and Travis. You ask Carson. Okay?"

"Um, sure, I guess I can ask Carson." I suppose a library isn't the worst place in the world to have your first kiss. It's kind of quaint, charming, even. Especially if we kiss by the Harlequin romance novels.

"Okay. Then that's it. Give me the camera. I'll meet you at your locker in the morning. Early. So we're not late for class." She holds up both hands and lobster-snaps. The librarian approaches us. "Someone asked me to give this to you." She hands me an envelope.

"What? Who? When?" I ask.

"I don't know, a boy. He wanted me to hold on to it for an hour before I gave it to you.

"What? What did he look like?"

"He was handsome. But not in a Mr. Darcy way."

"Right. Mr. Darcy." Mr. Darcy must be her husband. "Okay. Umm, anything else?"

"He was wearing a baseball cap that has the letter B on the front. Which in itself is fascinating."

"A letter B baseball hat?" None of the Idiot Boys wear baseball hats. Maybe I actually do have a secret admirer. Maybe it's not just a sick joke.

"Yes, and he also had a rather pretty rainbow bead on a string around his neck; it's probably deeply symbolic. I can look that up for you tomorrow."

"Hey! That's the same as your bracelet!" Susan is incredulous. "Quick! Open the envelope!" I want to save the envelope, but not opening it now wouldn't be right because best friends always open envelopes in front of one another. I slowly peel the flap, careful not to rip it.

"C'mon!"

I check over my shoulder. The librarian is aggressively crushing toddler biscuits into dust with her carpet sweeper in the L'il Readers section. Like Charlie, looking for the golden ticket, I am hold-your-breath careful. And there it is. We stare at it.

Thank you for supporting your public library. The library will be closing in five minutes. Please make your way to the front exit. The library will reopen tomorrow morning at 9:30.

We hear the announcement and go to the back of the FICTION R-W shelves, where we are hidden from view.

"Wow." Susan's eyes are wide and her mouth hangs open. "Are you going to use it? Do you have somewhere to go?"

"I did. But I don't anymore." It's a gift certificate to *La Belle Château*, the most exclusive and notoriously snobby bridal and prom dress shop in the city. There's no dollar amount written down, it just says: *Find something beautiful, like you*. Official Romantic Scale Level: off the charts. Slowly, so it won't crinkle, I replace the certificate into the envelope and carefully wedge it between the pages of my math notebook.

"Susan, do you know of any way that we can get enough money to buy tickets to the Winter Solstice Carnival dance?"

"Are you kidding? My mom tries forcing me to go every year, but I never want to. I have no one to go with, and me in a ball gown? Not really my style. But if you want to go, I'm sure she'd buy tickets for both of us. She thinks that a dance would motivate me to stop eating Oreos.

"Your mom would buy us tickets?"

"Yeah, no problem, if you really wanted to go."

"Yes, I really want to go! Do you know what this means?"

Susan shrugs.

"This means that my life could change. I could actually do something normal and amazing and I might not have to live the rest of my life as a total loser."

"You're not a loser, Aggie, you're a warrior."

The lights go out and we hear the beeping noises of an alarm, a door closes and is then locked.

We're trapped.

Neither of us has a cell, so we can't tell our parents that we're staying over at each other's houses. This is bad. The police will come and I'll never be allowed to go to the library again.

"Now what?" Susan sticks her hand in her coat pocket and takes out a well-used plastic bag full of sour soothers and hard foam bananas. She opens the bag and pops a handful into her mouth.

"It's too bad we don't know the combination to the alarm," I say. "It's probably Shakespeare's birthday."

"It's too bad ... *chomp* ... we didn't just ... *smack* ... leave when we were supposed to." A bit of saliva accumulates on the side of Susan's mouth. "Maybe there's ... *slurp* ... another way out."

"Genius!"

We check the windows but they're all locked from the inside. "Do you think the alarm would go off if we opened one?" I ask.

"I don't know. Probably."

"Well, even if it did, we could escape and run and no one would know that it was us who set off the alarm."

"Aggie, I can't *escape* out a *window*."

"Oh. Right."

"But you could go. You could get out the window."

"Yeah, but I'm not going to do that." And I wouldn't. I would never abandon Susan.

"Aggie?"

"Yeah?"

"I'm gonna be sick." Susan hobbles away like her shoes are on fire. She disappears. I follow the retching sounds.

"Susan, look!"

"I know! Tie-dye vomit! She makes a peace sign. "Peace and love baby, feelin' groovy!" She wipes the sticky kaleidoscope from her chin.

"No, look up!"

A bright red EXIT sign hangs above her head.

"Do you think we should try it?"

"It's the only way," I say. "Ready?"

We push on the heavy steel bar, the door opens and we're out. No alarm. No ride home in a police car. Just a dimly lit street and a distant barking dog. Susan catches her breath, "I'm kinda disappointed the alarm didn't go off."

"Yeah me too. Hey, where's your bag?"

"It's on the ... oh, no. Oh, no. Oh-no-no-no!"

"Susan, what is it?"

"I left my bag in there. It has the camera in it, and someone's going to steal it and our project will be ruined!"

"Oh," is all I can say. Susan turns pale. I try to play down how completely disastrous the situation really is. "Look, we'll come back in the morning."

"At 9:30? We can't skip."

"Right. What if we phone the library from school, and asked the librarian to keep the bag safe for us?"

"Or, what if we leave a note asking the librarian to hold the bag for us until we get there. That way we wouldn't have to wait until class gets out to make a phone call.

"Yeah, that should work."

I rip a page from my math notebook and write a polite and detailed note. I slip it through the overnight return slot and we hear the *thhhht* as it lands in the empty bin.

"I finally have something to write in my diary." Susan says and she hugs me again. That makes two on the hugometer. I wonder if there will ever come a time when I lose count?

JANE IS ZONKED out on the couch when I get home so I sort through a few of the inner core garbage bags and fill a different bag with what I consider are sellable items of Jane's "vintage" clothing. If she asks, I will tell her that it's a bag of dirty laundry that I'm taking to Susan's house to do for free. I think I have about fifty dollars' worth of stuff, and after Spendapenny takes half, I'll still end up with more money than I've ever had in my entire life.

11

I open my eyes, count to fifty (dollars), divide by half, count to twenty-five, and force myself out of bed.

Today I need to ask Carson if he wants to join what I've decided to call the Warriors Video Club. He'll probably think that the reason I want to talk to him is to settle the kissing thing, which I do, and I don't. I do because kissing a boy is inevitable, and I don't because I'm scared. I'm scared that I'll do it wrong, and I'm scared that he won't like the way I kiss, even though I don't even have a way of kissing yet. I grab another Sears catalogue for another mailbox.

The fresh air on my face is rejuvenating. I didn't eat breakfast, but I have Susan.

When I arrive at school and get to my locker, my heart stops.

Two naked Barbie dolls dangle from my locker door handle. They are tied together and hang by their necks. KILL THE DYKES is written in black across the top of my locker and ketchup is splattered everywhere. It drips, along with my self-esteem, onto the floor. I look around and, like the weirdos who wait for the eyeballs to pop out of the guy getting zapped in the electric chair, everyone watches in eager anticipation of my suffering.

I turn and walk away. Janitor Stan will clean up the mess, and then this will have never happened. Naked Barbie dolls. It's absurd. Barbie doesn't do naked; everybody knows that Barbie is all about the clothes. And why, why, why is it me who everyone tortures? What makes it okay to threaten me with ... *death*? I touch the rainbow bead that's around my wrist. I cling to the power of its obscure reassurance. The boy in the letter B baseball hat has probably already been scouted by the Boston Red Sox and because I'll be his fiancée, I'll be on the *Baseball Wives* reality series and because he's the youngest player on the team, we will be the most famous couple on the show. And even though all the other wives wear diamond bracelets, I won't let fame change me — I'll still wear my rainbow bead bracelet. In the meantime, I have to go to French. I have to suck it up, armor myself against them and pretend that I don't care.

"Aggie, do you want to have lunch with me?"

It's Joanie.

"Yeah, um, sure. That'd be great."

"Okay, I'll meet you in the caf. It's lasagna day. Do you like lasagna?"

"Yeah, but I don't have any money."

"Don't worry about it," she says. "See you at lunch."

I'm sure she's reaching out to me because she knows what pain is. I wonder what Susan is doing for lunch. I bet her locker was also trashed. I walk into class, and Myhell, who was at the library last night, announces my arrival.

"Bonjour, Barbie!" No one laughs this time, and because the teacher, Madame Clous, is bilingually oblivious, I say, "Aren't you a little too old to be playing with dolls?" Myhell doesn't have a comeback, and a hint of mortification crosses her face. Maybe I should say things aloud more often. Or maybe I should just keep my mouth shut. *Je ne sais pas* about that, but what I do know is that insulting Myhell doesn't make me feel any better.

Class is typically dismal. The bell rings and Myhell tosses a piece of paper onto my desk. In bold pink, she's written the misspelled French words, *Vous êtes mort*, which in English, is meant to say, *you're dead*. The fact that because we're in French class she thought she needed to write me a threatening note *in French*, strikes me as hilarious and I have to laugh. If we were in art class would she have finger-painted the note? If we were in math I'm sure her head would have exploded.

"What's funny?" It's Carson, and again, he actually seems kind of attractive. Maybe it's because I'm sitting and he's standing, and we're at eye-level.

"It's this note that Michelle gave me. It says I'm dead, but she's written it in French."

"Why?"

"Why? I guess, well, I guess because she's not *très intelligent*, that's why."

"So, have you thought any more about, well, you know." A deep shade of crimson floods Carson's face.

"Oh! Right! As a matter of fact, Carson, I have, and I think it's a good idea."

"You do?" His voice hits a high note.

"Yes, I do."

"Great. We should get together. Soon." He moves in closer to me.

"I actually wanted to ask you something. My friend Susan and I have started this sort of club, and we're wondering if you want to join."

"A club? What club?"

"You know, it's kinda hard to explain right now, but we're going to meet at the library tonight, around seven. Can you be there?"

"Unlikely. My mom has this thing about me going outside at night. She's so weird about it. She thinks that the dark stunts my growth. Like I'm an underachieving mushroom."

"Oh. Well it'd be cool if you could make it. Tell your mom that the lights in the library are really bright."

The next class files into the room, which means that Carson and I are late for our own classes.

"Okay. Maybe." He runs out, and I walk. Yale comes in, sees me, and looks away. I guess he's a little homophobic or something. Disappointing? Yes. Surprising? No.

"Miss Murphy, can you come with me to the office, please?"

Oh great, it's the Prince of Vice and, like a recently scolded puppy that's just peed on the rug rather than the designated newspaper, I follow him. We don't speak. He opens the door to his office and sits behind his I'm-really-super-important desk.

"Sit." He says and points at the chair.

I sit and wait for my treat. He lifts his more-Thermos-than-mug coffee mug to his face and stares over it at me, like he's trying to figure out if I'm actually an alien. I don't know if I'm supposed to be saying something here, so I just wait and will myself to disappear into the hole in my sweats, teleporting myself into my bedroom closet. I start to count: *1-2-3-4-* ...

"We had a call from your mother this morning."

What? Really? She got up off the floor? And *5-6-7-8* ...

"She wants to withdraw you from school. According to her, you are over-stressed with all the homework assignments you are expected to do at the library. She believes that the school has unreasonable expectations because you do not have a home computer and the other students have an unfair advantage." I say nothing. "Also, according to her, someone at the school is demonstrating inappropriate behavior towards you — a boy. He calls the house at unreasonable hours? Demanding to talk to you?" With notable urgency, he guzzles his coffee, like it's keeping him alive. "I have spoken to the school counsellor, Miss Strand, and she believes that home-schooling might be the best choice for you, and because we do not tolerate any form of student harassment, I need the name of that boy." He picks up a pen.

"Do you mind if I have a cup of coffee? With milk and lots of sugar? Is that okay? Are students allowed to drink coffee?" I ask.

His neck stretches and turns like an inquisitive ostrich. I don't want coffee, I just want him to do something for me. That's his job, right? To do *something* for me?

"Normally we don't give coffee to students."

"Yeah, I know, but obviously I'm not normal." He walks over to the coffee pot and pours me a cup, adds sugar and a white powder, and actually stirs it. He plunks it in front of me. "Thanks." I stand and take exactly four steps to the door. "You can't make me leave school, and coffee is bad for kids."

I don't bother getting a late pass from the secretary.

I want to send Susan a note to ask her about her locker, but the class is watching a video about Anne Boleyn and chopping off people's heads. I wish someone would chop off my head. Susan takes off as soon as the bell rings.

THE CAFETERIA IS chaos, wet-feet smelly, and filled with kids who get money from their parents *every* day to buy whatever they want, like fries with gravy. Unlike my enviable lunch: a hardboiled egg rolled up in a plastic grocery bag. I suck and my lunch stinks, but I have to eat the egg, it's what poor people do. We eat inappropriate food in inappropriate places. We bring homemade snacks to the movie theatre and public pools, like rice cakes with peanut butter in a Ziploc bag. I scan the masses. A few of Those Girls attempt to carve me open with sharp stares; my terror intensifies and my legs weaken under the sheer weight of it. Their hatred pushes me forward. An Idiot Boy stands in my way and says, "I bet you'd smell better if you took off your clothes."

I step around him. "What, you don't like me?"

"Aggie!" I look around. "Aggie! Over here!" It's Joanie, waving to me from the stairs, a.k.a., the Dead Zone where the Official Freak population hangs out. I hope I fit in.

"I got you that lasagna. And there's garlic bread, too."

It's like, amazing. *And there's garlic bread, too.* Joanie hands me a tray with real actual food on it. I want to save it because if I eat it, it'll be gone and all I'll have left is an egg.

"Go ahead, eat!"

Pummeling the noodles and cheese, I ruthlessly bend the plastic fork into the crispy crust. A small puff of steam escapes as I cut the first bite. It tastes so good that I could be on death row, eating my last meal before they inject me with a lethal dose of liquid life-sucker. I finish the lasagna in 35.4 seconds and soak up the remaining sauce on the soggy paper plate with the last crumb of garlic bread. Had I been alone, I would have licked that plate.

"It's good, hey?" Joanie smiles at me and for a whole minute I forget that I'm thoroughly despised by almost everyone.

"It's *really* good. Is the food here always this good?"

"Most of the time. I like Sloppy Joe Wednesday."

"There's a Sloppy Joe Wednesday?" The things I don't know. I might as well be living on the moon; I'm not an active participant in earthly traditions.

"So, Rat's having a party this weekend. The 'rents are in Colorado for one of those couples' sweat lodge detox retreats. It's a Halloween party, but nobody ever dresses up or anything. There's always tons to drink and stuff because Rat never gets ID'ed."

I guess "Rat" is the freak equivalent of "Hamster."

"Who's Rat?"

She points to a Torture Chamber *man* wearing a long black over-coat. A ton of heavy black eyeliner contrasts against his candle-white skin. What appears to be a shrunken head hangs from a rope around his neck and a thick metal hook violently pierces his left eyebrow.

"Oh. Maybe …"

"Will your parents care?"

"Um. It depends."

"On what?"

"It depends on how drunk my mom gets after dinner." There. I said it. I said something out loud that nobody knows. Being with Joanie makes me brave and less afraid of who I am.

"Yeah, no kidding. My mom wouldn't miss me, either. I'll come and get you, like at around ten. Where do you live?"

"I don't know if I can make it — I might be doing something already. Look, thanks for lunch, I have to go. I'll pay you back."

"It's no problem. You don't need to. Tell me later in Art if you decide about the party. And if you want to just show up, that's cool, too. Rat's house is the one right beside the abandoned fire hall. And don't worry about going home, most of us just end up sleeping in the yard."

"Yeah, for sure."

I want to run. They sleep in the yard. Like zombies. I want to find Susan. I want to apologize to her for the collateral damage that comes with being my friend. I'm going to stick a note in her locker to ask her meet me at the library after school.

I find the girls washroom and spew the lasagna and garlic bread into the toilet. I hate myself for this. My brain doesn't want to barf, but my body does.

"Goodbye, lasagna, you were good to me." I exit the stall and Nicole stands over one of the sinks, blotting her left armpit with a huge wad of paper towels. This is the girl who Susan wants to invite into our club. Coincidence? I think not.

"You're Nicole, right?" She doesn't look at me. "Is your name Nicole?" Nicole turns away and flings the paper towel pile into the garbage and quickly leaves, forgetting her really pretty white beaded fringe purse on the shelf. I guess she doesn't want to talk to someone who talks to toilets.

I wash my hands and accidentally look at myself in the mirror. Small chunks of noodle and meat cling to several sections of the longer side of my hair. If I had anything left in my stomach the sight of myself would make me hurl. I want to be back at The Dump. I attempt to wash the ends of my hair, but the bits that come off remain in the sink on top of the screened drain. I have to use my hand to remove them. I make a mental note: *never eat lasagna again.*

"I pushed the stupid bitch so hard that she actually broke her arm!"

It's them. Myhell, Bevy, and Chrissy Crop Top. I hold a bit of noodle in my hand. How appropriate that I would die this way: gross, alone, and smelling of barf. Myhell comes toward me, frog-legs her arms to shove me, but at the last moment she notices the vomit. It acts as a force field, a protective covering.

"Ewwww! She smells like puke!"

"Look! There's puke in her hair!" Crop Top holds up her pink bejeweled phone and yells, "Smile!"

I cower, hide my face in my hands and crouch flat against the tile wall.

"Video her!" Myhell says.

Crop Top starts her narration, "And here she is, looking as charming as ever, Miss Vomit U.S.A."

"Film the sink!"

"And this, folks, is the legacy of Puke Girl!"

"Get a close-up of her hair!"

I ready myself for a Jimmy Choo to the head.

"Take her purse!" Bevy grabs Nicole's purse off the shelf. "Dump it!"

And then suddenly, the Joanie voice comes. The voice that defends the weak, stands up for the powerless, and protects the sisterhood of Loserdom.

"Don't touch that!"

"Don't tell me what to do, chunk-face." Bevy dumps Nicole's purse and three things fall out: a stick of prescription antiperspirant, a maxi pad, and a book.

"Look! She uses deodorant on her pads!" It occurs to me that maybe Nicole *does* put antiperspirant on a pad and then sticks it to the inside of her shirt.

"You think a little deodorant is going to make you smell any less putrid down there? Not likely, skank!"

The door opens and we all look to see a frantic one-arm-drenched Nicole. She says nothing.

"Give me back my purse!" I say.

"You want your purse? How cute, little fugly slut wants her purse." Bevy approaches me and whacks me across my head with the purse, full force. My ear immediately rings. "Happy now?" She says in a deceptively precious princess voice. She walks into one of the stalls.

Sploosh

She flushes. "It's all yours. C'mon you guys, let's get away from this mutant reunion." They simultaneously check their hair in the mirror and walk victoriously out the door. So beautiful.

"Are you okay?" Nicole bends down to my level. "That was nice of you — what you did — not telling them it's my purse."

"Oh. Well, the funny thing is, I'd never own a purse that cute."

"Yeah, it's okay, my mom bought it for my birthday. She got it from *La Belle Château* so I sort of *have* to like it. Are you sick or something?"

La Belle Château! I forgot to take my gift certificate out of my math notebook.

"I was, but I'm done. You'd better go see if your purse is still there."

Nicole checks the stall.

"Yup, it's in there."

"Aren't you going to take it out?" Nicole looks at me and slowly shakes her head.

Maybe Nicole is a bit of a germaphobe. Myself, on the other hand, well, let's just say this sort of thing to me is mild.

"I'll get it for you." I look in the stall and it's floating, half in, half out of the bowl. I pull on it, the water splurts, the purse drips, a limp octopus out of the sea.

"Here you go." I offer her the offensive wet creature. She backs away.

"I ... don't ... I don't need it anymore. You can keep it if you want."

"But it was your birthday present."

"I don't care. It's not really my style. White leather reminds me of cheerleaders. Why were you asking me my name earlier?"

"Oh! You know Susan Williamson? Well she's my friend, too, and we're starting up this club, and ..."

"You're starting a club? Can I join? When do you meet?"

"Our first meeting is tonight at the library at seven."

"Who else is in the club?"

"Just us right now, but I've asked Carson Turndale, and we're going to ask Travis Tarkington."

"Carson Turndale?"

"You know him?" Nicole stares at the floor. "Not really. Well, we sort of kissed."

"You ... kissed?"

"Yeah, well, he kind of really wanted to, it was his birthday and I kinda felt sorry for him, and then I let him kiss me, and now he pretends that I don't exist."

"That's stupid."

"I think he's afraid of girls. I mean, he's only four feet tall. I'm afraid of girls and I'm a five foot seven. How tall are you?"

"I don't know."

"You don't know how tall you are?"

"No." I say a little defensively, like knowing how tall you are *doesn't* matter.

"Here, stand with your back against mine." We go to the mirror, but I don't look at us. "Hey! You're taller than me! I wish everyone was taller than me."

"Really?'

"Yeah. If I was shorter than everyone, no one would be able to see my armpits."

"Oh. Is that important?"

"Obviously it's important. If I had two normal armpits, maybe people wouldn't be so mean."

"But not everyone is mean."

"No. Not exactly everyone. But the people who ridicule me do it with such merciless efficiency that it feels like a lot of people." The bell rings. Lunch is over.

"So, tonight, okay, at the library, seven o'clock," I say.

"Maybe." Nicole picks up her pad and her antiperspirant and leaves the bathroom without her book: *Magic Spells for Teens*. I bend the purse in half so that it fits into my backpack, and open Nicole's book to a dog-eared page that's titled "Potions to Alleviate Physical Dysfunctions." Maybe there's a potion in here for me. I go to the index and look for "Potions to Alleviate Almost Everything."

12

I have to kinda run to make it on time to my next class, a double block of Art. I can't believe that I forgot about my *La Belle Château* gift certificate. I slide into my chair unnoticed. The teacher, Miss Ounet (no one knows how to pronounce her name, so we all call her Miss O — even other teachers), demonstrates the proper technique of papier-mâché. Our assignment is to create a sculpture of something that is important to us. Jay-Rome, the boy who sits at my table, says, "I'm gonna make a big pair of girl's boobs."

The things that are important to me can't be made out of papier-mâché. Miss O drones on, "… ensuring that you don't make your flour and water glue mixture too runny …"

Miss O is extremely particular about "proper listening skills." It's part of our overall mark. There's no way I can root through my backpack until she's finished her demo.

"… carefully placing each strip of newspaper onto the wire form …" It seems crude and messy and it reminds me of The Dump, and for some reason I can't breathe and Jay-Rome must have noticed because he discreetly unpacks his lunch and hands me the paper bag.

He whispers instructions, "Place the bag over your nose and mouth and breathe in, slowly and deeply."

Seriously?

"Trust me. You're having a panic attack. I get 'em all the time."

"… and wipe off any excess liquid …"

I place the bag over my mouth and nose and breathe in. The scent of warm salami fills my lungs, and I don't know what's worse, not being able to breathe, or breathing this.

"… and finally, allow your structure to dry overnight. Does anyone have any questions?" No one ever has any questions. We all know that asking a question exposes to everyone what a complete idiot you are.

"Good, then let's get creative."

I remove the bag from my face and hand it back to Jay-Rome, who is eating a salami sandwich.

"Keep it." He mumbles.

Wow. A plate of lasagna, a white squid purse, and a paper bag. The day is mine.

I find my math notebook and flip through the pages, waiting to gaze upon the *La Belle Château* gift certificate. I keep flipping, but find nothing. I turn a single page at a time, still nothing. Just to be sure, I rip out each page and my worst fear becomes real: I've lost my gift certificate! But how! Where? Think. Think. Think. When was the last time I saw it. In the library? I put it in my notebook, which I put in my backpack, and then we were locked out, and then I wrote a note to the librarian! It must have fallen out of my notebook and onto the street.

"You're supposed to use the *newspaper* provided, not your notebook. Proper papier-mâché is done with a *newspaper* medium. If you use anything but *newspaper*, I can't accept your project."

I look up and realize that Miss O is talking to me. My math notebook is torn apart, my gift certificate is gone, and I live with an alcoholic basket case. Proper papier-mâché?

I grab a piece of wire and twist and bend and wind it into a large

curve. Recklessly, I mix the water and flour and cover the wire structure with the ripped pages of my math notebook. How improper
of me! I frantically rip strips of *newspaper* until the pile in front of
me is so huge that I've created a sort of fortress around myself like
a hyperactive gerbil. I dip the strips into the wet mixture and wrap
the *newspaper* around the arched wire, and I start to hum. I hum so
loudly that Jay-Rome mouths *shut up* to me, but I ignore him because
I'm Dorothy, right before the big twister hits and Toto and I are
running away. I'd sing, but that would attract too much attention
from the evil flying monkeys, the ones we don't know about yet. I
keep humming and wrapping and splattering glue and when I can't
do any more without letting the thing dry, I stop. I stand back to
admire it: a dripping and starkly colorless newborn rainbow.

"What is it?" Jay-Rome scrutinizes my work.

Accessing my brain for a word that I learned from *Reader's Digest*,
I answer, "It's an *enigma*."

He pretends to know what that means,

"Oh. Yeah. Cool."

I carry my baby to the shelves by the window. I don't want to leave
it. I want to stay and protect it, to watch over it, to make sure no
one *accidentally* throws it out the window. School is over and I
should be running to the library. There are a few plants in containers
on the window sill, each marked with a tiny chalk board sign: *Cherry
Tomatoes, Kale, Beets.*

"I've got to lock up, Agatha. Time to go home." It's Miss O and
up close her face is a thick palette of artificial reds, blues, and greens.

"Miss O, can you teach me how to grow vegetables?"

"What? Oh those. I thought I could use those for still lifes. The
colors. But apparently I have a colorless thumb. They're destined for
the compost, I'm afraid."

"Can I have them?"

"Sure, if you think you'll have better luck."

I'VE LOST COUNT of the cracks in the sidewalk on the way to the library. I'm too busy playing What If. What If Susan never talks to me again? What If I've had my last friend hug? What If my camcorder is gone? And finally, What If I don't find my gift certificate?

Is anything real?

"Aggie!" I hear Susan's voice. I look to see her behind me, she breaks into a fast joggle, I meet her halfway and she wraps her arms around me. OK this is real.

"Oh my God, Susan, I didn't think you were ever going to talk to me again after what they did to my locker. Did they do anything to your locker?"

"Ha! So stupid."

"What?"

"You are *not* going to believe this. They took a thong, *A tiny black lacy THONG*, and they strung it on the outside of my locker and wrote PLEASE RETURN TO FAGGIE. The only good part is that people might actually think that that tiny thong belongs to me. I was tempted to leave it there."

"Faggie? I guess that means me."

"I guess that means you." Susan notes my distress. "What's wrong?"

"I don't like that name. It's so brutal. I hope Joanie didn't see it."

"Aggie — forget it. You're better than some lame-o nickname. Sticks and stones, remember?" Susan sucks in a gigantic breath and screams, "Pork and Beans!"

We burst out laughing and the outrageous momentum of pent-up despair-soaked happiness continues each time we try to stop, and I don't know if my face hurts from the laughing or the lingering sting of the purse. Susan somehow manages enough restraint to bring us back to our mission, "C'mon, let's get your camera."

We tiptoe-rush to the front desk. A different librarian from the one last night sits behind a computer, adjusting a neon orange bra strap, an outline of lace shows under a loosely buttoned pale pink sweater. We've come to the library during Singles Reading Afternoon, a fundraising concept that's by donation, and obviously it's wildly successful; the library is packed with people dressed in club clothes.

"Excuse me, um, we left a note in the bin last night about a camera?"

The librarian raises a thinly penciled eyebrow, double-checks her un-library-like cleavage, and says, "A note?"

"Could you look in the Lost and Found for us, please?"

Butt-first, she twists up and swaggers to the back. And then I hear it — the unmistakable humming of a show tune. I don't want to turn around. If she sees me, we'll both panic. I whisper to Susan.

"Susan, my mother's here. I have to go." I bolt for the door. Outside, I hide behind the FREE BOOKS TO GOOD HOME bin, find Jay-Rome's paper bag, and put it up against my nose. Is Jane looking for a man? She can't be. She hates them. The thought of Jane with a man is just gross.

I rummage through the bin: *Dogs Are People Too*, *Getting the Job You've Always Wanted*, *How to Lose Those Last Ten Pounds*, *The First Nine Months*, *Understanding Shakespeare's Tragic Characters*, and a Sears Christmas catalogue. I take every one of them but the catalogue and stuff them into the bottom of my pack, carefully replacing Miss O's plants on top. Someday I'll be looking for a good job that will give me maternity leave and while I'm pregnant I'll be so bored that I'll read Shakespeare's plays. After the baby comes, I'm sure I'll need to lose those last ten pounds, and my husband, a.k.a., the boy in the letter B baseball hat, will definitely want to give our kid a puppy. It's as though these books were selected for me personally and it's such a coincidence that it's almost *weird*.

"Got it!" Like she's trying to prevent someone from reaching it, Susan holds the video camera over her head. "And I saw your mom, she was filling her purse with crackers and cut-up vegetables."

"That's funny."

"It is?"

"Yeah — that's exactly what we had *last* Thursday for dinner.

"It's too bad she doesn't get you guys some cheese."

"Susan, there's no way anybody would want to eat cheese that's been at the bottom of my mother's purse. Look, I have to go to the alley where we opened my notebook. I think my *La Belle Château* gift certificate fell out when I wrote that note."

"Oh, crap, really?" Susan's voice carries the sincerity of her disappointment. She's a good friend and I want to tell her that, but I don't.

We're in the note-writing spot, and there's nothing. No gift certificate, no discarded fast-food wrappers, no empty pop cans. The street is immaculate.

"I'm sorry, Aggie. I wish I could buy you a dress."

"I know, Susan. Forget about it. I'm going home."

"Will you still come out tonight?

"I don't know. Maybe."

"But you're the club leader."

"Maybe."

I walk to The Dump and remove Miss O's plants from my pack and place them beside the Mexican donkey and baby Jesus ceramic figurines on our kitchen window. I lie down in my dark closet. I close my eyes and imagine nothing because my whole life is colorless, not just my thumb.

13

"**A**ggie, come and eat!"

I must've fallen asleep. I count to eleven and drag myself out of my closet because if I don't come out, Jane will be Jane. She's cleared a small area on the table where two paper plates sit. A cracked plastic poinsettia platter that she found in someone's garbage last January holds a stack of crackers and cut-up vegetables.

"No cheese?" I ask.

"Cheese? We don't need cheese. Cheese is fattening. These are good vegetables. Try the radishes."

I'm like one of those hungry-faced kids pictured in the black-and-white footage of a Torture Chamber social studies video about the Great Depression. Just looking at this dinner causes me great depression.

"Did you talk to the vice-principal today?" Cracker crumbs landslide from her mouth onto the paper plate.

"No. Why?" I say.

"Well, that's disappointing. I let him know in no uncertain terms that I plan to take you out of that hoity-toity school. I'll call him again tomorrow."

"Please don't. I don't want to leave school." Actually, I want to leave The Torture Chamber more than anything, but if the choice is to stay in purgatory with Jane, or stay in purgatory with friends, I choose the purgatory that comes with friends.

"Fine, Aggie, but if those teachers don't stop giving you so much homework, I'm going to pursue it."

Great. Now I need a new excuse to go to the public library.

"Yeah, good idea. Um, Mom, tonight I'm going to meet Susan at the library and we're going to go through the teen magazines, and maybe play some games on the computers and stuff for fun."

"Oh … I don't know about that."

"And then I was thinking that tomorrow, if you're not busy, we could have our own Games Night here. Spend some time together."

"Oh, that's super! I'll set up the games while you're out." She crunches a radish and chews it with her face all scrunched up. "Which games were you thinking?"

"You know Mom, why don't you pick."

"Okay! This is going to be *so much fun*!"

Oh yeah, *so* much fun. Ranks right up there with square-dancing.

"Clear the table and I'll start looking out the games."

I take what's left of the veggies (celery), and put it in the fridge with the other green things. I lift my plate and there's a dirty, folded piece of paper underneath it. My name is scribbled in pencil on the outside. It's obviously something Jane wants me to find, probably another list of new words she's copied out of a *Reader's Digest*. I unfold the paper and read the familiar script. *Buy something beautiful, just like you.*

"MOM! Where did you get this?"

"Isn't it great! I want you to have it! I found it on one of my regular scavenger hunt routes. I'm always amazed at what perfectly good stuff people just casually discard. I also found a Thermos. There weren't any *Reader's Digests* or free books. I did get this Sears Christmas catalogue that we should look through. You can make a list of the things you want."

"Oh my God! Thanks, Mom!" I go to hug her, and she freezes. Like she's guarding the king, her arms hang straight, her legs stiffen.

"Good. That's enough." She pulls away. "I have to find those games."

"I love it, Mom. Thanks."

"Okay. Already. Right? Don't make a big deal about it. There's people out there who have nothing. It can all be taken away from you, Aggie. At any moment. Everything can be taken away. Don't fool yourself into thinking that you have control over anything, because you don't."

I HEAD TO the library. Again. Not that it's my favorite place in the world or anything, it's just that I don't have a ton of choices. Tomorrow is garbage day and everyone except Jane and I have their garbage cans neatly placed outside their driveways. Sometimes normal people put bigger items beside their garbage cans. I like to check out everyone's stuff to see if there's anything awesome. One time I found a birdcage and Jane was so excited that the next day she somehow caught a bird from our backyard and stuck it in the cage. Five days later, the bird was dead. Apparently, birds can't survive on Fruit Loops. Jane insisted that it died because it wasn't used to living in such a palace.

There's something shiny, leaning up against a garbage tub across the street. I cross the street like I need to.

"Yes!"

It's a worn-out, slightly crooked, perfectly scootable scooter. I've always wanted a scooter, or *I used to* always want a scooter; it would have been super cool had I found this scooter four years ago. I check to make sure no one is taking my picture. I remove the scooter from its spot, and take it for a test drive. It's a little squabbly, and rusty, but other than that, and the remnants of half-peeled Hello Kitty stickers on it, it's fantastic. I don't care that it's kind of stupid; all I care about is that from now on, I don't have to walk, run, or spend money I don't have on bus fare, to get somewhere. I scoot myself to the library, and there's one thing I know for sure as the wind whips around my face: I love garbage day.

Nonchalantly, I wheel my scooter into the library, but the ever-vigilant librarian shoos me out. I hide it in the shrubberies that line the walkway.

"Hi, Aggie." It's Nicole. "So, is anyone else here?" She looks around.

"Nope. But we meet in the back where there's a long table and an electrical outlet."

"Why the outlet?"

"We need it to view the daily footage."

"Oh, right. Um. I'm useless at electronics. I should probably leave."

"Trust me. You'll be fine. And we only film certain things."

"What things?"

"Well, you know how people are mean to you, because, well, because they're just mean?"

"Yeah ..."

"Well people are mean to me, too. And Susan. And Carson and Travis. We decided that *documenting* the meanness is our way to fight back."

"They let you *video* them?"

"Not exactly. It's kind of *covert*. They don't actually know they're being filmed."

Nicole thinks about this for exactly one split second, "I love it! We have a video camera at home — I bet I could get it without my parents even knowing."

"Really?"

"Yeah, they stopped using it a few years ago when I developed my problem. It makes them mad at each other because I'm not trying hard enough to be normal. I am trying, though. I've got a few new potions that I'm working on."

"Oh. Hmph." I should say something supportive to Nicole, but she kissed Carson and that really bugs me for some reason.

"Hey!" It's Travis. He's wearing a suit.

"Hi, Travis."

"I brought supplies." He pats his NASA backpack.

"Ah, we're just waiting for Susan, and maybe Carson. Susan's kind of our official spokesperson."

"Okay, I'll get set up." Travis sits down and empties his backpack. He's brought a graphing calculator, a GPS, a box of waterproof matches, a satchel of dehydrated soup, and a pack of reinforced-toe panty hose. Beige. Maybe inviting him into the club wasn't the best idea. Nicole fidgets with her hair.

"Hi, everyone!" It's Susan. "Sorry I'm late. My mom wanted me to do a hundred sit-ups before I left the house, so I did three, lay on the floor for ten minutes, and left. So, hi, Nicole, hi, Travis. No Carson?"

"Nope, not yet," I say.

"Well, whatever, let's get started, anyway. First of all, I'd like to just say how cool it is that you are all here tonight."

Nicole raises her hand, the one attached to the un-sweaty armpit, "My parents have a video camera."

"That's awesome, Nicole. And really, you don't have to raise your hand if you want to say something. Really. Please, don't."

"What do we need video cameras for?"

"Oh, right. Sorry, Travis, well …"

"It's a video club!" Nicole is super excited. The sweat stain starts from the inside of the top her sleeve and Niagara Falls down to where her shirt is tucked in at the waist.

"A video club? I thought it was a survival club. That's what you told me, Susan, you said it was a school survival club."

"Yeah, but I didn't get into the details. It's a school survival club for those of us who are victims."

"Victims? Victims of what?" Travis scans the area, likely preparing himself against an attack by rogue librarian rebels.

Susan clears her throat and begins her oration. "Victims of everyday school brutality. Victims of the ugly reality that fear transforms cowards into mean people. Victims of the truth that lies hidden behind the malicious acts of every bully. The truth that mean people are actually total wimps who need to be cruel to others in order to fill a void and bolster their precarious power and insecure existence." Susan takes a breath. "Any questions?"

"I have a question." It's Carson. He's standing behind a short shelf and even though he's wearing a neon orange construction worker's vest, we didn't notice him. Nicole stares at the floor.

"Carson! You're here!"

"Yeah. Do you guys want to come over to my house? My mom said that if I was going to join a club, it had to meet at our house. Would that be okay?"

"Really?" I say. Even though meeting at Carson's house runs the risk of Jane finding out and randomly visiting Carson's mom to ask her for a background check to ensure that she's not an escaped convict from the local women's prison, it's perfect. *And* it'll be nice to get out of the library.

"Yeah, my mom is afraid that when I leave the house I'll be run over by a dump truck like a lost dog. She's waiting in the car."

"Now?"

Susan shrugs. Carson nods. We all look at each other.

Travis packs up and says, "I'm fine with it."

"Okay! Let's go!" I say. Carson's mom makes cupcakes, and, unlike The Dump, you don't have to maneuver through a thin and hazardous path in the hallway to use the bathroom.

We climb into Carson's mom's car. The clean smell is intoxicating.

Now I *definitely* want to kiss Carson … is that shallow? To want to kiss someone *more* because they have a clean car? And yes, the "incident" with Nicole is a little bothersome, but it's not as though they're full-on hanging out or anything. But if we do end up kissing, does that mean that I've been unfaithful to the boy in the Letter B baseball hat?

We stop outside the gate. Carson's mom pushes some buttons and again, the gate opens slowly, allowing us enough time to appreciate the moment. I feel like a rock star. A rock star who's forgotten her new scooter in the library shrubs!

"So you kids can stay until nine o'clock. That's when Carson has to get ready for bed."

I wonder if he has fire trucks on his pajamas. How am I supposed to make out with a guy who has an earlier bedtime than most five-year-olds? Official Romantic Scale Level: 0.

The downstairs of Carson's house is a miniature amusement park. There's a big screen TV room with little La-Z-Boy movie seats, a custom-made pool table with legs low to the ground, a crane-powered carnival candy machine that any one of us except Carson would have to get down on their knees to operate. There's even a minibar with a micro fridge. A white neon sign announces ROOT-BEER ON TAP and I wouldn't be surprised to see Sneezy, Dopey, and Doc sitting on the short bar stools.

Susan is the first to speak. "Wow, Carson, this is amazing."

"It's okay."

Travis goes to the pool table and starts setting up the balls to execute some sort of physics experiment, Susan can't take her eyes off the candy machine, and Nicole sweats. We only have an hour left for our club meeting, so I attempt to break through the collective dazzled trance.

"Hey, guys! Remember why we're here! We gotta figure out our strategy. Who gets the video cameras when, and what group of people we're going to focus on, and on what days."

"We're videoing *people*?" Carson is visibly confused.

"Yes, the people at school who are mean to us. We're secretly filming them when they're mean to us, and when we have enough footage, we're going to somehow show it at school. Maybe during a drama production or something, and then they won't be mean to us anymore. We are the Warriors Video Club."

Carson speaks quietly,

"I don't know …"

"Yeah I wasn't sure at first, either." Susan stares at the candy crane. "How do you work this thing?"

"I'll bring my video camera to school tomorrow." Nicole is committed. "How exactly do we film them without them knowing?"

"It's not as complicated as it sounds." Susan pries her eyes away from the sweet magnet and opens the embroidered sack she uses to carry her schoolbooks in and brings out her lunch bag, to which she has made a few alterations. "Observe." She unzips the top, and there sits my video camera. A Velcro flap is affixed to the side, and a small opening is the viewpoint of the lens. Her hands move as a magician's, as she opens and closes the flap a few times to demonstrate. "All I have to do is press the button, and *voilà*! It's recording!" We stand over the lunch bag in collective awe, admiring its clever components.

We don't hear her come in.

"What kind of club is this?" It's Carson's mother. She holds a tray of cold drinks and warm brownies. A red-polka-dotted apron that has strawberry-shaped pockets and a red-and-white striped ruffled hem is tied around her waist. Is this what a mom is?

"It's a videography club, Mrs. Turndale. We all have a vested interest in the documentation of the world around us and all its many wonders." Travis is surprisingly adept at talking in a parent-pleasing manner. I think it's the suit.

"That's a very appropriate club for you, Carson. I'm guessing there's nothing athletic? I'll ask Dad to pick up a video camera for you tomorrow. Enjoy your snack and Mr. Turndale will drive every-one home in twenty minutes." She disappears up the staircase. Drive us home? Who *are* these people?

"I don't have a lunch bag. Or a purse. But I *guess* I can *try* to figure out how to hide my camera," Nicole says.

Travis stands, adjusts his tie, and says, "Nicole, leave it to me. I'll design something for you and it'll be ready in the morning. Bring your camera to school, fully charged with an empty memory card." I guess inviting him into the club was a good idea after all, even with the panty hose.

"What about my camera?" Carson is the only one of us who doesn't eat a brownie.

"We'll think of something, Carson, but I'll work on Nicole's first. I also think we should upload daily. Aggie, we'll let you do that."

"Ah. We don't actually have a computer." The looks on their faces indicate their disbelief. Not having a computer is like not having indoor plumbing.

"Yeah, right! But seriously, if you upload and save at the end of every day, we're always prepared to edit and then acquire more foot-age the following day."

"Um, well, that sounds like a good plan Travis, but, like I said, I don't have a computer."

"Oh."

A long pause emphasizes the shockingly sad depth of what it means to not have a computer.

"I'll do it. And Aggie's camera is a little more complicated 'cause it uses tapes, not a memory card. But not that complicated." Carson says and looks over to a small room just on the other side of the pool table.

"Do you keep your computer in there, Carson?" Travis's eyes light up like someone just plugged him in.

"Uh-huh. You wanna see?"

Carson opens the door and Travis screams out something that I never thought I'd hear coming from him, "Dude!"

Unsurprisingly, Carson's computer is the most state-of-the-art-brand-new-top-of-the-line-world's-most-expensive piece of equipment that any of us has ever seen, and it sits, low to the ground, along with two kiddie chairs: Mr. Roaring Lion and Manic Zebra.

"I think you should be in charge of all the uploading and editing, Carson," Susan manages to say between bites of brownie number three.

"Okay, kids, it's time to go home!" Mrs. Turndale calls down the stairs.

Everyone grabs their stuff and heads up. I stop and pick up a few of the cups to take to Carson's kitchen. Carson waits for me on the top step.

"Is now a good time?"

"What?" I hold the cups in both hands. Carson leans in and kisses me, on the lips, slowly, like he's done this before.

"I wish I had *that* on tape." It's Susan. She saw the whole thing. She turns away and walks to the door where everyone waits.

"I ... cups," is all I manage.

"Oh, you didn't have to do that." Carson's mom says. Did *she* see the kiss, too? "And I want to invite all your mothers over for lunch. Make sure Carson has your phone numbers."

Carson looks at me, crosses his arms, and smiles. "See *you* tomorrow." Nicole notices the way he's looking at me and I feel like I've done something wrong, but at the same time, I feel extraordinary. Maybe that kiss is worthy of a Romantic Scale rating. It wasn't the worst thing in the world.

"Yup," I say.

The door closes behind me and Susan grabs my arm. I look at her and she's giving me the *what just happened in there?* gape. Carson's dad talks to Travis about why the electric car is not yet economically feasible. I'm dropped off first.

"Meet me at my locker before school," Susan insists.

"Okay. Thanks for the ride, Mr. Turndale."

There's something sitting in the middle of my driveway and it looks like a skinny dead dog. My heart sinks deep into my Converse when I get close enough to decipher what it is. It's my scooter and there's a sticky note attached to one of the handlebars, but it's too dark to read it so I walk to the street lamp:

I hope you can come to the dance.

The radiant hue of the street lamp shines on me like a spotlight. I leave the scooter in the driveway, because I don't know what to feel. It *seems* romantic, but it also seems a bit weird. I open the door to The Dump.

"Aren't you pretty? Yes, you are, you're so pretty." I know she's not talking to me.

I enter the living room, and I hear the slight mewing of a cat. For a second I think that I've totally lost it, but sure enough, there's a cat trapped in a plastic half-cracked cat carrying case. Jane is down on the floor. A hostage paw pokes through the little wire gate. The cat spies me and full-on-feral meows.

"Mom, what are you doing? Whose cat is that?"

"It's our cat, Agatha."

"Uh, we don't own a cat."

"We do now. It was lost, and I saved it. I saved it from the wild animals that roam the streets at night."

I peer at the poor thing. "Mom, it has a collar. It belongs to someone."

"Exactly. And whoever put that terrible contraption on her doesn't deserve to keep her."

"Mom, look ..." I get down onto the floor to read the dangly tin tag. "There's an identification number on here. And it says *Mr. Peanut.* We have to call the cat shelter."

"No. I won't abandon my duty to this defenseless animal!"

"Mom, remember what happened with that bird? Well, this is the same thing, and the bird didn't actually have an owner. An owner who is probably willing to offer us a *reward* for finding their cat."

"A reward?" Jane looks at me. A tiny light bulb switches on in her head.

"Yeah, a reward. A cat like this is probably worth at least fifty bucks."

Forty-eight seconds pass.

"Well, I guess if someone is willing to pay *fifty dollars* for Lady Gaga, then I guess that would make them deserving." Jane decides.

"Lady Gaga, Mom?"

"I thought it was a good name. Better than Mr. Peanut."

"Okaaay. We need to make posters and put them up around the neighborhood."

"You make a poster, and I'll get something for Lady G to eat."

I want to let the cat out, but I know that if I do it will get trapped in The Dump rubble and eventually starve to death like the rest of us. I look for some Sharpies to make a poster, but all we have is a box of broken wax crayons — the cheap kind that don't even work in the first place. A crumbled-up Pop-Tart sits on a plate that Jane carries from the kitchen. The last time I remember eating a Pop-Tart was in grade two. Seriously.

"Mom, I don't think cats like Pop-Tarts."

"Sure they do. I've seen them go crazy for them on TV." She places the dish outside the cage. Lady Gaga sniffs the tempting delicacy and retreats to the back of her cell.

"See! It's so special that she's saving it for later!" Jane has mastered the art of making sense of things that are so obviously wrong — a perk of being a total mental screw-up.

I finish the first poster. Jane examines it,

"You can't put our phone number on it."

"Why not?"

"Because, then people will *call*."

"Yeah, Mom, that's kinda the whole point."

"No. I don't want everyone knowing our phone number. It's a security risk."

"Then how are people going to get in touch with us to give us the fifty dollars?" I ask.

Jane thinks. "Put down my work number. I'm there almost every day."

Surprisingly, this is a good solution considering Jane's perpetually paranoid state of mind. I cross out our home phone number and add Spendapenny's phone number. Jane clears a spot on the floor beside the cage.

"Mom, what are you doing?"

"I'm going to sleep beside Lady Gaga."

"Why don't you just take Lady Gaga into your room?"

"Agatha! You've got to be kidding — that's unsanitary! You can't let a cat sleep in the same bed as you, you'll get a *disease*." She sets up her ratty blankets, a missing-its-stuffing couch pillow, her wind-up alarm clock, and the box of Pop-Tarts, "Just in case Gaga gets hungry in the middle of the night."

In my room I read over the note. I wish I knew more about boys and what is and isn't normal. If I were a princess and I accidentally left my horse somewhere and the prince returned it to me — that would be normal. I sneak outside, get my scooter, and bring it in the house.

14

"**H**ey, Corpse!"

It's Myhell, and she's wearing blue medical gloves like a forensic examiner. She is flanked by her entourage, who apparently, have done their hair especially for this occasion; they're all so *pretty*.

Susan has my video camera.

I face my locker and they stand behind me. If there were a bully alarm on the wall like those red fire alarms, I would pull it. Someone grabs my hair and jerks my head so hard that I drop my books. She doesn't let go.

Myhell speaks again, "I told you you're dead."

"Not exactly," I say.

"What's that? The douchebag speaks? You got somethin' to say before we kill you?"

"Well, technically, you said I was *mort*, remember?" Why, oh, why, do I get sassy in these situations?

"You know what I think? I think you need to shut your ugly decomposing mouth." And with that, she rams a tuna sandwich into my face, full on, and mushes it around. The tuna fills my nostrils and I can't breathe. She keeps the sandwich on my face. Two other girls hold on to my arms, making it impossible for me to fight back.

"You like that, hey? Tell me you like it and I'll let you go." How they expect me to speak is beyond comprehension.

"Come on, dyke, tell me how much you like cat food!"

Inaudible, muted, I attempt to mumble the word *no*.

"We can't hear you!" Someone kicks the side of my knee. I crumple, but whoever is holding my hair doesn't let go. It comes out in a large clump and I hear a muffled rip inside my head as it tears away from my scalp. I try to cry out, but incredibly, Myhell is still holding what's left of the sandwich on my mouth and nose. She gives the sandwich one final shove and full-force whacks me across the face with the back of her strange blue hand. I fall back and hit my head on the floor. I hear the *snap! snap!* of the gloves and they land by my cheek, I'm eye-level with their *really nice* shoes as they *clop-clop-clop* away.

My head feels as though it's been hit with a heavy club, but the cold floor is soothing. I touch the place where my hair used to be and my hand comes away covered in blood. So far, this has *not* been a good day. I make my way to my locker, open it, and on the shelf sits a demented group of happy faces smiling at me: Susan's lunch bag.

"Oh, my God." I say aloud. How did she get into my locker? I check the lunch bag, and sure enough, the camera is in there, and the power is ON. There's a note:

I had to go to Fat Camp this weekend, and my mother didn't tell me about it until right before school so I figured you should have the camera. I told her that I would go only if she took me to school first, to get my homework out of your locker. (Insert devious laugh here.) Have a fat-free weekend, and make sure you smile for the camera!

S.W.

P.S. I made sure the camera was on the exact right angle for the best view of you and Carson kissing. JK!

P.P.S. Destroy this note.

I'm bleeding and feel sick and I have tuna (at least I think it's tuna), in places where no one should ever have tuna, but Susan is a genius and, even though the Prince of Vice is always lurking, I go to the bathroom.

There's blood on my hoodie, my camo pants, and the small white plastic toe part of my Converse. I want to leave, but I'm not sure if Jane is at work. If I show up at The Dump looking like this, she'll definitely get me expelled from The Torture Chamber. I dab my head with the coarse brown paper towels in the dispenser, and it hurts. A lot.

The bathroom door opens and a shock of fear hits me. It's someone I don't recognize. She looks at me and immediately turns around and leaves. Great. Now *I'm* scaring people. I can feel a bruise forming on my left cheek, and I don't own any makeup to conceal it, so I'll have to tell people that it's part of my costume for the Hallowe'en dance tomorrow. I head to class.

The door to the Science room is locked. I glance in the window. The class must be writing a test. Awesome. I knock quietly, but Kraus doesn't look up from his desk. Maybe I really am dead, which might not be the worst thing in the world right now, because if I were dead, no one could hurt me. But I can't think about that right now because I won't be in The Torture Chamber forever. Maybe after I graduate people will no longer hurt me and I won't want to be dead. Maybe even tomorrow, I won't want to be dead. Maybe on my *dying breath*, I won't want to be dead.

I make my way to the cafeteria. Occasionally the kitchen ladies leave out free food that's only a hundred years past its best before date: weird stuff like plastic-wrapped maple walnut Danish with yellow string icing. I walk past the gym and a group of Gocks (girl jocks) are playing basketball and, even though they're all sweaty, they're clean and their gym clothes are substantially nicer than my regular clothes. I could rummage through the Lost and Found clothing bin in the hall, but that's risky — someone might recognize what I'm wearing as theirs, and then they'll make a big deal about getting it back. It would also provide Those Girls with another reason to embarrass me — no one wears other people's lost stuff and gets away with it. I sit on a bench at one of the long tables and, thankfully, the place is empty. I fold my arms in front of me and put my forehead down on top of them. I am even too sad and too tired to try to imagine a place that doesn't hurt. A place where I am no longer afraid.

I WAKE UP to the sound of a group of French exchange students laughing with a distinct French accent, which seems impossible, until you hear it. There's a massive line of people waiting for chocolate milk and cardboard cutouts that pass as hamburgers, and either there's a tall slice of lemon meringue pie sitting in front of me, or I'm hallucinating from the blood loss. Maybe I've gone to heaven. At least I know I haven't gone to hell. I'm pretty sure there's no lemon meringue pie in hell. Well, maybe at the gates of hell they try to lure you inside with a piece of lemon meringue pie, but as soon as it's in your mouth, it transforms into a bran muffin.

A white plastic fork rests on the thin Styrofoam plate, and even though initially I'm hesitant to eat it because it might be laced with arsenic, I devour it in under twenty seconds. Mrs. Turndale's baking comes close, but for me, there's nothing more beautiful than a slice of lemon meringue pie. The first time I tasted it was in grade two when Myhell's mom, of all people, made it for Myhell's birthday and she brought enough pie for the entire class. But now, I don't even look around to see if I can figure out who bought me this pie. I don't care anymore. I don't care anymore about romance or kissing or mystery boys in Letter B baseball hats. It's hard to care when you've been scalped, kicked, and hammered in the face, just because you exist.

Forget about *The Pig Mask Chronicles*.

I'm out.

It was an impossible idea in the first place. From now on, I'm off the grid. And what's the one thing that you should do when you decide that you're no longer mainstream? You go to a party hosted by a guy named Rat.

15

"**W**hat the hell happened to you?" It's Joanie. I'm painting my rainbow, and I still haven't come up with a good explanation for my new look.

"Um. It's kind of a long story. I think I might go to Rat's party."

"Yeah, you should. What do you drink?"

"Ah, the usual."

"Vodka?"

"Yeah. Definitely. Vodka. But … I can't really um, afford it?"

"Don't even worry about it. Like I said, there's always lots." She takes a closer look at my face. "Are you sure you're okay?"

"Yeah, it kinda hurts, but whatever, I'm fine."

She holds up her papier-mâché project. Like fashion accessories, the glint of freshly stapled staples shine off both of her arms, oddly complementing the ripped parts of her jean vest that have also been stapled. She's made a giraffe and she's painted it sky blue and its spots are white clouds and it's beautiful.

"Whaddya think?"

"It's amazing."

"Yeah, I like giraffes. Do you know why their necks are so long?"

There's probably some official scientific explanation for it, but because I don't really know anything, I reply, "No."

"Giraffes' necks are so long because they're trying to hide themselves behind the clouds. That's the thing — giraffes don't even know how cool they are. The last time I saw a giraffe was the last time I saw my dad. He took me to the stupid kiddie zoo, but now it seems like it didn't even happen, you know, so I have to keep reminding myself that it did. I sort of have a giraffe obsession."

"Nice. I sort of have a rainbow obsession." Joanie looks at my project and says nothing. I suck at art, and compared to a cloudy giraffe, a rainbow is pretty juvenile — it ranks right up there with liking unicorns and purple ponies.

"So, I guess I'll see you tonight." Joanie doesn't wait for me to say anything; she just takes her giraffe and walks back to her table. Maybe I should have told her why I like rainbows.

The rest of my day is spent in strange silence. No one talks to me, and I don't see Carson or Nicole, which is good, because I'm not feeling particularly social and I don't have the courage to tell them that I'm out of the club. I passed by Travis, who was discussing a chemistry hypothesis with a teacher and because he was so engrossed in the overwhelming fun of it, he didn't even notice me.

LOST CAT
Answers to the name Mr. Peanut. Reward.

I rip the poster off the telephone pole and stuff it into my pocket.

I get to The Dump and go straight to my room to get a toque to cover my blood-caked head. The only one I can find has a snowman on it. I change out of my wretched clothes, and Jane stumbles in. It's four o'clock in the afternoon and she's totally cooked. She holds a Pop-Tart in one hand and a clear plastic slushy cup filled with red wine in the other.

"What's wrong with your face?" She flops down on my bed. I don't want to talk to her and I don't want her on my bed.

"I accidentally walked into a shelf at the school book fair."

She dips an edge of the Pop-Tart into the cup, and, with as much gross and disgusting effort as possible, sucks the corner and starts to drunk-sputter tears.

"It doesn't even hurt, Mom, don't worry about it."

"I can't find Gaga!"

So that's it. It's not because her daughter looks like the loser of a twelve-round boxing match.

"How did she get out?"

"I only opened the cage for a second, and she was gone!" She flails her arm and the wine slops over the lip of the cup. "I've been calling her all day, and nothing! Maybe she's under your bed!" Jane leans over to look under my bed, falls on the floor, drops the Pop-Tart and the wine and doesn't move. Rehearsing for her zombie movie audition, she lies lifeless, but still alive. Perfect. Now I can go to Rat's party, drink vodka if I want to, and Jane won't even know that I've left the house.

I look in the fridge, but there's nothing recognizable. I want a hamburger. I fill a couple of plastic bags with pop cans that we've extracted from the neighbors' recycling boxes, and last-drop-empty booze bottles that rapidly accumulate in our kitchen. The table is covered with board games: Scrabble, Snakes and Ladders, and Trivial Pursuit: The Movie Edition. So much for Games Night. The bag of clothes that I've prepared to take to Spendapenny has been opened and dumped onto the floor.

A faint mewing comes from the corner of the room, but because of the mounds of crapbage, there's no way I can gain access to the spot. I'll save part of my hamburger for Mr. Peanut. I put out a small bowl of water for him so at least he won't die of dehydration, the way Jane will. I'm bringing Susan's lunch bag so when I see Joanie

I can tell her about the club and give her the camera. She's the real warrior, anyway. Vile-lific snorts resound from my bedroom. Bye Jane.

I balance the six bags of empty bottles on my scooter handlebars and the lunch bag hangs over my shoulder. I love this scooter and if I ever get to own a real cat, I'll call her Scooter and I'll love her even more.

The bottle recycle place is packed with basketball Gocks. Two of them hold a banner: *Girls Play to Win*. Another fundraiser for shinier uniforms. Mrs. Toeplicky, the gym teacher, unloads a large truck filled with bags of plastic water bottles. I attempt to remain invisible, but one of them sees me and texts the others. It's probably about my trendy toque, or my bruised cheek. I'm having trouble seeing out of my left eye, so I guess I look pretty bad. Oh great. An intensely hyper Gock-mom radars me.

"Hi! I'll take those for you. The girls are happy to sort them." She holds out her arms and wiggles her fingernail scythes at me.

"Um. Yeah, okay. Thanks." I hand over my dinner fund and turn to leave.

"Don't forget your tickets!"

"Tickets?"

"Everyone who contributes to our fundraiser receives two free passes to the Championship State Finals. This year it's in Wisconsin!"

And that's that.

So now I have to go to the fast food place to see what the lazy people (God bless the lazy people!) who don't throw away their garbage may have left on their trays. Sometimes I can get almost an entire box of fries, maybe a bite of a mini apple pie. The rarest of all leftovers is chicken bits 'n strips, and the only way you get those is if a skinny kid orders a large. Once I even got most of a fudge sundae and even though it was totally melted, it was melt-mazing.

The best way to achieve this delicate form of exquisite dining is to find a corner and secretly observe people while they eat, and wait for them to leave. You can't openly appear to be eating other people's scraps, because that's embarrassing, so you have to be patient, but fast. If you hesitate, the opportunity is lost because one of the workers comes out and cleans up.

I enter the Burger Stop and quickly look around to make sure there's no one here who knows me. If there is, I have to terminate the entire mission and execute plan B, which I don't want to have to implement because the B in plan B stands for "bin," as in *garbage* bin.

Recognizing no one, I grab one of the complimentary grease-stained newspapers and find a quiet corner in which to "read." Things are looking favorable, as a large family comes in. Maybe today is a chicken bits'n strips day. I can't hear what they're ordering, but families usually have a couple of kid's meals. If the parents are over-weight, they'll blow the whole deal and finish off whatever the kids don't eat. If the parents are at all fit-looking, they won't even touch the kids' food. The funny part is, it's either all or nothing, every single time. This particular group appears health-conscious, which means a potentially good outcome for me. Sure enough, they carry three (!) trays of food, and it looks like they've ordered the works. I can only hope that Mom and Dad aren't trying to teach their kids good citizenship, and they don't clean up after themselves. I wait, seemingly fully engrossed in the "Making the Most of Your Home-grown Herbs" article.

A pack of construction workers come in. Men in hard hats never have leftovers. Two one-thousand-year-old ladies also come in, and there's really no hope there, either, because old ladies have about as much money to spend on this stuff as I do, and they never order an actual meal, only a couple of small coffees and a strawberry sundae to share. One more person comes in. Do I know him? He's wearing a letter B baseball hat. He looks in my direction, wait, *there's a rainbow bead choker around his neck!* I peer over at him out of my one good eye to get a better look, but he's gone. I guess he doesn't want to talk to me? I can't follow him because if I don't eat I won't be able to walk upright, let alone drink vodka. But he must be *the guy*, which is pretty amazing since he's not bad-looking and he goes to my school, but I think he's in grade twelve, which is weird, because unless you're one of Those Girls, or you have erroneous and flagrantly double-standard designated tramp status, the grade twelve guys want nothing to do with the grade ten girls. Maybe he doesn't know how old I am, and, as far as I know, I don't have a reputation as a tramp.

The family gets up. Oh please, please, *please* don't throw away your garbage. Dad picks up the mostly full pop cups and mom neatly arranges the garbage in a pile, but they don't take it to the garbage. I look around. Conditions appear optimal. I saunter over to their table and sit down with my newspaper. To the untrained eye, it would appear that I have just finished my meal and I'm relaxing.

"Are you done?"

Jay-Rome, the paper-bag guy from my art class stands over my table. He wasn't in class. I thought he was ditching.

"No! I mean, almost. Don't worry about this stuff, I'll do it."

"Did you actually have three kid's meals?"

"I was hungry."

"So, did you finish your eggamma?"

"Sort of. Did you finish your ah, project?"

"Nah. Do you know how hard it is to make a nipple out of papier-mâché? I hate art. I'm only taking it is because we can't afford a therapist. I'm pretty sure it's not working. I still have three hundred panic attacks a day."

"Yeah, I don't like art much, either, probably because I totally suck at it." I rummage through the fry cartons while he awkwardly stands at my table.

"Do you want a milkshake or something?" He looks around. "I can get you one for free."

"What?"

"What kind do you want? Chocolate?"

"Yeah, sure, that'd be … cool." Jay-Rome disappears and I actually find about five french fries left in one of the boxes. I stuff one of the fries into my pocket for Mr. Peanut. I don't know if cats eat fries, but at least it's not a petrified Pop-Tart. My left eye is now completely closed, and I'm wearing a Christmas toque, but the day just keeps getting better. Maybe Rat's party will be fun.

Jay-Rome returns with a very large chocolate milkshake and wet droplets of milkshake sweat cover the outside of the waxy cardboard container, just like the ones on TV.

"Here you go. I thought you might be having a bad day."

"Thanks, Jay-Rome. How long you been working here?"

"Today's my first day. You should apply. You get free food when the manager's not around, and even though you have to wear this suck-up uniform, it's not the worst place in the world."

"I don't think they'd hire me. I'm kind of a mess."

"Who cares? There's lots of weird people working here."

I'm not really sure what to say to that, so I just drink my beautiful, beautiful shake.

"Just a minute." Jay-Rome leaves, and I dig through the rest of the scraps on my table.

"Here you go. Do you need a pen?" He hands me a job application form and a pen.

"Thanks."

"You done?" He picks up the tray.

"Yeah. Thanks." Jay-Rome cleans the tables around me, and I fill out the form. I'm stuck at the place where it asks for personal references. I write down Carson's mom. I don't know their phone number, or even her first name, just *Mrs. Turndale, High Knoll Road*, but it doesn't matter because I'm not going to get the job, anyway. I walk to the counter. Behind a cash register a jack-o'-lantern-toothed woman with a sunken-junkie face grins at me.

"Hi," I say. "I wanted to hand in my application form." She stares at me like I'm speaking a foreign language.

"Are you a pirate?"

"What?"

"For Halloween?"

"Yup, that's it. I'm a pirate."

"Good one! I'll get your ice cream."

"What?"

"Every kid who comes in here wearing a costume between now and Halloween gets a free small cone!"

"Oh." A pirate. Whatever, free ice cream. I think I'll come back every day wearing a different "costume." She hands me the ice cream, and I hand her the form. I wish I could save this ice cream for Mr. Peanut.

"There ya be, matey! Yarrrrr!" She swoops her arm like a buccaneer.

Okay, that was weird, but I really don't mind, as matter of fact, I prefer it because in my experience, the "weird" people aren't compelled to hurt the other "weird" people around them.

I leave the Burger Stop and sit on a rock and think about rainbow-bead Baseball B guy. I wish I knew what was going on. Why doesn't he talk to me? Does he want me to be his girlfriend? I'm not exactly the kind of girl that boys pursue because having a relationship with me will improve their social status, and I'm not exactly the kind of girl who has a lot to offer in the sex department. I can't even look at myself in the mirror when I have my clothes *on*. I don't want to be like Jane, though, suspicious of everyone. He's probably just really shy, so it'd be mean of me to not at least give him a chance.

16

"**W**here's Waldo!" Anonymous party guy tries to maintain his balance. His right hand grips a mostly finished bottle of Jack Daniels.

"What?"

"Your toque, man! You look like Waldo." He takes a large gulp from the bottle and offers it to me. I take it from him and pretend to drink. I lift the bottle up to my lips, knock it back, and keep my mouth closed.

"Thanks." I hand it back.

"Do you have any smokes?"

"No, sorry. Hey, have you seen Joanie?"

"Noooo. But have you seen Molly?" He moves in closer to me.

"No. I don't know a Molly." I take a step back.

"I could introduce you to Molly. Sometime. Maybe even tonight."

"Maybe. Right now I'm looking for my friend. Rat's friend. She goes to my school."

"Your school! That's total bullshit! Do you know where I can get a smoke?"

"No, sorry."

"Why are you just standing there? You should come sit on the

couch. With me." He jabs his right pointy finger into his chest, slosh-
ing the cowboy amber liquid.

"I just wanna wait for my friend first."

Not letting go of the bottle, he leans over into the bushes and
pukes right onto my hidden scooter.

"Let's go inside. It's cold!" He knocks the bottle back again and
then holds it out to me. I shake my head no. It was a stupid idea to
come here by myself. "How *old* are you?"

"Sixteen."

"No, you're not! You're thirteen.

"I'm almost sixteen."

"When's your birthday?"

"March."

"So, that makes you 15.7. That's how old you are. I'm 17.2. That's
how old I am. From now on, that's who we are. We're not *names* here,
we're numbers. Do you get it? We're all anonymous statistics and
we will only be identified by our numbers. Do you have a smoke?" *We
will* only be identified by our numbers. It makes perfect sense. Why
didn't I think of it? It's total genius. "Why did you bring your lunch?
Are you on like a *field* trip or something?"

"Oh, no, it's my purse."

"Shit." He takes another swig and moves in very close to my face.
"Were you in a fight or something?"

"No. I fell." I want to get away from this guy, but I don't want to
go in the house. My rough estimate is that there's probably sixty-four
people in the house, all of them older than 15.7, all of them drinking.

"Holy crap!" He recognizes someone coming up the walk and
stumbles toward him. They stagger up to the front door together, the
new person holds him up.

"My buddy, 17.5, this is 15.7, 15.7, this is 17.5, he has smokes,
don't you 17.5." Then 17.2 one-arm strangles 17.5 who takes a pack
of cigarettes out of his pocket, gives one to 17.2, and offers one to

me, 15.7.

"No, thanks," I say.

"Aw, 15.7 doesn't smoke. Cigarettes, anyway. Did Mommy pack you any bud for lunch?"

"Unfortunately not. No bud. No smokes, just an egg salad sandwich."

"Ewww. That is seriously ..." He thinks. "Seriously wrong."

"I'm goin' inside," 17.5 says. "You comin' or what?" He finishes his cigarette and tosses it in the same bush that 17.2 threw up in and it fizzles out. I might have to ditch my scooter, and as much as this depresses me, I really don't want to deal with any more difficult stuff today.

"Hey. Shithead." A hooded man stands in the doorway. It might actually be the Grim Reaper. "Where's my money?" He grabs 17.2's hair, quickly wrenches his neck back and then releases it.

"Relax. I got it. Jesus. Don't get so hyper." He leans down to me and whispers, "You got any money, Waldo?"

It's time to go back to The Dump.

"Look, I gotta go," I say. Halfway down the walk, a bottle of Jack Daniels narrowly misses my head and smashes on the sidewalk.

"You shoulda come in the house, 15.7!"

Yeah. Too bad I didn't go in the house with that total zero.

I WALK PAST the Torture Chamber and loud music vibrates from the gym. Right. Halloween dance. I cross the street. Those Girls are around here somewhere, and it would be best if they'd just get it over with, whatever it is. Hit me, throw something at me, run me over with a tank, *just get* it over with. It's like winding a jack-in-the-box, you know it's coming, and you just keep winding and winding the little lever, fully expecting the *sproing*! of the puppet to pop out at you at any second, and when it does, you jump, even though you knew it was going to happen. You just didn't know *when*.

I turn on the camera — I may be out of the club, but I'm sure the others will want to keep the project going. I keep the flap open where the lens is set up, and press *record*.

"Combustible maybe, flammable, unlikely." I hear.

A group comes around the corner, but it's too late for me to turn around, so I just keep walking. If I die, at least I'll have died on a day that I had a chocolate milkshake. Three skeletons walk toward me like anonymous assassins, their costumes covering their faces. One of them stops and speaks to me, "Hey … you should come to the dance."

"No, thanks," I say.

"Aggie, it's *me*!" One of the skeletons removes his skeleton face. It's Travis.

"Travis! You're going to the dance?"

"Yes. We're conducting a scientific experiment on anonymity. We want to see if girls are more likely to dance with us if they don't know who we are." The other skeletons take off their masks and two of Travis's techie friends full-face grin at me.

"The human skeleton is made up of 206 bones, from the skull to the metacarpus."

"And the shoulder is made up of three different bones."

"Yes, the humerus, the scapula, and the clavicle."

"Interesting," I say.

"We've been practicing our small talk." Travis notices the lunch bag. "Are you filming this?"

"I don't know what I'm doing, Travis."

"Are you hurt?" He takes a closer look at me.

"I'm fine."

"Yeah, right. Who did this to you?"

"It's fine. I'll tell you about it later. Just go to the dance and shake those bones."

All the skeletons laugh. Happy, harmless geeks: loveable, but not exactly boyfriend material.

"Do you want us to walk you home?" This is one of the nicest things anyone has ever offered to do for me.

"No, that's okay, you guys go. I'll see you on Monday."

The two other skeletons look at one another. The skinniest of the three says, "I think we should walk her home."

"Yes, it's not good for a girl to be out on the streets alone when the center of the sun is fifty arc minutes below the horizon. We would like to walk you home." They stand, awkward-skeleton-like, and wait for my reply.

"All right. That'd be great. And here I thought you guys were just a bunch of lazy bones." They laugh again and for a minute I feel like I'm not actually as hideous as I look. When we get to my house I want to invite them in for a hot chocolate, but that, of course, is impossible.

"Well, thanks, guys. Have fun at the dance." I hand over the lunch bag to Travis because I don't need it anymore. "Be careful."

"Oh, a skeleton is nothing if not careful."

I imagine him winking under his costume, which is totally absurd because Travis is way too studious for that.

I need to go to bed, but Jane remains passed out on my bedroom floor. I'll crash in the living room. I start moving stuff to clear a place to lie down amid the gloppy slime-filled bottles of bath oils, broken ceramic goats in kilts, and ratty-tatty Christmas garlands. I lift one of the cardboard boxes full of moth-eaten sheets, and a colony of silverfish catch my eye. I have to get out of here. I grab a sheet, shake it, and head out the door.

The night is coffin-dark and the harsh cold bites against my bruised and broken face. I feel heavy with the loneliness of being alive. Exhausted and with nowhere else to go, I lie down in the high grass of my front yard and, just like Dorothy in the field of poppies, I close my eyes. Fifteen point seven, fifteen point seven. We're all anonymous statistics, and we will only be identified by our numbers.

16.5

The waves crash over me. I'm drowning. I can't breathe. I can't breathe!

"Maybe she's dead!"

I open my eyes and it stings.

"Don't waste all of it!" Dark figures stand over me. I cower.

"Hey, cockroach!" Someone kicks me hard in the leg.

"Get her clothes!" They pull at me, at my clothes, they grab my top and I hear it rip around the neck.

"Get her pants!" Two people grab my legs and tug on my pants. They come off easily. Fortunately, my underwear stays on.

A distant voice breaks their assault, "FBI!" They stop.

"Look, it's the crazy bitch's crazy mom!"

"Holy crap!"

I sit up and in the dim light of the street lamp, a wild demented beast approaches, swinging two bats and running towards us, Jane screams, "FBI! Drop your weapons! Now!"

My assailants run. Jane reaches me, crouches to my level, "Oh, my God, Aggie, what happened to you?" I guess she's now sober enough to notice that I'm a total mess. "Those girls, they hurt you! I'm phoning the cops! I'm phoning their mothers!"

"No, Mom, don't. I'm fine. They're drunk. Just let it go."

"Aggie, stop protecting them."

"I'm not protecting them, Mom, it's just not important. It's over, okay?"

"Are you kidding me? I saw them and I can identify them to the police — there was a cat, Dorothy from the Wizard of Oz, and a bunny. They *hurt* you, Aggie, they can't just get away with it."

I shiver violently like an overloaded washing machine on the spin cycle.

"Mom, can we go inside?" Jane attempts to help me up, but she doesn't know where to touch me, so it's just awkward. There's a large, almost empty bottle of gin on the ground.

Jane picks up the bottle, but leaves my pants. I have to limp and my leg throbs.

"I guess I'm just a bad mother."

She wants me to say, *No you're not — you're not a bad mother*. But I don't.

"It's fine, Mom." I say, ending the conversation.

I stick my head in the bathroom sink and wash off the gin, dirt, and remaining blood. I try to avoid the gouge in my head where my hair was ripped out, and I wince from the pain. It's still the middle of the night and I lie awake and think about how I'm going to tell everyone that I've quit the club.

17

"Aggie! Phone! Hurry up!"

It's two-thirty. I've slept through the morning and I'm guessing Jane has, too, otherwise she would have woken me up long ago to get me to eat some grossamundo breakfast that would sicken a ravenous dog.

"Hello?"

"Hi, is this Aggie Murphy?"

"Yeah."

"Hi Aggie, this is Donna from the Burger Stop. You filled out an application form with us yesterday?"

Oh wow.

"Ah, yeah."

"Can you come in for an interview today?"

"Today?"

"I know it's fast, but someone quit on us yesterday, and I need to fill some shifts. How's four o'clock?"

"Uh, sure, yeah."

"Great. Just come to the front counter and ask for Donna."

"Yeah, okay, see you at four"

"Who was that?" Jane hovers over me accusingly, like I've just made an appointment with the official white coats at the mental institution who will take her away today at four o'clock. Not a bad idea.

"It was The Burger Stop. I have an interview. I applied for a job yesterday and they need someone to fill some shifts."

"What? How did they get this number? Did you give out our number?"

"You sort of have to give out your number if you want people to phone you, Mother."

"Mother? Since when do you call me *Mother*?"

"Okay, *Mom*."

"Well you can't work on weekends. I want you home."

"Sure, *Mom*. I'll let them know which shifts are the most convenient for you."

I go to my room to look for something, *anything* to wear. I find a three-buttons-missing shirt to wear over a т-shirt and a pair of corduroy pants that are thrift-store short. Maybe they'll let me work *today* and I can get something to eat — if the manager isn't around. Unsuccessfully, I attempt to comb my hair over the gash in my head. I remember Jay-Rome's words of encouragement: "There's lots of weird people working here."

Jane has gone back to bed. I suppose she's trying to sleep off the effects of an entire box of Interlude: Fine Red Table Wine for the Price of Beer. Now's my chance. I put the cat cage on the table and make squeaky noises and call out very quietly, "Here, Mr. Peanut. C'mere. It's okay, C'mere, Mr. Peanut." I hear a tiny mew. "Come on, Mr. Peanut, it's time to go home." I walk slowly to where I think he is and I see the tip of his ear. "There we go." He lets me pick him up and he's so beautiful that I want to keep him. I encourage him into the carrier. It only takes us eighteen minutes to find his house. I knock on the door and an old, old, old lady, approximately eighty-seven-point six, answers it.

"I think I found Mr. Peanut." I hold up the carrier and she looks inside.

"That's him, all right." She talks to the cage. "Mr. Peanut, you old Tom! Wait here." she says to me. I put the carrier down and play with Mr. Peanut's paw through the wire door. "Here you are. Thank you. He's a bloody hooligan and I was starting to worry this time." I consider not taking the ten dollars she wants to give me, but old, old, old ladies like to make things right.

"Thanks!" I say. I take the money, open the door of the cage, and the bloody hooligan runs into the house.

I leave the cat carrier on her stoop after she closes the door. I don't need it. I have to try to remember that: *I don't need* it. Whatever it is, I don't need it, and it feels good to give it away. Besides, it can't be taken away if I give it away.

I make my way to the bus stop and even though my leg hurts and my head throbs, I'm feeling pretty optimistic. If I get this job, my whole entire life will change. I'll go to the movies, buy something from a vending machine, and go to the caf on Sloppy Joe Wednesdays. I will no longer be the world's biggest loser who doesn't use tampons because pads are marginally cheaper.

A shiny white SUV slows to a stop.

"Aggie! You want a ride?" It's Carson.

"Yes!" I climb in and immediately I'm raised up into a better world. If we owned a car like this, I would sleep in it.

"Where are you going?" Carson asks.

"The Burger Stop. I have a job interview."

Mrs. Turndale looks through the rear-view mirror at me, "Aggie, I have a niece who lives in Oregon, and I want to buy her some Christmas clothes and she's your size — would you do me a big favor and come try on some things? It would help me out."

"Ah, I guess. I don't have a lot of time, though."

Carson's mom pulls into the mall and we head straight for Route

66, a hip clothing shop that I've never actually been in. Mrs. Turndale skillfully selects an armful of things and leads me to the change room. I try them on as fast as I can without hurting.

"Let's see the next one!"

I have to "model" the clothes for Carson's mom. There's a pair of cool, randomly ripped jeans, a flannel Western-style snap shirt, a т-shirt that has tiny blue flowers on it, a jacket that's made of actual leather, a sweater that has an embroidered horse on it, a blouse that's black with lace on the back, a long-sleeved pullover that hangs at the shoulders, and a baby-blue hoodie that says *Surf's up*. With each item I try on, I feel increasingly depressed. Even if I do get a job, I still won't be able to buy any of this stuff.

"Carson, go get me a skinny, half-sweet French Vanilla 180-degree, no-foam cappuccino." Mrs. Turndale hands Carson a twenty-dollar bill. Carson disappears and I picture the people at the coffee shop wondering why a six-year-old would order such a thing.

"Aggie, I want to thank you. You are a good friend to Carson. He's talked about you for years, about how nice you are to him, even when everyone gangs up on him, you stick by him. I want you to do me another favor."

"Sure …"

"I want you to accept these clothes as my gift to you. Please. It would make me happy."

"I can't let you do that."

"Aggie, please."

"You don't understand, Mrs. Turndale, it's not that I'm not grateful, because I am, it's just, that … it's just that my mother would freak. She'd never let me keep any of these things and if she saw me in them she'd either take them and wear them herself or set fire to them in the backyard. Really Mrs. Turndale, thanks, anyway."

"Oh. I'm sorry." Mrs. Turndale sighs. "Well, then, can I at least buy you a late lunch?"

"I have to be at The Burger Stop in ten minutes. I gotta get changed." When I come out there's no sign of either Mrs. Turndale or Carson. I go to the front counter. "Hi. Did you see that woman I was with?"

"Oh, yeah, they announced something on the P.A. and she booked it outta here."

"Do you know what it said?"

"Something about a lost kid."

Great. I need to leave *now*. Do I go to the coffee shop? Do I go to the car? Do I make an announcement? I decide to sit outside Route 66 and wait. Yale (Only Boy) walks by with a guy I've never seen before. They're both wearing short-shorts and Yale has ankle weights Velcro-strapped around his *hairless* orangey legs. They're walking really close together, and the boy he's with puts a thumb in one of the belt loops around the waist of Yale's cutoffs and kisses Yale on the neck. Whoa. Yale looks behind him, sees me, and aggressively pushes the other boy away.

An unhappy Carson and his mom return. "Aggie, I'm so sorry. They thought Carson was lost and they took him to a little room for missing children and I had to fill out a bunch of forms, what a mess!"

"It's okay."

"But it's four-thirty — you've missed your appointment."

"Yeah. I guess I have." And I guess I've screwed up again. I bet even the weird people who work there showed up on time for their interview. I bite down hard on my tongue to keep from crying.

Carson takes my hand.

"My dad will give you a job, Aggie."

"Oh, sure, like I can work for your dad. Doing what? Cleaning his office?"

"You could do that, or you could organize all his papers — there's *tons* of stuff to do. And he'll pay you lots, won't he, Mom? What do you think Dad would pay Aggie to work for him? Like, ten dollars an hour?"

"That's a good idea." She lifts her cappuccino 180 degrees to her lips to get the last drop. "Let's go eat."

I order a double cheeseburger with *bacon*, a medium fries (I don't want to seem too hungry), and a megaton Coke. We sit and eat like normal people, out for a normal day of shopping, and you know what? I *really* like it.

18

It's Monday morning and I'm excited to see Susan and to hear about her weekend. Tonight we meet at Carson's house again and even though I have to tell everyone that I'm done with the project, maybe Mrs. Turndale will make chocolate chip cookies. I haven't had a homemade chocolate chip cookie since kindergarten, and no, I'm not kidding.

"I'm going to walk you to school today," Jane announces. She puts on her coat.

"No, Mom, I'm fine. Really. Maybe you should stay here and relax before work. It's been a tough week for you."

"You're right, it's been stressful. And I'm still emotionally drained from the loss of my little Gaga."

"I'm sure he just found his way home, don't even worry about it anymore."

"But Aggie, this was his home."

"Okay, I'll see you after school."

"If you're sure." Still in her coat, she turns on the TV and efficiently fades into the Land of Self-induced Coma.

I'm wearing the toque, but I don't own a winter coat and I can't borrow Jane's because, first of all, she's in it, and second, it's a hideous burgundy with peeling pleather sleeves. If I get a job working for Carson's dad, the first thing I'll buy is a coat. And one of those expensive coffee drinks. The kind that I've only tried once when I found a third of a leftover one in the gym change room. It was cold and there was lipstick on the cup, but I could tell just from that little taste that when it was fresh, it was *really* good.

I get to school and go straight to Susan's locker, and when she sees me, her mouth drops.

"What happened to you?"

"Ah, just another close encounter of the Michelle kind."

"Oh-my-God! I hope you fought back!"

"Yeah, well. How was camp?"

"Unbelievable! They totally starved us for three days. We had to eat kale and whole grains and yetch, *cottage cheese*. It was disgusting. We hated it." I wish I had some kale and whole grains and any kind of cheese, cottage, village, barn-floor.

"Ew, that's awful." I'm just about to tell Susan how much I missed her, but a girl I don't recognize walks up to us. She's almost as big as Susan.

"Hi!"

"Hey!"

Susan and this new girl hug.

"Aggie, this is J.J. We met at camp. She actually goes to our school and we've never even seen each other before! J.J.'s in grade eleven."

"Oh. Hi, J.J." Grade eleven? Maybe she knows the boy in the baseball hat.

"Do you want to have lunch with us?" Susan and J.J. stand side by side and together they await my reply.

"Ah, no, that's okay, I have stuff to do."

"Okay, but if you change your mind, we're going to The Sub Cafe to get the 2-4-1-Deli Meat Delight."

Should I go with them? That would be awkward: it's 2-4-1, not

3-4-1. We'd have to get 6-4-3 and that'd be way too much.

"And a jelly roll! Don't forget the jelly rolls!" They look at each other and burst out laughing.

"Anyway, I guess I'll see you tonight, at Carson's house," I say.

"Oh, shoot! I totally forgot about that. Fat camp brain fog."

"My dad's out of town so we're going to my house to watch old rom-coms from the eighties and eat cheesy-butter-smothered pop-corn. My mom makes the world's best popcorn — way better than at the movie theatre. You can come, too, if you want." J.J. offers.

"Maybe next time."

"And I'll be at Carson's for sure next time. Maybe you and Carson want some alone time anyway," says Susan.

"What's *that* supposed to mean?"

"Kidding!"

"Maybe we could go to *La Belle Château* this week and look for dresses?"

"Oh, yeah, about that. My mom said that she would only buy us tickets to the dance if I lose ten pounds." Susan might as well have announced that we could only go to the dance if a helicopter picks us up on the moon. "Anyway, I'll see you later, we have to get to the caf before class."

Now I'm worried that Susan won't reach her passive-aggressive mother's ten-pound goal and there won't be any dance. If her mother would just let Susan be Susan, rather than what she thinks she should be, Susan might not feel so bad about herself. I slowly walk to my locker, and before I see him, Travis yells out to me.

"Where have you been? I've been waiting here for six minutes! You have to see this!" Travis holds out my video camera so that I can see the screen. He presses *play*. It's dark, but I can make out the faces of Bevy, Myhell, and Chrissy Crop Top.

"I bet she ate that cat food after we stuffed it in her face!"

So it was actually cat food. Sick.

"She looked like roadkill!" Like thirsty camels, they take turns swigging greedily from a bottle of gin.

"That clump of her hair totally grossed me out! We should probably actually kill her."

"No, I have a better idea. We should just *almost* kill her. That'd be more fun. And then we can keep doing it. Come on, let's get this party started!" Myhell stashes the bottle in the bushes that flank the back door. Bevy, dressed as exotic-dancer-Dorothy (the blue gingham dress barely covers her butt) puts on the red sequined shoe that is wedged in the door and they disappear into the gym.

"Can you believe that? We have to show this to the principal."

"No. We can't."

"But Aggie, this is serious. I'm … I'm worried about you." And at that precise moment, Travis turns into a real boy.

"I'll think about it, okay? I have to go to class. Give me the camera and I'll bring it to Carson's tonight." I say quietly. Our hands touch when he passes me the camera and a massive bolt of energy zaps through our fingertips. Oddly, Travis is unfazed. You'd think the guy who gets 900 percent in chemistry would notice that some sort of *reaction* just happened between us.

"Fine, but if you don't do something about it, I will."

And that pretty much seals it. Someday I will be Mrs. T. Hamster and we'll travel to all sorts of places for physics conventions. Places even better than Wisconsin.

WHEN I ARRIVE at Carson's, Nicole, and Travis are already here and Travis is showing Nicole how to use the camera holder that he's made out of a microscope carrying case. Like Susan's lunch bag, he's set it up so the side has a hidden flap that, when opened, exposes the camera lens. It's ingenious and annoying because he doesn't move away when Nicole's long billy goat chin hair touches his arm as he explains to her how it all works. Official Romantic Scale level: -100.

"And no one will ever know it's a camera, Nicole." Travis stares into her eyes and she stares right back like it's some sort of contest. Maybe she's cast a spell on him.

"Okay. Can we do this?" I blurt. Everyone looks at me like I've totally lost it.

"I thought we were waiting for Susan," Carson says.

"Susan's not coming tonight. She's indisposed."

"Oh. That's terrible!" Nicole says this with such concern that she must think that something serious has happened to Susan.

"So, I've got something to say and I want to just get it over with so don't interrupt me until I'm done."

"How will we know when you're done?" Nicole asks.

"I don't know, I'll say I'm done, I guess." Nicole nods in understanding. "Okay, here's the thing. I can't to do this anymore. I'm quitting the club."

"But we're just getting started!" Nicole interrupts.

"Let her finish!" Carson says.

"Sorry. It's just that I don't think we can win."

"Hmm." Travis grabs hold of his chin and nods. "Plausible."

Carson stands and walks to where I'm sitting, very dramatically takes both of my hands in his, and stares straight into my one good eye, "Look, the whole entire world of misfit people like us needs you. You're our one brave person, our revolutionary. And obviously we haven't protected you enough and I'm sorry, but we see that now. Right, everyone? We'll watch out for each other more? We have to do this, Aggie. We've been called. And if we quit, we lose for sure."

"Thanks, Carson, but honestly. *I can't do this* anymore," I say.

"Okay, but nothing's official until all the club members are present. It wouldn't be fair. I'm currently involved in another project, anyway," Travis says.

"What other project?" I ask, thinking that it might have something to do with me.

"I'm working on an aluminum chloride compound to help Nicole. It's a new type of antiperspirant. No more of that hocus-pocus, right Nicole? This is science."

Oh, great, I should have known that Travis would find a strange chemical imbalance romantically inspiring. Maybe I should develop an inexplicable rash or grow a horn out of the top of my head.

"Dessert time!" It's Mrs. Turndale. She's made a video-camera-shaped cake. "I thought the videography club should have a special treat!"

We gather around the little table and sit on the little chairs. We even have little plastic safety sporks, but Mrs. Turndale cuts a double-sized adult slice of cake for each of us, like she knows that cake is sometimes the answer to everything. It's too bad Susan is missing out. I would ask to take a piece home with me, but if Jane saw it, she'd have a surge of Inadequate Mother Syndrome and buy another box of wine.

"When do the parents get to see your movie?" Mrs. Turndale asks, we stop mid-sporkful.

Travis takes over. "Well, you must understand the creative process, Mrs. Turndale. As artists, we protect our work from the general public until it represents the message we desire to portray. Exposing the work before it's time would mean imminent disaster!"

"Oh, I didn't realize …"

"Yeah, Mom, don't ruin everything!"

"Oh. I'm sorry, ah … who wants eggnog?"

"Eggnog, Mom? It's November."

"Carson, I'm bringing the eggnog."

"And Coke." For some reason, Carson appears to be showing off.

"Carson, you know Coke is number one on the *Not Allowed* list. You can have apple juice."

Not wanting to embarrass Carson, we focus on the cake. I've never tasted eggnog, so I'm excited to try it, even in November. Carson cuts

another piece of cake for everyone but himself, and to let him know
that we're on his side, we all eat as quietly as one possibly can when
eating a piece of homemade chocolate cake: It's hard to not audibly
"*mmmmmm.*"

"Carson, I want to speak with you!" Mr. Turndale's voice crashes
down the stairs, and by the panicked look on his face, Carson knows
what's coming. He leaves the three of us alone and awkward, each of
us a contender for Social Idiot of the Year award.

"So how long is Susan indisposed?" Nicole asks.

"I don't know, maybe forever." I don't even want to talk to Nicole.
Not only has she kissed Carson, she's also stolen one of my few future
husband candidates, a.k.a., boys who have the potential to get me
out of The Dump. She's definitely cast a spell on him. I try to think
of something to say to Travis to diffuse the magic.

"So, Travis, what kind of instrument does a skeleton play?" I ask.

Entirely unamused, Travis replies, "Um, I wouldn't know."

"The trombone. Get it? Trom-BONE?" He doesn't laugh. It's not
like it was the other night. I guess things just aren't as funny when
you're not in a costume, and now that Nicole is with us, the romantic
ambiance has shifted.

I see Carson's tiny feet, followed by the rest of him, slowly coming
down the stairs. He looks at the floor. "You have to go home.
My mom said I was rude. My dad's in the car waiting, and I'm
grounded from the club for two weeks. No one can come over, and I
can't go out."

Matching Carson's tone, Travis speaks kindly, "Don't worry about
it. We're taking a break, remember?"

"And my mom is going to get me from school at lunch and bring
me home, and then bring me back for the afternoon."

"It's like she's your babysitter," Nicole says.

Carson runs into his computer room and closes the door. I guess
because they treat him like a four-year-old, he sometimes acts like

a four-year-old. Travis, Nicole and I head upstairs. There's nothing more to say, and obviously this is not a good time to ask about working for Mr. Turndale. Carson's even more of a prisoner than I am. At least I can come and go whenever I want — another benefit of being raised by, well, no one.

"MATH-I, HUMANITIES-I, P.E.-I, Art-c-, French-I. What do all these IS mean? How is this a report card?"

Apparently Jane went into my room and rifled through my school texts and found my unopened report card. I didn't want to know how sucky I was doing in my classes, but I know now: my highest mark is a C-, everything else is an "Incomplete."

"Oh, that's the new reporting system, 'I' stands for 'in progress.' It just means that the course isn't over yet." A definite high-five for that lie.

"I've never seen this before."

"Yeah, I know, it's *new*." Why only a C- in Art? Maybe my papier-mâché was too improper.

"Well I don't like it. That school isn't doing its job. You should come and work with me at Spendapenny. I'll recommend you!"

"But, Mom, if I drop out, I won't graduate, and then I'd be like you."

"What's so bad about being like me? Huh? Is there something bad about being like me that I should know about? Tell me, Agatha, what's so bad about being like me?"

Walk away. Now. Don't say anything.

"Well, you kinda limited your options when you dropped out of school."

"Limited my options? Who in hell's bells do you think you are? Did it ever occur to you to think about why I dropped out of school?" She stands and upends her chair. It tumbles and knocks over a pile of lethal rusted garden tools that we found teetering into our yard on the mootable edge of our old man neighbor's planter box. "You're the reason I dropped out of school. I could have had so much more than this." I tug on an eyelash. "I was beautiful and all the boys wanted me to be their girlfriend." Jane opens the fridge and removes a familiar box, takes a coffee mug out of the cupboard, and jet-streams wine into the mug. She holds the mug up to her mouth, drinks the entire contents, and fills it again. "All the boys. Everything I dreamed of was gone because of you. It's you who *limited* my *options*." She drinks. "You stole my dreams." Jane finishes another cup full and refills a third time. "What's that feel like? To steal someone's dreams?"

Because I don't have an answer to that, I go to my room, shut the door, and sit in my closet. Something hard and sharp jabs into my leg. Nail clippers. I roll up the sleeve on my left arm and cut tiny sections of my skin and it hurts. The blood is brightly tinted and honest. It's actually *really* beautiful. My arm is the canvas and I use my finger as the brush and paint a one color rainbow. I'm a dream stealer and dream stealers don't need friends, or a mother, or a job. This is the only thing a dream stealer needs, because this is the only thing I that I want to feel.

19

Mrs. Washington, the principal, stands in the front doorway of The Torture Chamber. She's talking to a woman in a pointy-lapelled business suit. They see me and their conversation abruptly stops. Are they talking about me? Like a guy in tights balancing on a high wire in a windstorm, my legs wobble as I pass them and slink to my locker. I ditched the toque. I made a sort of headband from a disintegrating T-shirt. I cut the end off a sleeve and it was just big enough to fit around my head, and, in my fashion-maven opinion, it looks good. Jane would kill me for ruining a "perfectly good piece of clothing."

I reach for the books for my first class and my arm hurts just to lift it, let alone carry around my two-hundred-pound highly fascinating textbook: *A Brief History of World Geography*.

"WOULD AGATHA MURPHY PLEASE REPORT TO THE OFFICE IMMEDIATELY. AGATHA MURPHY TO THE OFFICE IMMEDIATELY."

That's weird. It must be time for me to pick up my trophy for Outstanding Academic Achievement.

I approach the secretary who sits diminutive behind the imposing and extraordinarily long counter that I imagine they play shuffleboard

on after school, and tell her my name. She doesn't smile. The door
to the principal's office opens and Mrs. Washington summons me in.
The suit woman stands when she sees me, tightly gripping the top of
a chair.

"This is her?" She addresses Mrs. Washington.

"Yes."

They both stare at me, so much so that I want to pick up the decorative ruler on Mrs. Washington's desk and force the sharp corner of
it into my skin.

"And she doesn't know?" Asks the woman.

"Not yet." Again, they stare.

I have to ask, "What's going on?"

"Sit down, Miss Murphy." Mrs. Washington takes a deep breath,
"We have some sad news, a school friend of yours has taken her life
over the weekend."

"Who? What? Taken her life?"

"Joanne Charles — Joanie. Mrs. Charles noticed your name in her
journal."

*Joanie's dead? Nah! Joanie can't be dead! Did she even finish her
giraffe? She bought me lasagna. She was so nice to me. To everyone. Joanie
can't be dead!*

Shedding her well-dressed dignity, the businesswoman's skirt rips
as she bends down to me, "Miss Murphy, please, if you know *anything*."

"Who are you?" I ask.

"I'm Joanne's mother. Please help me to understand. Did she say
anything to you? Did something bad happen to her here at school?
Were kids being mean to her again?"

Again? It never stopped. I hate this. I hate this place. I hate
breathing.

"I'm sorry. I'm so sorry. The last time I saw her was in Art. She
made a giraffe. Out of papier-mâché. It reminded her of her dad."

Sudden and unexpected tears come from Joanie's mom and I

want to cry, and I'm sure Mrs. Washington would cry if she didn't have to adhere to the mandated level of professionalism, "Go on," Mrs. Washington says.

"She invited me to a party but I didn't go inside. And I was only there a few minutes. There were tons of people there. People I didn't know. I only went because Joanie invited me. I didn't know anyone else. Except for maybe Rat."

"Rat?" Mrs. Washington abruptly opens her desk drawer, grabs a pen, and quickly scribbles something in a notebook.

"Yes, Rat. The party was at his house."

"What's the address?"

"I don't know. It's the house by the fire hall." Mrs. Washington writes frantically, but it's too late to save Joanie.

"Do you know his real name?" Mrs. Washington pauses, pen ready.

"No, but he's really tall and he has long black hair and he wears a shrunken head around his neck. And a long black trench coat. He always wears a black trench coat."

"Yes, I know him. He's in the alternative program. Thank you, Agatha. Someone from Victim Services will be here this afternoon to help you navigate these difficult times. We can set up an appointment for you."

Navigate these difficult times? Who am I, Christopher Columbus?

"No, thanks." I say. "Can I ask you something?" I look at Joanie's mom.

"Do you mind telling me the month of Joanie's birthday?"

"Agatha, how is that relevant?" Mrs. Washington says.

"January. She would have been sixteen in January," Joanie's mom says.

"Thanks." I say, and leave the office. Joanie only made it to 15.9.

I TAKE ALL the papers out of one of my binders and, even though I'm afraid to go into the bathroom, I open the door. The lights are off and the place is empty and cold, like a morgue at midnight. Faint daylight shines through the wire over the windows. Paper cut-out snowflake shadows fall upon the floor.

I lock the door of the last stall and squat with my feet on the toilet seat, which isn't easy, but it makes me unseeable. I unfold my plastic binder and the spine creaks. I snap open the metal ring. Using my left hand, I force the thick blunt edge of the metal claw into my right forearm. The blood doesn't come and the pain alone isn't enough. Heavy sorrow crushes my heart. What if I were to angle the binder so that all three of the rings could penetrate my skin at the same time? I try to fit my entire right arm into the rings, but only my wrist and part of my lower forearm are gripped by the first two rings. The third ring just pinches about an inch of skin on my upper forearm. I secure my arm in the binder and then with as much strength as I have, I push the rings shut and all three of them pierce my skin. I don't hear the bathroom door open.

"Oh my God, only a total loser kills herself."

"I know, right?" It's Myhell and Bevy. "Hey, give me the answers to dickhead's math quiz, I have to memorize them."

"Memorize them? What, are you serious? Just take a picture of them with your phone."

"Shut *up*! You *do* that? And all this time I've been cheating the hard way!"

"That's cuz you're retarded!"

And then, silence. I push the metal rings farther into my arm. Joanie's dead and it's Myhell, Bevy, Chrissy, and the people like them who killed her. And they don't care. They'll go shopping together and they'll laugh and tell each other that Joanie killed herself because she was weird and messed up in her head because *only a total loser kills herself.*

That's it. I remove the binder from my arm and throw it onto the ground.

This is war.

And I won't stop until it's over. I won't stop until it stops. I won't stop until no one else has to die. I kick open the door of one of the stalls, "THIS!" I yell and the door bangs against the stall wall. I go to the next stall and kick its door. "IS!" I scream. I get to the third stall and kick even harder. "WAR!" I shout, and the door bangs against the wall.

I cover my arms with my hoodie and leave the bathroom. I get to the art room and even though there's a class working on their projects, I walk straight to the back shelves and take Joanie's giraffe.

Susan is at my locker writing on a piece of paper. Her face is moist from half-wiped tears.

"What's going on?" I ask.

"Oh my God, Aggie, did you hear about Joanie?"

"I know."

Susan puts her arms around me and we share one of those friend hugs that manages to make you feel better even after you've flatlined. "Look, I'm sorry about the dance. I've been thinking about it, and I feel like I broke a promise to you, sooooo, I started a new diet today, and I can walk on my mother's treadmill. I'm going to lose at least ten pounds! Let's do that *La Belle Château* trip this week, okay?"

"But what about J.J.?"

"Oh, I doubt she'd want to come to the dance. What's with the giraffe?"

"It's Joanie's. We have Art together. Had. The last time I saw her she was holding this giraffe."

"It's beautiful."

"Hey, STUPID BITCH!" A man's voice booms in our direction. Rat's long black trench wings around him as he walks, an evil creature of the night. We stop breathing. He stands six inches away from my face and screams, "You told them about my party! You told them where I live! I will end you! They're gonna kick me out again!"

My only chance for survival is to lie.

"I didn't say anything — I didn't even know you had a party! I don't even know what you're talking about!"

"Right. Chug said he saw you coming out of Washington's office, and then they call me in and start asking me questions. I saw you with Joanie in the caf last week."

I have no idea who Chug is, but I'm guessing he didn't earn his name because of his ability to rapidly consume massive amounts of milk. My voice warbles, "No way. I was in the principal's office because I'm failing all my classes. We didn't even talk about any party."

Rat opens the top of the skull that hangs around his neck and pulls out a broken kitchen paring knife crudely wrapped in black electrician's tape. He calmly trims the dirt-encrusted thumbnail on his left hand, and then suddenly whips the knife at my face,

"Look, *bitch*, if I find out you're lying, I'll scalp the other side of your ugly bitch head."

I think bitch must be his favorite word.

"Which do you prefer, Pepsi or Coke?" I sputter.

"What?"

"You know, *the drink*." Oh God. Please don't *end* me.

Rat looks at me and frowns. A few kids walk in our direction.

"Shut up, bitch." The evil creature of the night turns and swoops away.

"That was close. What the heck happened? You were in the principal's office?" Susan asks.

"Yeah, I, well, Joanie invited me to Rat's party, and I went to his house, but I didn't go in. It was stupid."

"Oh wow. Were people drinking? Was there a fight? Did the cops come? I've never been to a house party."

"There was drinking, there weren't any fights when I was there, which was only about ten minutes, I didn't even see Joanie."

"Did *you* drink?"

Not technically.

"No. I didn't even want to. I was by myself and it was super weird."

"Do you want to drink at the dance? My dad has *tons* of booze in a cupboard. *Real* booze, you know? French brandy. I'm totally sure he wouldn't miss it. He doesn't even lock his booze cupboard, the only cupboard that's locked in our house is the one that stores the crapalicious semi-sweet chocolate."

Is Susan asking me if I want to drink because she thinks I want to drink, or is she asking me because *she* wants to drink?

"I don't know. Do *you* want to drink at the dance?" Susan shrugs. I continue, "Umm. You know what, no. I don't want to drink. I think that would sort of ruin it."

Susan lets out a sigh of relief.

"Good. I thought that maybe because you've been to a house party you might have become, I don't know, cooler, lol."

"Susan. Seriously? You, of all people, should know that there's no way that I can get any cooler, as a matter of fact, I'm so cool that no one has even noticed how cool I am."

"Oh, right, that explains it. So, we're at Carson's house tonight?" Susan asks.

"Oh, right. You don't know. Carson is grounded, total lockdown — not even allowed to have friends over. And when you were at J.J.'s I sorta told everyone that I was quitting the club, but that's ancient history now because I changed my mind."

"You? Quit? There's no way. I won't let you quit. We'll meet at my house. I'll tell my mom it's a video fitness club. She'll make us a decadent tray of raw vegetables with fat-free yogurt dip."

"Really? That'd be awesome. You tell whoever you see, and so will I. And let them know that I'm back in."

"Sounds like a plan. Hey, do you want to go for a walk today at lunch, or do you have to study?"

"A walk? Are grade tens *allowed* to leave the school grounds?"

"You know what, Aggie, Joanie's dead. I think we can do whatever we want today. At least I think that's what she'd want us to do."

"You're right. We will honor Joanie's memory and do more of the stuff that *we* want to do, the way Joanie would have."

"It's too bad that what she wanted to do was die."

We stand beside one another and mourn for a minute and then I say something that I don't think I've ever said to anyone in my entire life. It just comes out, like it's the most natural thing in the world, "I love you."

"Oh my gosh! I love you, too!"

And this time, I hug Susan.

20

"So tell me ... what's going on ... you know, you and Carson?"

Although the incline is vaguely discernible, Susan struggles with each step. I try to count (3) the cracks on the sidewalk and talk at the same time.

"Oh, that."

"Yeah, that."

"Well, he asked if he could kiss me. (7) And I wasn't totally sure about it. I don't exactly have tons of experience with that sort of thing. Then it just happened, the way kissing does. I think. I haven't had a chance to talk to him about it. (11) I'm not sure what to say."

"What was it like?"

"Um, well, it was over pretty fast."

"Yeah, but what was it like to have a boy *kiss* you?" Susan stops, waits for my reply, catching her breath.

"It was ..."

"I bet it was great."

"It was sorta great." We continue walking. "It's just that I'm still not sure if I actually *wanted* to kiss him, or if I kind of just went along with it because he wanted to kiss me." (14)

"Oh. Yes. Love is always complicated."

"I know, but it's not like I'm dying to kiss him again." (16. Or was that 17?)

"Well, then I think that's your answer. If you're not sure about a re-kiss, then you probably don't really like him in *that* way."

"Yeah. Probably not, but I think I also like Travis."

"What? You mean *like*-like? Why?"

"I don't know. He was nice to me?"

"Aggie, that's a stupid reason to like-like someone. Besides, I think it's pretty obvious he's crushing on Nicole. The two of you have more in common, though. You're both trees, and I think Nicole's probably a shrub.

Trees? Shrub?

"What?" Susan bends down and plucks a long-stemmed pieced of weedy grass and holds it out toward me.

"Okay. Tree or shrub? What do you think this is? You have to pick one."

"Umm, okay, how about tree." Susan shoots her hand up the stem and a few of the little branches break off. What's left resembles a miniature tree.

"There. Tree it is. You were right."

"So, what does that have to do with me and Travis?"

"Everybody has a choice, Aggie. You either choose to be a tree, or you choose to be a shrub. A person either chooses to do the right thing: to speak up and be a tree, or to remain quiet and be a shrub. You and Travis are trees, and I think Nicole is a shrub. I think that when it really comes down to it, she will choose to be a shrub, and shrubs stay low to the ground. Trees stand tall. Everyone has a choice. Hey look!" Susan shuffles up in front of me and from out of the long grass, she produces a cellphone. It's pink and shiny, and familiar to me.

"Whose do you think it is?" Susan asks. She taps the screen.

"What are you doing?"

"I'm going through the contacts. We know all of these people." We stand over the phone while Susan taps and pictures appear out of nowhere. A jillion pictures of people from The Torture Chamber. Susan stops on one. Her hand rests on the phone. It's the picture of me rummaging through a garbage can. Susan says the only thing in the world that could diffuse my escalating shame, "Your hair looks good in this picture."

"Thanks. That was before most of it was ripped out. But now at least we know whose phone it is."

"How do we know that?"

"Because I know who took that picture."

Susan looks at me like I'm six years old and she's just about to tell me that Santa's a hoax.

"Aggie, people share pictures, send each other pictures on their phones. This picture might have been sent to a hundred different people. Maybe a thousand."

"But I saw her delete it. She couldn't have sent it!"

"Did she delete it immediately after she took it?"

"What? No. It was the next day."

"So then she had already sent it around. Who was it?"

"Mandy Kronk."

"I know her. And my mom sees her mom at the gym. I could tell my mom and she could talk to Mandy's mom and then ..."

"Forget about it. Just throw the phone back in the bushes."

But she doesn't. Susan carefully puts the phone on the ground, walks to the edge of the sidewalk and finds a large rock. She passes the rock to me.

"Okay. It's your turn."

I take the rock from her, raise it high in the air, and, with one massive blow, I smash the phone. It cracks and small glass shards splinter into the air. I lift my arm and smash the phone again, breaking it apart even more. I keep smashing, and with every violent blow, the phone becomes more unrecognizable, and I start to cry. The tears blur my vision and I have to stop. Susan kicks the larger bits off the sidewalk. "That phone was a real piece a shit."

I smile up at her and she offers me her hand. I throw the rock into the bushes and wipe my rock-dirtied-palm on my pants.

"Hey, did you find out who that boy is? The rainbow-bead baseball hat guy?"

"Not exactly," I say. "But he goes to our school. He kind of … watches over me?"

"Isn't that, ah, you know, *strange*?"

"It's different, but I think it's romantic."

"Yeah, maybe. As long as he doesn't turn out to be a creeper. You know that some boys just want to have sex, right? And it's not because they like you or because they want to be your boyfriend or anything. It's because they want to have sex."

"Yeah. I know. But I think he really likes me. And I can't wait to see him at the dance."

"Mmm 'kay. I'm just sayin'. And, what dance?"

"Oh, right, you don't know. He sent me a ticket to the Winter Solstice Carnival dance, but I had to give it to Mandy in exchange for deleting that picture.

"Well, that worked out well. So he's going to be at the dance?"

"I think so. Are you mad?"

"Mad? Are you kidding? I want to meet this guy just as much as you do. I'm totally jealous, though. You have one guy who wants to kiss you, and another guy who wants to dance with you. I wish I had a boyfriend. I don't even have an affectionate dog."

I can't tell her what I wish I had, like, more than two pairs of pants. Instead I say, "So, when will you know if it's okay for us to come over tonight?"

"Huh? Oh, don't worry, it's totally fine. My dad will be sleeping and my mom will be steeping."

21

"It's Vivaldi! The symphony!" Jane yells.

She found a toddler-friendly pink bunny-armed turntable at Spendapenny. We had the exact same one when I was five years old. The two of us would listen to records all the time together and do the hokey-pokey and shake it all about, but this record is so scratched that it sounds like a dog's funeral.

"Yeah, that's great! I have to go!"

"What? Where? No! Come dance!"

"I have to go to Susan's! To work on something!"

"What? Susan works?"

I lift the paw-needle off the record and speak calmly and without emotion. The gin-bottle encounter on the front lawn gave Jane a good reason to further her paranoia.

"I need to go to Susan's to work on a project."

"No. I want you home tonight."

Jane replaces the paw and dances on the spot like she's at a grand ball. When she gets to this point, there's nothing I can say to bring her back to the land of the living. The only way that I can leave now is to sneak out. I have to yell again, "Okay, fine. I'm really tired, anyway. I think the best thing is for me to go to bed early!"

"What?"

"I'm going to bed!" Jane continues her ghost-partner waltz — not an easy undertaking considering there's no room to move. She'll knock something over and it'll be my fault. "Good night!" No reply. I can't leave until I know that she's heard me, otherwise, she'll check on me before she goes to bed. "GOOD NIGHT!"

She snaps out of the place where garden gnomes rule the earth and yells, "You don't have to yell!"

"I'm going to bed! Good night!"

"You're ruining the moment! For Pete's sake, good night!"

She's heard it. I go to my room, climb onto a pile of boxes stacked beneath the window, hold my breath, and jump.

I'll stop by Carson's on the way to Susan's. Maybe Mrs. Turndale will help me hire a garbage truck to come and clean out The Dump. I hate Jane more now than ever. I'm going to surround myself with friends instead of garbage. The only thing worth keeping is Joanie's giraffe.

Carson's gate is closed. I press the buzzer. Nothing. I press again. A quiet voice trickles through the microphone, "Hello?"

"Hi, it's Aggie, is that you, Mrs. Turndale?"

"Carson's grounded."

"Oh, yes, I know. I'm actually here to see you."

"Not tonight. We have … guests. Another time. We'll talk another time."

And that's it. I'm not invited in, the gate doesn't open, not a cupcake in sight.

I look over my shoulder every twenty-three seconds on the way to Susan's. I carry them with me — Those Girls.

I tap-tap-tap the Buddha-head knocker on Susan's purple front door. Susan's mother is dressed in a velvety yoga ensemble.

She lets me in and whispers, "Welcome to our refuge, a house of quiet. Please, when here, no one speaks above a sigh."

Wow. Susan could have warned me. No wonder her dad wants to sleep all the time; the place is one big bedroom. No real furniture, just piles of enormous embroidered pillows, dark candles, and exotic incense. I love it.

"Can I offer you some non-GMO fruit and yogurt?"

I'm thinking YES! but in my most Zen-ish voice I say, "Yes, please. I like your purple door."

"It's *aubergine*. Please, relax."

With a prima donna open arm gesture, she indicates to me that I should enter the "place of many cushions." After a whole two minutes of lounging, I start to doze off. Susan's mother returns with a Japanese calligraphed ceramic bowl that's filled with thinly sliced strawberries and thick vanilla yogurt. I quietly whisper a *thank-you* and, balancing on one leg, Susan's mother slowly lowers herself beside me. She lifts each foot onto an opposite thigh.

"Mom! I told you to *tell* me when people got here." Breaking our meditation, Susan talks in a loud voice, "Sorry, Aggie."

"No, it's fine. It's nice. I'm good."

"Well, come *on*."

I get up and bring my bowl of smooth, fruity *ohm* with me. I don't want to eat it because when I do, it will be gone.

"Mom, just send the next person upstairs when they come, okay?"

Susan's mother closes her eyes and silently nods. When we reach the top of the stairs, Susan turns to me. Her face reveals an unprecedented level of annoyance, "It's all an act. She pretends to be all lady-monk, but really she's the Evil Fitness Queen. I wouldn't eat that, if I were you, it's probably poisonous. And stay away from her home-made tea."

"Oh," I say, and peer into the bowl.

Susan's room is the same size as the entire top floor of my house. Clothes are strewn everywhere and Susan huffs and puffs as she bends to pick them up and then drape them over a disappearing chair. When she's not looking, I take quick scoops of non-GMO and chew. Like it's against the law.

"Don't clean up for me," I manage, between bites.

"A *boy* is coming over."

"Oh, right." I comb my fingers through my hair.

Nicole and Travis stand in the doorway, Travis holds a Japanese calligraphed ceramic bowl and he's wearing his suit, but this time he's put on a Professor Clown polka-dot bow tie. "Did you guys try this yogurt?" He takes a scoop. "The club's back on?"

"Yes, Travis. And I promise that I won't ever quit again."

"That's good, 'cause I got some footage. Just a sec."

Travis plunks himself down on Susan's big bed and sets up Carson's video camera. We hover around him, the sultan with his harem. I wish Carson were here. He may be small, but he's still a boy. Travis stops the tape as it rewinds and presses *play*. We see Idiot Boy Grant, whose locker shares a wall with Travis's.

"Hey, mutant, give me the test."

"What test would that be?"

Travis is obviously setting him up. Grant grabs Travis's face with one of his hands and digs his fingers into his cheeks and mouth.

"You know it'd only take a second to rip your stupid face off your stupid face."

"Fine. I'll give you Mr. Gibbs's math test, but only because you're threatening me."

"Whatever, Dumbass."

Then there's a shot of linoleum, and then nothing.

"The battery ran out. But there's still enough there to use."

"That's really good footage, Travis. Were you scared?" Nicole smiles at him.

Apparently, Nicole is attempting to flirt with Travis, which is commendable, seeing as how her armpit sweat is leaking quite unattractively through her "sweatshirt."

"Nah. How can I be scared of someone whose career in a few years is going to be cleaning out the park Porta Potties?"

"I want to see her now!" A frantic voice screams from downstairs.

It's Jane. She's yelling. In the House of Zen. My instinct is to leap out Susan's bedroom window, but there's no time. She's already at the door in all her magnificently deranged glory.

"Get over here now! You left the house! You lied to me!"

Susan's mother makes the unfortunate choice of trying to calm her. "She's fine, Mrs. Murphy. Let the kids have their club meeting and I'll make you some tea."

"Mind your own beeswax! A club meeting? What club meeting? Agatha isn't allowed to belong to any clubs."

"The Keep Fit Teen Club? You don't know about it?"

"Of course I know about it. Let's go Agatha, the van is running."

Susan's mother looks genuinely concerned. "That's not good for the environment," she says.

Feeding off her crazy-person adrenaline, Jane clenches her fists. "Do you want to know what else isn't good for the environment?"

Susan's mother thinks Jane is actually having a conversation with her. "Yes, of course."

"Teenage obesity."

No one speaks. I look at Susan and mouth the word: *Sorry*.

I hear Travis's voice from upstairs, "Bring all your tapes to school tomorrow!"

THE SHEET OF ice on the inside of Turdle's windows makes it difficult to see the road. I watch my warm breath rise against the cold in front of me, empty clouds filled with the things I cannot say out loud. Jane scrapes the window with the hard end of a hairbrush. As soon as I get to 16.0, I will run away to somewhere warm — probably the Mediterranean. I'll work for a French family as an *au pair* to three little girls who wear satin ribbons in their hair and curtsey when I ask them to get ready for bed. I'll teach them how to do papier-mâché.

It's not until we're almost home that Jane says, "I forbid you to see that fat girl again. She's a bad influence. And those other kids — stay away from them. Any friend who would be an accomplice to a lie that you tell your mother is not a real friend. You have to understand this. Those kids are *not* your friends. Do you understand me?" Preparing the dough for an invisible pie crust, she emphasizes her point by slapping her hand on the dash in front of her. "They are not your friends."

"Really, *Jane*? They're not my friends? They're more my friends than you are my mother."

She jerks the steering wheel sideways and we spin around with such force that the contents of the van hurricane. A Burger Stop takeout bag lands at my feet. We've never once gone to the Burger Stop together. We smash into a bulky metal mailbox, which is probably a federal offence. She reverses the van without checking behind her, thrashes back into drive, speeds forward, and drives dangerously close to oncoming traffic. Cars honk at us as we speed by. She's trying to scare me, but I don't care. There is nothing she can say or do that will have any effect on me whatsoever.

"You're grounded. Forever. You may not leave the house ever again. Not even for school."

"*Aubergine*," I whisper.

Miraculously, we arrive at The Dump alive. I go to my room and slam the door. The walls shake. I put on my yellow terry towel shorts that I've owned since I was seven, and I look through a stack of bags. I need something sharp. Six bags later, I find the perfect item: an electric can opener. I plug it in and place the blade close to the inside of my left thigh. I turn it on. It doesn't work. I throw the can opener against my wall and it makes an impressive dent at the place of impact.

I lie on my bed and stare at the ceiling. And that's when I see it. My overhead light. It has two light bulbs in it, one of them not burned out. I stand on my bed and manage to unscrew the burned-out bulb. I take the bulb and put it on my floor, then smash my heavy *The Wonders of Math* textbook onto the bulb. Do I use just a piece of the glass, or the end part of the broken bulb? The end part will allow me a better grip. I hold the sharp edges close to my skin and draw a long line down my thigh, and it cuts beautifully and precisely; a soothing and perfect revelation of bright red blood. The incision isn't too deep that it's a problem, but just deep enough to feel right. I can finally breathe. I cut another line parallel to the first one and I let go of the bulb and close my eyes. *This* pain is good. *This* pain I control.

22

🕷

I wake up early enough to sneak out. I'm going to ask Susan to go to *La Belle Château* with me today. If I don't get a dress soon, all the good ones will be gone, especially since I need one that will cover my arms — there's not enough time for them to heal before the dance. From now on I will only cut my legs — so much easier to hide. I look in the fridge and find a couple of small plastic plum sauce, mustard, and vinegar packs, all from takeout restaurants, and a nutritious box of wine. I grab five of the plum sauce packs, open them, and suck out the sweet-and-sour paste. It'd be nice to have an egg roll.

When I get to The Torture Chamber, Carson is at my locker and the anxiety on his face would scare a ticked-off Tyrannosaurus.

"Why did you come to my house? What were you going to tell my mom? You weren't going to tell her about ... about ..."

"How you kissed me?"

"You're not going to say anything, are you? You can't."

"Apparently I'm not the only girl you tell it's your birthday, and that you've never kissed anyone before. What about that?"

Carson's face turns ketchup-bottle red. "Oh."

"Yeah, oh."

"It's kind of a long story."

"I've got aaaall day."

"I'm not sure you'll want to hear this."

"Just tell the truth Carson. That's all I want to hear."

"Well, I kinda, kinda ..."

"Kinda what?"

"I kinda kiss girls who, well, who I think that a kiss would make them feel better about themselves." He stares at his feet, which isn't difficult, seeing as how they're so close to his head.

"You *what*?"

"I kiss girls so that they think that someone wants to kiss them. And I do want to kiss them, in a way. It's just something that I think is a nice thing to do. Like a good deed."

"A good *deed*? You kiss us because you think you're doing us a *favor*? Are you *kidding* me?"

"No, it's not a bad thing. It's meant to be nice."

"Carson, you don't know the first thing about girls. If you kiss a girl, she's obviously going to think you *like* her, she's not going to think, oh, this guy is doing me a big favor. Lucky, lucky me, I guess I'm not as hideous as I thought."

"So, you're saying you didn't feel good after I kissed you? It didn't feel good that someone, even someone as ... even someone like me, wanted to kiss you?"

He's right, of course, but the reason behind the kiss sucks. I hate that he lied, but at least he's trying to be nice, even though it is pretty weird. Carson motions to me to bend down so that he can whisper something, "*I liked kissing you. It was more than just a good deed.*" And then, magically, our lips touch and we're kissing. Again. And we keep kissing for what seems like forever (a full forty-eight seconds, to be exact). We stop and he turns to leave, but before he runs away, he looks up at me and says, "You make me feel taller." I think about that all morning and for some reason I can't pinpoint which level to assign it on The Official Romantic Scale. I guess because I know that the boy in the

Letter B baseball hat is around here somewhere and if he saw Carson and I kissing, he'd for sure get the wrong impression about me.

When lunch break finally comes, I want to go for another walk with Susan, so I go to her locker. She's talking to J.J. who's devouring a Jumbo Tron bag of Nacho-Cha-Cha chips. Susan isn't eating any.

"Hey!"

They look at me, Susan smiles, J.J. crunches, creating a visually pleasing combination of complimentary colors; orange crumbs stick to the front of her *aubergine* sweater.

And then, as though they've been in love for a hundred years, Yale and Chrissy Crop Top walk by, arm in arm, almost exactly the same way he was walking with that boy in the mall. They stare at each other's hit-the-gene-pool-jackpot faces, entirely oblivious to the world around them.

Chrissy Crop Top speaks. "Do you want to go to Spa Hollywood after school to get our eyebrows waxed?"

And Yale replies, "Awesome."

They saunter away, so into how the other one is so into them.

"When did they become a thing?" Susan asks.

J.J. catapults chip shrapnel. "This morning!"

"Well, that's worth celebrating," Susan says. "Let's all go into town after school and get a non-fat cinnamon latte, my treat!"

"I can't go. I have an Alateen meeting," J.J. says.

It must be some fat-camp follow-up or something. I have to ask, "What's Alateen?"

"Oh, it's for kids whose parents are alcoholics."

"You mean … for you?" She doesn't mean me, does she?

"Yeah, my dad is what they call a raging alcoholic. He drinks, we duck. He's either throwing something, kicking something, or punching something. One night he got into a fight with our fireplace and broke his foot. Miss Strand, the school counsellor told me about it. She's so nice."

I think about Jay-Rome's family not being able to afford a therapist.

"Does it cost a lot?" I ask.

"Nope, it's totally free. And they have good snacks. Anyway, I'll see you guys later. Have fun downtown." J.J. leaves and Susan looks at me like she has something to say.

"What?" I ask.

"Not that I think that I can tell you what to do or anything, but maybe you should find out where that meeting is."

"Maybe. Sometime. Not today. Today, before we get lattes, maybe we can stop by *La Belle Château*?"

"Hey! That's a great idea. I'll meet you at the bus stop after school. Do you have bus money?"

"Yes." I do. I have ten Mr. Peanut dollars.

"Okay, great. I have a bunch of math to do in the library. Do you want to come? You could go on the internet."

We get to our new-books-are-not-in-the-budget school library and it's empty. There's not even a teacher-librarian around. I want to rummage through the big oak desk because to me, teachers' desks have a Narnia-wardrobe appeal. Susan sits at a table and points me in the direction of the computers.

"Just use your student number and log in."

"Student number?"

"Yeah, we all have them." I look at Susan like she's asked me to figure out the square root of 6,729.43. "You can use mine for now." Susan logs me in and leaves to work on her math. I Google Alateen.

Alcoholism is a family disease. Those of us who are closest to the alcoholic suffer the most ...

Got that right.

... the meetings are a place for people to share their personal experiences and stories ...

Forget it. There's no way I'm going to *share personal experiences and stories.*

"Susan, I'm done. I have to get my books for my next class." She gives me a thumbs-up and stares at her textbook.

A piece of paper is taped to the outside of my locker. It's a drawing of a rainbow, but there are two dots over it, so it looks like a sad face. That's it, then, he saw me kissing Carson. I've ruined everything. Sure, I like Carson, and I like Travis, but this boy could really change my life. Get me out of here. *Marry* me. Why did I kiss Carson like that? *In public.*

I open my locker and take out my camera and immediately press rewind.

Brrrrring

I turn off the camera and put it back inside my locker. I'll try to think of an excuse to get out of class. Maybe I'll say that I have to puke. Teachers hate that.

The cytoplasm consists of plasmasol surrounded by a more viscous plasma gel …

This stuff is mesmerizing, I raise my hand. Thrilled that someone wants to ask him something about the plasma gel phenomenon, Big Head Kraus's furball eyebrows lift in ecstatic anticipation. "Yes, what is it? We have a question!"

"Um, I think I'm going to be sick?"

"Fine. Go."

Mass loathing permeates the room and everyone stares me. I wish I were surrounded by a viscous plasma gel.

The halls are vacant. I look over my shoulder to make sure no one is following me with an X-ACTO knife, ready to slash my face or make me eat the dirt from the bottom of my own shoe.

There's a Sharpie stick-man drawn on my locker and the part between his legs is exaggerated and grotesque. Four words are scribbled underneath:

Bang bang you're dead.

Now I *do* feel like I'm going to be sick. Unfortunately, my camera wasn't recording, so I have no idea who defaced my locker. Probably Rat, aggressive, threatening, crude. I reach for my lock but I have to stop. There's a thing covering it and I only recognize what it is because we all had to suffer through sex-ed classes in grade five. It's a stretched-out condom. Great. Now what? Do I tell the principal? Obviously not. What about the janitor? I'm not going to touch this … thing. J.J. said the counsellor is nice. Maybe I should tell the counselor. Maybe I should have told the counselor everything a long time ago. All of Those Girls combined are nothing compared to one Rat and before today I thought I could handle this alone, but now I know that I can't.

I walk to Miss Strand's room, but there's already someone in her office, so I sit on a small hand-knitted afghan-covered couch and wait in the "holding" area. I look around at the posters: *Love Doesn't Hurt. Tell Someone. To Make a Friend, Be a Friend.* Lots of flowers and kittens. It's like life is all pretty and precious and cute. Right. I stare at the trapped scuba diver whose oxygen tank releases tiny bubbles in the small aquarium in the corner of the room. The door opens and Myhell and her just as remarkably red-haired mother (I'm guessing), whose left arm is covered by a wrist-to-elbow cast, exit the room.

"Oh, hello. Are you waiting for me?" Miss Strand asks. I nod. "Go ahead inside, I'll be right in."

Miss Strand's voice is so soothing that I feel like I'm floating inside one of the little scuba diver's air bubbles. The room is cozy and very warm, furnished with two green leaf-patterned upholstered chairs. A thin decorative Asian rug covers the floor and a heavy wool-spun picture of a willow tree hangs on the wall. The obligatory box of Kleenex sits on her desk, along with a yellow notepad. A glass bowl filled with colorful unwrapped flat marble candies sits beside a gold macaronied tin of sharpened pencils.

"Would you like one?" Miss Strand offers me the bowl. To be polite, I choose a green one, not the one I want, but the one closest to me. She probably thinks I'm here because of Joanie, and I feel bad because I'm not. "So, tell me, Agatha, right?"

I nod.

"What's going on?"

And that's it. I break. Streaming gasps of pain release from my gut. I would be all-out wailing if it weren't for the candy that I'm trying to not spit out. "Take your time. It's okay, you're safe here." Her saying that makes me cry more. That word. Safe. So simple. So impossible. A Kleenex Kilimanjaro takes shape on my lap.

Miss Strand waits quietly as I sniffle-catch my breath. "I can't get into my locker."

"Oh. Well, we can fix that." She waits. "Is there anything else?"

"I can't get into my locker because ... because ... because someone has stuck a condom on my lock and I don't want to touch it and they drew a rude picture on my locker and they want to kill me."

"Just a minute." Miss Strand picks up her phone and presses a couple of buttons. "Hi, it's Judy, could you send me Stan when he has a moment, please. We have a code 42. Yes, a code 42." She rolls her eyes. "A *locker* cleanup." Quietly, she hangs up the phone. "You said they want to kill you. What do you mean by that?"

"The people here at school. They want to kill me, but I can't tell you who because then they'd kill me."

"You must be scared."

I can barely speak. I manage a "Yup."

"Okay, listen, I'm going to enlist you in our new Victim Protection Program."

"What's that?"

"It's a new program we're starting. I'm very excited about it. I assign a group of older students to look out for the younger kids."

"Oh, wow."

"I know. It's very innovative. And you know how the sports teams have uniforms? Well, the members of the v.p.p. will also have uniforms. Jackets and t-shirts that they'll wear so that everyone can identify them. It's going to be very visual. Very high-profile. Your friend Michelle just joined and I've already assigned her three grade eight students to watch over."

"Michelle Hastings?"

"Yes, that was her mother with her. The Hastings family is funding the program."

Seriously? That's messed up. *Click*. Just like that, someone turned on the big LIFE SUCKS neon light switch. I want to cry again. I want to push over the aquarium and lie on the floor, gasping for breath like the stupid naive fish that don't deserve it because they never did anything to anyone.

"We just need to fill out a few forms ..." Miss Strand shuffles through a file. None of this makes any sense. I hold back a scream. I want to pick up my chair and throw it at the wall. Jackets and t-shirts — yeah, that will make it stop. I need that soft cut of quiet relief against my skin. I take a deep breath,

"You know, um, can I think about this for a coupla days?"

Disappointed, she stops and looks at me and waits for me to change my mind. The only sound is the clickety click of the hard candy hitting the enamel of my teeth. I purposefully crunch it. Grind it into nothing.

"Of course. Oh, here he is."

Janitor Stan holds a black plastic bucket and a coarse green scouring pad. His grey braided pony-tailed hair matches his long grey moustache, a red lizard tattoo crawls up his neck. The kinda guy you'd expect to see ride in on a chopper, not a floor polisher.

"Stan, this is Agatha. She'll show you where her locker is. Agatha, take Stan to your locker, and get back to me with your decision on the program. Would you like another candy?"

I reach into the bowl with an open fist and take about thirty. I have so many that I drop a few on the floor on my way out the door; I feel bad that she'll have to pick them up after I'm gone, but maybe she'll just leave them for Janitor Stan.

We walk quietly to my locker. I hold out my sticky, dye-stained hand and he takes a candy and says nothing. After examining the damage, he takes his work gloves out of his back pocket, along with a tarnished silver cigarette lighter. He holds the lighter up to the condom, flicks it, and the offending thing shrivels into nothingness. He lets out an exasperated sigh and goes to work on removing the stick-man using a strong-smelling spray and a bristle brush. I should have taken some footage of my locker.

Janitor Stan removes his gloves, looks at me, and says, "They do this to you because you have something that they'll never have, and they know it. Don't let these jerks get to you." He takes out a pack of cigarettes. "You want one? For later?"

"Ah, sure," I say. I take one and then he takes one and puts it in his mouth and walks away. The work gloves half-stuffed in the back pocket of his coveralls wave goodbye to me.

I open my locker, take out my camera, and rewind to the spot where, sure enough, I see the boy in the letter B baseball hat and the note. Why the heck does he even like me? Maybe he just feels sorry for me. But that's not at all romantic. Maybe he wants to be my hero. Yes, that's much better.

I get to the bus stop but there's no Susan yet, so I sit on the bench and stare at my knees because I'm too excited to do anything else. *La Belle Château*! I am Neil Armstrong, my foot hovers inches above the surface of the moon. I look at the crumpled gift certificate: *Buy something beautiful, like you*. Why do I kiss Carson? Because I'm a moron, that's why. The gift certificate goes into my front pocket, close to my heart.

A pack of students walk toward the bus stop, and I should probably get up off the bench and hide behind something.

Oh no.

Turdle zooms into the parking lot. I guess Jane is here to permanently remove me from The Torture Chamber. It's surprising that she has the energy to do anything, seeing as how I tripped over another empty box of wine outside her bedroom door this morning.

A bus pulls up and everyone gets on but me. Undoubtedly grateful that he has one fewer teenager to deal with, the bus driver ignores me and drives away. Where is Susan? More people come to the bus stop. I dig my fingernails deep into the palm of my hand, but it doesn't hurt enough to distract me. I stand up and gawkily sprint to the side of the school, and accidently drop my backpack (of course) on the way. People laugh and I bend down to pick it up. I'll watch for Susan from around the corner of the building.

"Hey! No trespassing, Derp!" someone yells.

This side of The Torture Chamber is the smokers' exclusive territory: the so-called cool people, the people who wear a lot of heavy dark makeup, pierce each other's body parts at home using a needle and an ice cube, and always smell like weed. But they've never hurt me — I guess they're always too relaxed to bother. Three people stare at me: Two cool girls and a very cool boy.

"What the hell are *you* doing here?" One of the girls asks, a halo of smoke escapes through a hoop-pierced lip.

"Oh, I just needed a light." I take out my Janitor Stan cigarette and, as awkward as a turtle with a chopstick, I put it in my mouth.

"You're *smoking*?"

I nod. If I speak, the cigarette will fall out, which is decidedly *not* cool.

The boy takes his red, white, and blue marijuana-leaf-adorned plastic lighter, flicks it in my face, and just like that, I'm smoking. It's gross and I hold back a cough. I feel a little dizzy, a little woozy, but not a whole lot cooler. I guess if I took up smoking it would give me something to do with all that extra cash I'm always carrying around.

Finally, I see Susan, hiking toward the bus stop. I call out to her. She turns and makes her way to me, struggling for air, but not because she's smoking. She stares at the cigarette, "Aggie? *What are you doing?*"

"Just waitin' for you, takin' a smoke break." Like a pro, I drop the cigarette onto the ground and crush it with my shoe. "Let's go." Susan has to jog to keep up with me, because if Jane sees us, I'm dead.

"What the heck, Aggie? You *smoke* now?"

"No! Not at *all*." I look over my shoulder. "I'm avoiding my mother. She's here and I'm not allowed to leave the house ever again, so I had to hide. She went inside, and I — oh my God, there she is!"

We stop and stand motionless like we're playing a game of freeze tag. Jane mumbles to herself and stomps to the parking lot. We're about as subtle as a couple of hot-pink flamingos on a snowbank, but she doesn't spot us because she's too caught up in her own drama. She gets in Turdle and screeches out of the parking lot. I let out a huge sigh and start to cough.

"You really should quit smoking," Susan offers.

"Yeah, you're probably right."

"I'm so excited about this," she says.

"Me too! *La Belle Château*! Who woulda thought?" I say.

"Oh. I kinda meant the cinnamon lattes."

"Right! That, too!"

"So, what? You can't leave your house?" Susan asks.

"I'm grounded forever. Not even allowed to go to school."

Incredulous, Susan gapes. "But that's *illegal*."

"It is?"

"C'mon, you can't just not take your kid to school. It's in the constitution or something. I wish I didn't have to go to school. I wish they'd invent a school just for fat kids. Half the time I'm not even hungry. I just want something and I don't know what it is." The bus rolls up, Susan gets on first. "I'm paying for both."

Chink a link, chink a link, chink a link, chink a link, chink a link, chink a link, chink a link.

The evil bus driver purposely lurches the bus forward. We topple and grab on to the steel bar. We take the seats that are normally reserved for old people types with broken hips, because it's the best place for us. The best place for Susan, her having to squeeze down the aisle and all. I can't stop smiling because nothing can ruin the rest of this day.

23

"Tinkle tink."

A fairy bell announces our arrival.

A woman who could be anywhere between her thirties and sixties sorts through puffy stacks of sequined, pearl-beaded wedding dresses. She holds a cream-colored satin-covered hanger and as soon as she sees us she drops the hanger and rushes toward us, "The public washroom is down the street, past the drugstore in the coffee shop," she says.

"Oh!" I bellow. "We're here to buy dresses!" The excitement in my voice is nowhere *near* cream-colored satin.

"What is your upcoming event? Your bat mitzvah?" The store woman frowns.

"It's the Winter Solstice Carnival dance!"

The woman bites her lower lip, "*This* year's dance?"

"Yes, in December."

"Oh, I know when it *is, ma chérie*. But for us to order you a dress in time, you would have had to reserve it last spring."

"But I have a gift certificate." I present it to her. It's crumpled, stained, and the left corner is slightly torn. "I have to use it for a dress from here, for the Winter Solstice Carnival dance."

"We're new at this," Susan says.

"You don't say." The store woman picks up a white clipboard and an ostrich-plumed pen and asks, "Size?"

Susan says nothing. I have no idea what size I am so I say my age, "I'm a 15.8."

Susan frowns at me, "You're not a fifteen. I'm a twenty-two. There's no *way* you're a fifteen. You're probably a two. A four at the most."

"Oh. Right. I'm not exactly what you'd call a frequent shopper. Do you have anything with long sleeves? I get cold."

"Long sleeves? Oh, *merde*." She looks at Susan. "And what are your specifications?"

"Big," Susan says.

"I'll see what I can do."

The store woman leaves us. We sit and play Rock Paper Scissors. No hand grenades allowed. After an infinitesimal twenty-seven minutes, she returns with two plastic garment bags. She hangs them on a metal rack and unzips the first one.

"This may need to be altered. It's our only plus-size gown. I don't even know why we have it. We're *not* a plus size store." She takes the dress out of the bag.

"Wow." Susan whispers.

The dress is a light purple, er, *mauve*. Black velvet ribbon bows sit on the short, ever-so-slightly puffy sleeves, and a small black velvet ribbon adorns the waist.

"Come with me." The woman leads Susan to a gold-tasseled curtained change room. She hangs the dress inside and closes the curtain for Susan. She unzips the second garment bag. "Now, we don't have any dresses with sleeves, but this one comes with a little lace bolero jacket." She pulls out a sleeveless, black-lace floor-length gown. There's a slit in the front and the lining is a light pink and it's the most incredible dress I've ever seen. I gasp. A moment of girl-shopping-bonding happens between us as she says with exaggerated Parisian flair, "*Elle est très chic, oui! And* it's marked down."

Susan's curtain flies open and she stands Disney princess confident.

"Fashion show!" I say. Susan walks out slowly, and with red-carpet skill she holds up the front part of the dress, exposing a peek of darker mauve tulle. "You look beautiful, girlfriend!" I belt out.

And then, with a snuffle and a crack in her voice, Susan manages, "I-can't-believe-it. I just can't believe it."

"Turn around!" A ballerina in a jewelry box, she turns, and the black velvet ribbon around the waist comes to a bow in the back and the girl who hates herself has vanished.

"Your turn!" Susan shouts.

The saleswoman walks my dress to another change room and closes me in. There's a floor-to-ceiling three-way mirror in the room. I take off my clothes and choke at my reflection: conspicuous and alarming bright red marks radiate from the slowly healing cuts on my arms and legs, along with bruises around the punctures from my school binder. My ribs, knees, and hip bones are jagged sticks stuffed in a plastic grocery bag. I ease the dress over my head, and with much horror, I realize that I don't have the lace jacket. I pull my hoodie on over the dress and come out of the change room.

Susan laughs. "What the heck are you doing! Take your stupid hoodie off! Let's see the dress!" Susan pulls at the hoodie.

"No!" I yell. She stops.

"I need the bolarea thing."

"Oh, of course. The bolero." The store woman goes to the rack. "Here it is." She hands me the jacket and I disappear back into the change room. I'm sure Susan thinks I'm horrible, but when I accidentally see myself in the mirror again, my astonishment overpowers the moment. The dress is a size two and it fits me as if it were custom-made. The jacket covers all of my cut marks, but I am aware that I have to take very small steps, otherwise the slit in the front of the dress reveals the damage I've done to my legs. I draw back the curtain.

"You look amazing!" Susan says.

"*Très magnifique!*"

Susan turns to the saleswoman. "Good job picking dresses for us!"

"And with the right shoes, you girls will be the belles of the ball!" she replies.

The right shoes? She points to a pair of high-heeled black strappy shoes that sit in front of the mirror. I slip my sneaker toes into the chic sandals and the dress becomes even more spectacular.

"Do you loan these out?" Like cheap perfume, my question hangs in the air, a vulgar cloud of gauche.

"Oh, ah, no one's ever asked to borrow the display shoes. I'd have to check with the owner," she says.

And because I don't want my obvious faux pas to ruin everything, I say, "Just kidding!"

Both Susan and the store woman let out a laugh, and the store woman, offers her opinion of my little joke, "You girls are *très* humorous!"

Yup. *Très* Humorous. No doubt about it. I'm so lacking all the stuff that everybody else has that the thought of not having it isn't just humorous, it's *très* humorous.

I take off the dress and see the $385.00 price tag. But she said it was marked down! There's no way I can spend that much. I thought it'd be more like $89.00. Even $89.00 is too much. I come out and Susan looks at me and asks, "What's wrong?"

I whisper to her, "*It's three hundred and eighty-five dollars.*"

"I know, I think it's half price! What a deal, right?"

"Susan, it's too much."

"But you have a gift certificate."

"I know, but …"

"All right, ladies, let's wrap these up for you."

And my genius friend says, "Actually, we'd like to put the dresses on hold. We have a couple other shops that we need to check first." The saleswoman frowns. Susan continues, "It's not because we want to. It's our crazy mothers. They're making us. I guess you meet lots of crazy mothers? Working here?"

"Oh, *c'est incroyable*! Just the other day there was a woman here with her daughter, picking up the daughter's dress, but the mother herself had to try on a dozen dresses and she had a broken arm! I'll hold the dresses for a week." She whispers, "It will be our *petit* secret. After that, I have to ship them back to the supplier."

Susan gives her phone number for the both of us. We leave the store and all I want to do is manage my overwhelming disappointment; these feelings I don't want to feel, but I can't. Not until I'm alone.

"So, tell me again why can't you get that dress?" Susan asks.

"It's a gift, right? I'm sure he's not expecting me to spend *four hundred dollars*."

"Aggie, he's given you a gift certificate with no fixed amount, from *La Belle Château*. He must know what stuff costs there. He'll probably be shocked at how *little* you spent."

"I doubt that."

"Aggie, give me the gift certificate and I'll come back later this week with my mom. I've already lost two pounds. By next week, I could lose at least three more. I think she'll be happy with that. Three hundred and eighty-five dollars is *not* too much to pay for a gown."

It's more money than Jane makes in a month at Spendapenny.

Susan holds out her hand. "Let's go get those lattes."

Reluctantly, I hand Susan the gift certificate.

We walk a couple of blocks to the coffee shop, the one I've never actually been inside. It's a hangout for the normal kids at school who think that getting a five-dollar coffee drink several times a week is no big deal. If I had fifteen dollars a week to spend on something, it'd be on other luxuries like food, deodorant, and toothpaste. I'd no longer have to brush with baking soda and use a dry bar of soap as deodorant because *It's better than that* TV *stuff, it won't clog your pores.*

"Okay, what do you feel like?" Susan and I stare up at the imposing looks-like-a-foreign-language-to-me coffee menu. The man in front of us orders a six-shot long-pour Americano. His back is bent and crooked and when he turns I see that he's not that much older than us. He smiles at Susan and she smiles back and for one brief moment, I see a Susan who is noticed by the opposite sex.

"Um, I'll have the same as you, is that okay?"

"Yeah, for sure. Two skinny cinnamon lattes, please. Extra hot. Medium." Susan turns to me, "Cinnamon is good for regulating the blood sugar."

"Oh, right," I say.

The girl behind the counter smiles. "Sounds good, that's nine eighty-six, please." She's from Australia, and her accent is so charming, that I want to thank her for charging us so much. "They'll be ready for you over there." She points to a different area of the counter and we have to pass a surreal display of baked goods under glass (it looks like what I imagine Christmas looks like at the Turndales') and product (logoed tea cups, logoed travel mugs, logoed coffee grinders), to pick up our drinks. I didn't care about this place before, but now I want to own something with a logo on it. I'll keep the cup that my drink comes in and carry it around with me for as long as I can.

"Comfy chairs!" Susan locomotives over to the dark orange velvety chairs by the giant window that frames the street. I'm out of place and I'm tempted to bolt, but I force myself, for the sake of all that is normal, to stay. "So, your mom's a drinker, Carson's mom's bipolar, and my mom's just totally weird."

"Carson's mom is bi-whater?"

"Bi-polar, manic-depressive, chemical-dependent, call it whatever you want. She's either really really up, or really really down. You didn't notice she was kinda, you know, strange?"

"I noticed she's kinda amazing."

"Yeah, sure. When she's *happy*." Susan holds up her hands and makes little air quote marks around the word happy. "I've never seen her when she's depressed, Carson's told me about it, though. He said that she doesn't get out of bed, and he's not allowed to leave the house. She's on medication, but they have to keep adjusting it. I feel sorry for Carson, he already has enough to deal with, being kind of well, you know, *tiny*." She slurps her drink like it's a race and the people around us offer us a subtle flash of disapproval. "Turn on the camera! Turn on the camera!" Susan blurts, spilling her latte as she puts it down on the little table that sits between us. I fumble for my video camera. Myhell and Bevy walk toward the entrance, dressed in matching floral-print summer skirts, and Myhell is wearing her Victim Protection Program shirt. I put the camera on the windowsill and prop it up with a cardboard cup sleeve so that the angle of focus is just right. Bevy sees us first and nudges Myhell, who spies me and looks away. This is going to be rough. I try to maintain my composure. Susan is also very agitated. My hands shake. Bevy and Myhell get their giant-sized ice-blended drinks and, because they find us irresistible, they walk toward us. They stand at the side of our table.

Myhell speaks directly to me, "I guess you think you're pretty cool, don't you?"

I'm not really sure how to answer this one, because no, I don't think I'm cool at all, but I don't want her to know that, so, because I am really very *un*-cool, I say,

"I'm not as cool as say, a penguin."

Susan snorts comically.

Myhell continues, "You *could* be as cool as a penguin."

And because I'm clueless, I say, "Really? That'd be great."

With that, Myhell takes the lid off her drink and pours it over my head.

"*Now* you're cool," she says.

Bevy leans over me. "And now you have to buy Michelle another drink, because you made her spill it, clumsy bitch."

And then, something remarkable happens, Susan stands up, toe-to-toe with Myhell, and says, "You need to apologize."

"Apologize? Okay. I'm sorry you're such a fat-ass." And she pushes Susan, but because Susan is stronger than her, she doesn't move. Bevy throws her drink at Susan. It bounces off her, hits the floor, and explodes.

"Hey! Knock it off!" someone yells. We stop.

Flash-frozen in our disgrace we see our school counsellor. Horrified, Miss Strand asks, "What's going on here?"

No one says anything. I'm covered with frozen coffee-whipped-cream mess, but I feel great because we have more footage.

Miss Strand points to an empty table, "Get over here and sit down. NOW."

Reluctantly, we grab our stuff. Preparing herself for an impromptu counseling session, Miss Strand pulls her hair back into a pony-tail and wraps it tightly with an elastic that she removes from her wrist.

"Okay, who wants to tell me what happened here?" We stare at the surreal baked goods crumbs on the floor.

Bevy speaks first.

"It's nothing, really, we were just, I don't know. I guess it got a little out of control. We weren't actually trying to hurt each other."

Miss Strand looks at me, "Is that right, Agatha?"

"Oh, yeah, we um, someone spilled a drink and then I'm not really sure what happened after that."

Miss Strand looks at Susan, "Susan, what can you tell me?"

"Oh, ah, it was kinda an accident. You know, honestly? I don't even know."

Miss Strand continues, "Right. If that's the way it is, you're all getting an assignment."

Oh, great, here we go, another essay on Why Honesty Is the Best Policy or something equally worthwhile.

"Your assignment is to spend time with each other. To get to know one another, as individuals."

"But Miss Strand, we have nothing in common. Look at them," Bevy whines.

"You can't make us do this. I'll tell my mother," Myhell says.

"I *can* make you do this, and you go right ahead and *tell* your mother. I'd be interested to hear what she has to say. So, this is how it's going to work. After school on Fridays for the next month, the four of you will sit together in the library and *dialogue* with each other."

Bevy scrunches up her nose. "Dialogue?"

Miss Strand continues, "Talk to each other. Get to know each other. As friends."

I almost choke on the, *as friends.*

Myhell's face turns corpse-pale, like she's been anchored to the bottom of the ocean for a couple of weeks. She protests, "This sucks! First my mother breaks her arm and I have to help her wash her hair, which is the grossest thing in the universe, and now this!" She breathes heavily, like she's having a panic attack. I would offer her my Jay-Rome paper bag, but I don't want her DNA anywhere near it — I can't risk contracting Mean People's Disease. We watch as Myhell Darth-Vader inhales.

"Are you okay, Michelle?" Miss Strand asks.

Myhell rifles through her purse and takes out a weird plastic contraption that she puts into her mouth and pumps a couple of times. Her breathing slows.

Miss Strand removes the elastic from her hair and says, "Susan and Aggie, you can go. I'll stay here and watch Michelle, but we'll see you Friday."

Susan and I say goodbye to one another outside the coffee shop. I hold my coffee cup in front of me with the logo facing out and pretend to drink from it, all the way home.

MY SKIN IS a jigsaw puzzle, but I'm really trying to cut myself less. I found a pair of saw-toothed pinking shears in a mouse-nibbled wicker sewing basket that sits buried in a corner of my bedroom and the edges are just jagged enough. I've removed the little screw that holds the two sections of the shears together and I'll keep one side here and the other side I'll keep in my locker for emergency Torture Chamber use. I'm going to cut my stomach today; my legs and arms are pretty messed up.

I lift my shirt like I'm about to perform surgery on myself and I place the notched edge of the shears just below my left rib. Take a deep breath. Press down. Hard. I zigzag back and forth and the sharp pierce of the serrated edge breaks through and the blood comes. Efficient and reliable, the pain takes over. I close my eyes and rest.

Something scurries across my feet. I crash out of my closet and a horror movie rat comes with me, but it doesn't run away. It stops, perched on top of a pile of rancid bedding, and looks at me like I owe it an apology.

I push the two life-size toddler dolls that are for some reason tucked under blankets on my bed like they're real children (creepy), onto the floor, and lie down. "*You have something they'll never have.*" Really Janitor Stan? Is it the rats?

Bur-ing Bur-ing.

The phone. I don't want to answer it. Yes, we only have the one because according to Jane, the more phones you have in the house, the more money the *evil bureaucratic* phone companies charge you. Like a search-and-rescue dog looking for a snowboarder under an avalanche, I dig toward the sound. The ringing stops. I go back to my room.

Bur-ing Bur-ing

Shoot.

Dig. Dig. Dig. Aha! It's trapped under an exploded can of botulistic tomato Pokémon pasta. There's no way I'm going to touch it.

I want to sit and watch TV like a normal person, but there's no-where for a normal person to sit. Time to throw all this stuff out the window.

I pick up a pile of torn and disintegrating newspapers. My arms are sore and it hurts to bend over. I walk to the place where I remember the window is supposed to be, but it's heavily concealed by bags and rapidly decaying encyclopedias. A crumb-filled toaster and a mold-infested blender sit on the top, the cords intertwine like two snakes on a date. Oh, God.

I sit down on a pile of whatever it is. A tiny city of activity erupts by my shoe. Beetles. They scuttle away. *I have to get out of here.* Maybe I could live with Miss Strand or Janitor Stan. Maybe I could live in Carson's basement, or Susan's resort and spa. Maybe I have a grandmother who needs a companion. Maybe when I get to 16.0 I can go live with Mr. Peanut and approximately 87.6.

I return to my bedroom, lie on my bed, and close my eyes. I've been kidnapped. My real family is on their way to save me and take me home to our potato farm in Idaho where my mother hangs the wash outside on the line to dry in the warm summer wind and the spotted whippoorwills perched in the black cottonwood trees sere-nade me to sleep.

24

✦

"To help you out with your interviews, I've made up worksheets with various *get-to-know-you* questions." Miss Strand stands at the edge of the library table and hands us each two pieces of paper. It's Friday. Jane hasn't been home for three days. I don't miss her. I can't even guess what has happened to her, and there's really no one I can tell about her disappearance, except maybe Susan. I've spent all of Mr. Peanut's reward money on emergency cafeteria food, so, as of today, I start living off cafeteria condiments: small packets of peanut butter, jam, honey, and salsa. "And I will be back in exactly two hours to collect them."

"*Two hours?*" Bevy protests.

"That's right. Unless you think you need more time, I could …"

Susan interrupts, "Nope. Two hours. Perfect. See you in two hours."

Miss Strand gives us each a neatly sharpened brand-new blue pencil, smiles, nods, and exits the library.

Susan takes over. "Okay, look, this is what we're going to do. We'll fill out our forms, you guys fill out your forms, and then we'll hand them in like we've actually asked each other the questions. And in the meantime, you two —" she looks at Bevy and Myhell "— should go sit at a different table."

And then Bevy, mustering up all her intellectual savvy, says, "Why should we have to move to a different table? Why don't you two …" She holds up the middle finger of each hand. "… move to a different table?"

Susan pinches her pencil like it's a dart and aims it at Bevy, "Because if you don't move, I'm going to stick my pencil in your eye."

Myhell gets up and grabs Bevy by the sleeve. "C'mon. This is bullshit."

The worksheet is made up of questions that teachers think we care about, like what our favorite dessert is (lemon meringue pie), where we want to travel (anywhere there's no school), and who's our favorite rock star. Like that's how we actually talk: *Hey, Susan, who's your favorite rock star?*

There's eighty-seven minutes until Miss Strand returns. Susan walks around the library and looks at books. Bevy and Myhell text. I sit at the crudely student-carved *F.U.'s* and words-that-I-hate table. I could stick this table in a museum of modern art, title it "High School," and win some big award. I break my pencil off at the tip and go to the librarian's desk to look through the drawers.

Bevy notices, "Hey scrounge, what the hell do you think you're doing?"

I hold up my pencil. "Broken pencil?"

She snarls at me and returns to her texting. Librarians get all the cool stuff: kitten Post-its, neon highlighters of every color, stickers that say *You're a Star!*, animal-shaped erasers, a retractable knife, polka-dotted paper clips, and a pair of first-aid gloves. I take a pencil, the gloves (just in case the phone rings again), and the knife. I sit back down and start carving. My hand works the sharp edge of the knife into the hard surface of the table and I feel the compelling tug of it as it subtly urges me to pierce my skin. I scrape a picture of a tree in the surface and then just as I finish the H-E-L- of the word H-E-L-P (the words HELP and HELL are just one letter away. Actually, not even a whole letter, just a kind of bump), in walks Miss Strand with a pink cardboard box.

"Okay, girls. Time's up." Miss Strand collects our sheets, quickly shuffles through them and a look of gratification crosses her face. "Well done." She smiles. "This week's homework is to write a paragraph about the two people you interviewed, summarizing what you have learned about them."

Crap.

It's like hearing the principal announce that the fire alarm is just a drill. Miss Strand notices the mood change,

"But the good news is, I brought doughnuts!"

Maybe Miss Strand does know something after all: food brings people together, not homework assignments.

Between chews, I think the most brilliant thought I think I've ever thought.

"Miss Strand, could we maybe take home the interview sheets that we filled out so that we can write our paragraphs using the information that we've recorded? Otherwise, I doubt I'll be able to remember everything about Michelle and Bevy, and I don't want to leave anything out." We wait seven seconds.

"I guess that's okay. Yes, it's a good idea. Help yourselves to another doughnut," she says.

I choose a white-powdered one that oozes a lemon filling. Detentions are awesome.

I'M GREETED BY the unmistakable smell of roast turkey. How is this possible? Wrong Dump? Jane sees me and rushes toward me. She's wearing her denim miniskirt and she's holding a leaky gravy boat in one hand, and a coffee cup filled with red wine in the other.

"Agatha Angela! You're home!"

She looks like she might hug me, but because she's made of brick, and I repel her with my mind, it doesn't happen.

"What's going on?" I try to make sense of the unfamiliar scene.

"It's Thanksgiving!"

Thanksgiving was over a month ago.

"I've made us a turkey with all the fixins. Even gravy!" Three plates and three sets of knives and forks sit stacked on the table. She's assembled a collection of random occasion candles, half-burned and mostly wickless.

"Who's *us*, Mom?" I know it doesn't include Lady Gaga.

"I've met someone. He's wonderful, and he loves me, and he'll be here in a few minutes." She surveys my appearance. "Go brush your hair."

"What? What are you talking about?"

"Burt. He paid for all this nice food, and he's coming over to eat with us, so go get cleaned up."

Burt. Like something you do that you have to excuse yourself for.

"Mom, are you crazy? He's coming over? Here?" I guess she can't see it anymore. She's having one of her *I'm not really from this planet* moments.

Jane laughs. "Yes he's coming over here. He has this super-luxurious camper van and we're going to take the food into his van and eat. Like we're on holiday. Besides, he just has a small burner, and there's no way to cook a full Thanksgiving dinner on *that*. Honestly, Aggie, sometimes I just don't know about you."

I leave the room to "get cleaned up." Cold water comes out of the hot-water tap.

I carefully change into last week's unwashed shirt. I need more long-sleeved T-shirts. I want to try out my new knife, but there's not enough time. I shove it under my pillow.

Jane yells from the kitchen, "He's here! Hurry up, Aggie, I need your help with the food!" She hands me a sharply chipped glass bowl filled with what looks like instant mashed potatoes. Yup, all the fixins. I purposefully run my thumb along the chip and a slight tinge of blood appears on the bowl.

"Take these outside with me, come on!"

Jane grabs the plates and I hold the ambiguous mix. We walk to the front of The Dump and there, standing beside a rust-eaten camper van, is a scrawny old man, dressed entirely in black. A black cowboy hat is pushed so far down on his head that his ears poke out in such a magnificent way that he could be a troll. The veins in his skin protrude like lakes on a relief map. He struggles as he holds out a frail hand to shake mine. His shrink-wrapped face is scrunched up, and his back is bent — a broken tree under a heavy snowfall. I can see why he's in love with Jane. He's gotta be thirty or forty years older than her, which makes him at least sixty-five. What is she thinking? Oh right, *he paid for all this nice food*. I don't want to touch him. We kind of shake hands, and his skin is extraordinarily cold. He offers me a yellow-toothed smile and I almost gag.

"I am honored to meet you, Agatha. Your mother has told me great things about you," he says.

"Is that right? Well, she's been gone awhile, so I'm surprised she remembers me at all."

"Agatha! Do not talk back! Burt is a guest! I tried phoning you. More than once. You were probably out with your no-good friends."

Talk back? No-good friends? Jane is attempting to say things that she thinks a mother might say.

"Your mother says you're fifteen."

"I'm 15.8."

"Right. I have something for you." He reaches into the frayed pocket of his pants and offers me a black sock that has something hard in it. "Sorry it's not properly wrapped."

Not exactly wanting to touch it, I hold my breath and reach into the sock. I feel a cardboard plastic thing and cautiously pull it out. "Do you like it?"

Wow. Yes, I like it. Burt, the least hip man on planet earth, has gifted me with a stick of Lady Eloise mascara. How unfortunate that I no longer have eyelashes.

"Thanks, Mr. ..."

"Burt."

"Thanks, Mr. Burt."

Jane waits for her sock, but when no sock appears, she hands Burt the dishes and the potato mush and snaps, "Put these in the van." She turns and stomps back into the house. I guess sometimes love *isn't* enough. I follow her into the house and put my mascara on the table.

Jane scowls, "Well! It's too bad you're too young for makeup. I'll just take it and put it with my things. Here." She hands me a plastic Bugs Bunny bowl that contains a soggy mass of frozen corn, peas, and ... carrots? "Take this outside. And this." She picks up a tin pot filled with instant stuffing. I carry the things to Burt's super-luxurious camper van and he leans out the door and I pass them to him.

"Your mother loves you, you know."

O-K ... this isn't awkward, not awkward at all.

"Oh. Right." I say. I turn and go back to The Dump. Jane passes by me with the turkey, fork-chopped-up and piled in an aluminum-foil-lined cardboard box. We sure know how to celebrate around here.

"Bring the fortune cookies, they're beside the stove."

I guess the fortune cookies are dessert — pumpkin pie is just way too ordinary for our refined tastes.

I look in a grocery bag that still has a few things in it, and along with the cookies, I find something else and it sickens me: a box of Party Girl! condoms. I consider opening the box, taking them all out, and replacing them with crayons.

The back door opens and Jane yells at me, "What's taking so long? The turkey's getting cold! You're going to ruin Thanksgiving!"

I so don't want to participate in this.

"I'm not feeling well," I manage.

"What? Oh, no. You're not doing this to me, young lady. You get yourself outside right this minute and get into that van and put on your nice-girl attitude."

I remind myself that I'm not a young lady, nor am I a nice girl. I remind myself that I'm a tree. "Or what? What are you going to do? Leave me alone again? Ban me from school? What are you going to do, *Party Girl*?" I hold up the box of condoms. Jane lunges toward me and I throw the box into the living room landfill, potentially lost forever.

"You little shit!" She climbs over the mounds of crap hoard, a cyclone of garbage swirls around her. I calmly watch and will myself to grow eyelashes. A loud rap almost breaks through the thin wood of our back door.

"Hello?" We hear Burt's fragile voice and freeze, "Everything okay in there?" Jane practically kills herself bounding over the piles to stop Burt from coming into the house.

"We're coming! You go back to the van! I had to help Aggie find the dessert!" Like a smack-talking wrestler, Jane stands with her face three inches from mine, her eyes pierce through the back of my brain and she says, "Either you get in that van now, or I'm going to invite all your little friends over for a play date." I pick up the bag of fortune cookies and walk out.

"THIS SONG REMINDS me of you," Burt says. During dinner he showed us his Johnny Cash record collection. The inside of his van is covered in Johnny Cash memorabilia. Johnny Cash posters, Johnny Cash concert photos, Johnny Cash on the cover of *Life* magazine, fridge magnets, a bobble-head, and a Johnny Cash ashtray. Before tonight, I didn't even know there was a Johnny Cash. "Do you want me to play it?"

Jane doesn't answer — she's too busy trying not to spill wine all over herself and the floor as it sprays out of the wine-box hose.

"Sure," I say, not caring one way or another.

Burt lifts the heavy square lid of an old turntable, and then carefully takes a record out of an old cardboard record cover and holds it for a moment. He doesn't touch the actual record, only the inside part, and then he delicately places it on the player, all the while handling it like it's worth a zillion dollars. I hear a guitar, and then the words. The song is about a girl who is in love with the boy next door. She goes to Hollywood and becomes famous, but she ends up coming back home to be with the boy. It's a nice song, and I'm glad that Burt chose it for me, especially because of the part where it says that she's pretty.

Jane takes a gulp of wine and offers her opinion, "That's a stupid song. There's no way *any* girl would leave Hollywood and go back to some small town just to be with a boy."

Burt says nothing. Just as carefully as he put it on, he removes the record from the turntable, and replaces it inside the cardboard holder.

Jane blows out two of the dozen or so candles. "Go get ready for bed, Agatha. Take some dishes with you." I take Bugs Bunny and the turkey box.

Burt opens the van door, "It was good meeting you," he says kindly, sadly.

"It was good to meet you, too. Thanks for letting us use your van."

Burt smiles at me and Jane says, "Hurry up and shut the door! I'm cold!"

I REACH UNDER my pillow. There it is. I hold the librarian's knife. I lie on my bed and count: *1-2-3-4-5-6-7-8-9-10-11-12-13-14*. That's 14 hash marks on my left arm. Some people count sheep.

25

It's just before the afternoon bell. Travis, Nicole, Susan, and I stand by my locker.

"Okay, watch."

Travis presses a button on the video camera. His left arm is in a sling and finger-shaped bruises wrap around his neck.

"Well, look who's here, it's the geek and his sweaty little ho."

Idiot Boy Grant and Idiot Boy Duker come into view. Travis is at his locker and someone is filming, I'm guessing Nicole.

"Leave her alone." Fear resonates in Travis's voice.

"You want me to do *what* to her? I don't think so dude, she's *nasty*." Grant and Duker laugh.

Travis says, "Don't talk to us that way."

"What, freak? Did you say something?"

"You can't speak to us like that, it's disrespectful." Grant grabs Travis by the neck and throws him up against the locker.

"Stop!" Nicole yells.

"Don't tell me what to do, clown."

Travis chokes and we hear Nicole's best Hermione Granger impression in the background, "I call upon Minerva! Transform the power to reversa!"

"Okay," Grant says and drops Travis. He lands on the floor and immediately gets up and throws a clumsy swing at Grant. Grant grabs his arm and twists it behind Travis's back.

Desperation cracks open the back of Travis's throat. "Ahhhhhh!"

"I should beat your head in." Travis's face twists with pain. Duker stands watching, a dopey grin covers his face. Grant releases Travis's arm and then pushes him with such force that he falls back onto the floor. And it ends there.

"Pretty good, hey?" Travis says. "We need to start compiling. How long before we're allowed back to Carson's?"

Susan takes out a pack of sugar-free bubble gum, unwraps five, and pops all of them into her mouth. "Don't know." She smacks noisily. "But let's Minerva this thing into action."

I look over at Nicole. She closes her eyes and whispers something to herself that probably rhymes with I-am-so-misunderstood-by-everyone.

I READ OVER the interview answers. Myhell's hero is Ghundi, but I think she means Gandhi, and she wants to be a famous lawyer like Elle Woods. The most interesting things about Bevy are that she has a dog called Toby, she wants to see the Eiffel Tower, and she likes peanut butter cheesecake.

I'll write a paragraph on them, but seriously, what's the point? Me knowing their favorite dessert won't change anything. Picture it: Bevy is about to kick me in the head and I scream "Peanut butter cheesecake!" and of course, she stops.

"Whatcha doin'?"

"Carson! You scared me! Hey! We've missed you at the meetings. Are you ungrounded now?"

"You missed me?"

"We all did."

"Oh. Yeah, anyway, I guess now that I'm such a rebel, my parents think they need a way to contact me, at all times, so they gave me THIS." Carson holds up a very cool, very sleek-looking cellphone.

"Wow. That's amazing."

"You're amazing." He presses the screen. "And I'm recording you being amazing, right now."

"Carson, you're a genius! Every kid should do this. If people could see what *actually* goes on at The Torture Chambers around the world, then it would stop. Make the mean people famous! Recognizable! Accountable! A cellphone should be a required school supply, and every Torture Chamber should have a website where the footage can be anonymously posted. Wow. Nothing hidden, *everything*, every-*one* exposed for who they are."

"The torture chambers?" Carson asks.

"Carson, I can't kiss you anymore." Carson looks up at me like I've broken his tricycle. "Oh. Is it because I'm ..." he trails off.

"No, Carson, whatever you were going to say, it's not that. It's that I like someone else, and I think he likes me and if I keep kissing you, then things will get totally messed up, and I don't want to hurt you and I'd rather you kiss someone who ..."

"It's fine. I just really like you, and you're really cool, and if it doesn't work out with this other guy, then, well, then, maybe ..."

"I don't know, Carson. I really like what we have as friends."

"Okay then, friend, can you ask Susan if she'll come over to my house after school? It's my birthday."

"Carson!"

"Kidding!"

"Hey Carson, what size are your mom's feet?"

"I dunno. Why?"

"Well, I'm going to the Winter Carnival dance and I like your mom's style and I don't have the right shoes. She wanted to buy me some clothes and I thought that maybe ..."

"Yeah, she might have a spare pair. She only has about three hundred. What color? I could bring them to school, but it might be easier if you just try them on at my house at our next meeting."

"That'd be great. Black. Just plain old high-heeled black shoes."

"Okay, what size?"

I bend over to look inside my Converse. The size is worn off. I don't know what size my feet are. I'm probably the only person in the free world who doesn't know her shoe size.

"Um, how about I just try them on when I get there."

"Sure. What happened while I was grounded?"

"Well, a few things. Travis was attacked by Grant and my mother has a boyfriend.

"Is he okay?"

"Well he's old, but he seems all right."

"No, Travis. Is Travis okay?"

"Oh, yeah, he's fine. And they recorded it all." I smile and give him the two thumbs-up.

"You're beautiful," he says. And there it is, that feeling that makes me think that the stuff he says and does actually qualifies for a rating on the Official Romantic Scale. One compliment and I'm a snow cone in the Sahara. I better get out of here.

"Thanks, Carson. Um, I have to go do homework. I guess I'll see you later?"

"Yeah, okay. Hey! Maybe my parents could get you a phone, too."

Like everything else that's good in my life, if I had a cellphone, I'd have to hide it from Jane.

"Carson, let's just work on the shoes for now."

"Yeah, you're right." He holds up his phone and takes a picture of me, looks at it and says, "Yup, definitely gorgeous. Oh, and speaking of clothes …" He takes off his backpack and unzips it. "We went back, my mom and I, to that store. Anyway, here's some stuff that you tried on. We thought it would be okay if I brought them to school." Carson hands me a bag from Route 66.

"Wow. Thank you. Thank your mom for me? Please? Wow. Can I give you a hug?"

"Aggie. You never have to ask."

I SIT AT one of the library computers to work on my dumb assignment that I guess will make Miss Strand feel better because she's doing something proactive. It's difficult to concentrate. Everything hurts. I Google "cutting."

Whoa. Where do I start? I type: *How to stop cutting yourself.* Hmph. It says to draw butterflies on the spot that you want to cut. Maybe I'll try that. Let's see, here's a list of nineteen steps. That's way too many. Scroll down to number nineteen: *Remember, it will get better.* Will it? *How* will it get better? How do I stop the stuff that I can't control? Joanie stopped. It'd be easy to let the knife go in a little deeper, a little longer. Let the blood come faster. It's probably like falling asleep. Effortless.

26

"Okay, it's decided, December twenty-first," I say. "The last day of school before the Christmas break, at the Christmas assembly."

Travis smiles. "It's perfect."

"Yes, and it's also the day of the Winter Solstice Carnival dance," Susan adds.

"Carson, you could volunteer to help out with the sound system because you're the most technologically competent, and when the whole school is in the gym and the words to the Christmas carol sing-along are up on the big screen we'll interrupt the show with our footage."

Carson nods. "It's bold."

"We'll be heroes," Travis says.

"We'll be trees," I say.

"Travis, you and I will finish editing, and we can have a pre-screening here next week."

Travis holds up the pointer finger of his right hand, a distinct note of pride in his voice when he says, "I can't edit this weekend. I'm participating in the Young Mensa Tournament."

"I'm scared," Nicole says quietly.

Travis puts his good arm around her and speaks to all of us,

"We're all scared, Nicole. But you have to remember that this is our obligation to inspire all the other kids around the world who are warriors like us. We have to be brave and carry out this thing to the end, despite the fear."

"I know. It's just so real now."

Maybe Susan was right about Nicole being a shrub.

We hear the door open from the top of the stairs. Mrs. Turndale arrives with a plate of mini pizzas and just as I'm about to help myself to one, she says, "Agatha, can you come upstairs with me for a minute?"

Sure ... but I haven't had a pizza yet. I get up and follow her.

Carson's mother closes the door behind us. She takes me by the hand and leads me into the living room. "I am so happy that you came to me for this."

I look around. A kazillion pairs of black fancy shoes are laid out on display in front of me. The tour begins. "Now these are Versace, and these I wore to last year's Christmas party, these I haven't even worn yet, these I only wore once, these ones are fun, but they give me blisters, these would be adorable on you and these, well they're a little squeaky, but if you're somewhere where there's music it won't matter." She takes a breath and continues to lead me around the room. "These are just like the ones Jackie Kennedy wore in the sixties, don't you just love that era? These are great with a long gown, these are comfortable, but I think a higher heel might be more youthful. These are too big for me, these I plan to give away so if you wanted to keep them ..."

"I like those, the ones you're giving away."

"Good choice!" Carson's mom picks up a pair of high-heeled black suede pumps. They have a tiny rhinestone bow on the front and they're too beautiful for me. I try to fit my foot into the shoe, but I have my sock on. I'm too embarrassed to take it off because my feet always stink and I've never in my life had my toenails done. Carson's mom looks at me. "Hang on." She leaves and I look around. Jackie who? "Here you go." Mrs. Turndale hands me a pair of black knee-high panty hose. I pull my socks off and quickly cover my feet. They reek, and Carson's mother is too polite to say anything. I slip my foot into the shoe and it fits like I'm, well, obviously, Cinderella.

"Wow," is all I can say.

"They look better on you than they ever did on me. And they fit you so perfectly — how serendipitous! I'm thrilled they're going to a good home." I look down at my feet and back at Carson's mom. She looks genuinely pleased. I want to hug her, but I know that the rest of me probably smells just as bad as my feet and because we have no hot water, I haven't washed my hair in a while. Mrs. Turndale's seventh sense, a.k.a., the *mother* sense, kicks in, "Agatha, I've run myself a bubble bath, but I have a headache so I don't want to go in a hot tub right now. Would you mind? I hate to waste a good batch of bubbles." A *bubble* bath? I can't even remember the last time I had a *regular* bath.

She smiles and leaves me alone in the bathroom. I slip off my clothes and check to see where my cut marks are healing. I haven't cut myself for a few days, which is a major accomplishment. I carefully lower myself into the bath and the water engulfs me in compassion. The bubbles cover me and make their little popping bubble noises and I am astounded by the simple magnificence of it. A peach-colored razor sits on the edge of the tub and it kinda wants me to pick it up, but I don't touch it. I close my eyes and settle into the warmth. *This* is good. *This* is better.

I allow myself ten minutes to soak and to wash my hair. I pull the drain and a shocking dark ring Saturns the inside of the tub. It's greasy and stubborn and doesn't wash off with my hand. After using Mrs. Turndale's special conditioner, Forever Spring, my hair easily combs through. I've never in my life smelled this fresh, and I feel good. It's too bad I have to put on dirty clothes. I'll wash a shirt in our sink tonight so I'll have something semi-clean to wear to The Torture Chamber tomorrow, and then I'll change into one of my Route 66 shirts when I get there.

I come out of the bathroom. Mrs. Turndale sits at a delicately carved antique white vanity that has an oval-shaped mirror, and heavy glass princess-worthy knobs adorn each drawer. She looks up at me. "Here, let me help you." We return to the bathroom and, like I'm five years old, she blow-dries my hair. She doesn't mention my bald eyelids or the place on my head where the hair is just starting to grow back. She's gentle and her kindness makes me sad. She speaks to me quietly, "You know you're really very pretty."

I don't know how to respond. I'm more comfortable when someone is mean to me. "Thank you," I say. "And thank you for the clothes. I have to keep them at school for now."

"You do whatever it is you need to do. Okay, we are done! Go have a snack and Mr. Turndale will drive you and your new shoes home in about five minutes."

"Thank you," I say again. I head downstairs and the conversation stops when they see me.

"Hey! What did my mom want? Oh, wow, look at your hair!"

Susan looks up at me, "You look awesome! And those shoes! Did Mrs. Turndale *give* those to you?"

"Yup." I help myself to a mini pizza. "She sure did."

Carson winks at me.

In the car on the way home I give the most beautiful shoes in the world to Susan to take care of. If I bring them into The Dump, Jane will either wear them to work or use them as candlesticks.

Burt's van is in the driveway, which means that I have The Dump to myself, except of course for the usual weevil welcoming committee, and whatever else has taken up residence in my bedroom. Maybe today there's a grizzly bear or a pack of coyotes.

I put on my hoodie and wash my shirt in the sink with cold water and without soap.

It's time to get rid of all of the *Reader's Digest*s and rodent feces that sit in the bathtub. I put on the rubber gloves that I took from the librarian. I'll stack it all in the living room. Or in the kitchen, it doesn't matter. It's just more garbage on top of garbage.

"WHAT THE HELL is going on?" Jane tries to steady herself in the doorway. I've been working for over two hours.

"I'm cleaning up. I want to take a bath." I walk past her with an armful of magazines. She violently pushes them out of my arms and they land on the floor. I wince.

"You're not allowed to touch my things! Put them back! I want everything back where it belongs!"

I really hate her, but I remain calm. "If you want it back so bad, then *you* put it back. Can't you see how disgusting all of this is? Can't you smell it? It's not normal. Normal people take baths. Normal people don't have to eat in a van because their kitchen is too gross to sit in. It's sick. *We're* sick. Even the *rats* are probably sick. I don't want to live here anymore! I want out of here!"

"You want out of here? Then go! Get out of here! If you think someone else will put up with you! You have no idea what it's like out there, missy. The world's an ugly place filled with ugly people. You won't last a day. And by the way, Burt and I are getting married."

"Well that's just great, *Jane*. I hope he doesn't mind living like a *pig*," I say.

"Don't you call me Jane! I'm your mother!"

"No, you're not. I don't have a mother. You're just some crazy person who happens to live in the same pigsty as me." She slaps me hard across the face and neither of us says another word. I turn, walk away, go to my room, and close the door. Time to adjust number nineteen: *Remember, it will get better: but not for very long.* I find *The*

Muppet Family Christmas video and stomp on it with all that I have and it splinters into tiny, irreparable pieces.

"HI, SUSAN, IT's Aggie. Good, yeah." I cup the phone with one hand and hold it close to me. I have to speak quietly because after three trips from the living room to the bathroom with her treasured *Reader's Digests*, Jane sat in the bathtub on top of the stack of magazines, and passed out. "Listen, I was wondering if I could come and live with you for a while. My mom and I had a fight and she sort of kicked me out."

Susan pauses. "Can I call you back?"

"Thanks, Susan, and you don't have to call me back tonight, just tell me at school tomorrow." It's a lot to ask, and I don't really expect Susan's mom to allow me to disrupt the House of Zen. She hangs up and I'm alone again. Always alone.

I roll up my sleeve and look at my arm. Butterfly? I take the multi-colored art pens that I found in the art room garbage, and, instead of a butterfly, I draw a rainbow, and this time, instead of it being just red, I make it many colors, the way it should be.

I look out the front window. Burt's van is still parked in our driveway and the lights are on.

I stand in the driveway and hear music and singing coming from inside the van. Johnny Cash, of course. I'm reluctant to disturb him, but I need the company.

I quietly knock on the door. His frail voice breaks the night, "Jane? Is that you?" A skeletal silhouette of a man and a cowboy hat stands in front of the dim light of the doorway.

"Sorry, I was up and I can't sleep and …"

"Well, hello, Aggie. Why don't you come in? I'm not much of a sleeper, either."

His face seems so kind to me now; maybe it's the lighting, or maybe it's just because he's old.

I get in and he shuts the door. Steam rises from the Johnny Cash cup of tea that sits on his little wood table, along with a Johnny Cash teapot and a small glass dish with some cookies on it. Ginger snaps.

"Have a cookie. Can I pour you a cup?" He goes to a small cupboard and brings out a cup from the Big Moose Truck Stop.

"Thanks." I say. Burt takes an empty box of wine off the table and edges the cookie dish toward me.

"So, what's going on today?"

The way he asks, the tone of his voice, makes me believe that he truly wants to know.

"Are you and my mom getting married?"

Burt takes a cookie and dips it into the top of Johnny Cash's head.

"Did your mother say we were?"

"She just told me." I take a cookie. I'm not a dipper. I'm an eater.

"Ah, well, we haven't talked about it. I *like* your mother."

"So, you're not getting married?"

His hands tighten around Johnny Cash's neck. "Marriage is a pretty big deal, Aggie. We haven't known each other very long, and I'm a bit of a drifter. I don't tend to put down a lotta roots. Your family — you and your mother — you need someone a little more, ah …" He dips another cookie and it slips out of his twig fingers into the cup. "Damn!"

"So, no wedding on the horizon. That's what I thought," I say.

Burt looks at me like he's sorry, and now for some reason, *I'm* sorry. I'm sure he'd be a better parent than Jane.

"Do you have any more songs you think I should hear?"

Immediate calm overtakes the small space as the conversation moves into the Burt Zone. "Oh, you bet. I'll just top up your cup first." He picks up the teapot and pours the hot liquid, his wrist wobbles under the heaviness of the pot and the tea spills on my arm and instantly scalds the flesh. I wince from the pain. "Darn it, I'm sorry," Burt says.

The sleeve of my hoodie is wet and, without thinking, I roll it up slightly. Burt sees the recent cut marks, the scars on my arm. I try to cover myself, but he takes my hand, slowly turns my arm, fully exposing my handiwork. He then asks the question that sounds so wrong when I hear it. "Aggie, are you … *hurtin'* yourself?" He takes off his cowboy hat, rubs his old face, looks me in the eye and says, "Pain ain't no good thing. Ain't nobody out there gonna hand you a prize for storin' shit in your heart." He puts his hat back on, reaches up into his collection of albums, chooses one, and carefully places it on the turntable and we listen. And that's what we do. We listen to song after song after song and by the end of the night, I am Johnny Cash's second-biggest fan.

27

*

"I'm so sorry Aggie, but my mom said that we can have a sleepover tonight, but you can't live with us because it's against the law." Susan unwraps a cold, cooked pork chop and I would give almost anything for a small taste of it. "Personally? I think she's afraid of your mother."

"Yeah. I get that."

"Only because she hasn't figured out how to save her from herself yet. So just come home with me after our detention with Strand. Did you finish your paragraphs? Do you want to go to the Eiffel Tower and play with your dog Toby? Have you ever read anything more *vacuous*? Great word, hey? I learned it yesterday at the mall when my mom was trying to return a sweater because I said the color reminded me of a Milky Way. I guess she thought I might eat it. Anyway, they wouldn't let her return it because she was a day over the *two-day limit* for returns and she called the woman behind the counter *vacuous*. And then the woman said, "Ma'am, we don't sell vacuous here." So now it's my favorite word. I plan to use it every day." Susan takes a bite so big out of the pork chop that it's half gone. Cold grease covers her fingers.

"That's pretty funny, actually." I try to think of what it might be like to go to the mall with your mother and return things. The only things Jane and I have ever returned are empty wine bottles and foot-stomped Coke cans that we've found on the street. "Yeah, I finished the stupid paragraphs."

Susan examines the pork chop and when she's certain she's devoured all the meat, she licks each finger so clean that she might be on her way to perform an appendectomy.

"I wonder what Miss Strand will think of our video."

"She'll probably hate it," I say. "But I think its debut will be the end of the detentions." The loud growl of my stomach goes unnoticed. Burt gave me the bag of ginger snaps last night when I left and I finished them all this morning on the way to the Torture Chamber. That's the trouble with eating — it makes you hungry.

"ALL RIGHT, GIRLS, instead of having you read out your paragraphs, I want you to *paraphrase* what you've learned, and, to be fair, we will do this alphabetically, so Agatha, you will be first." So *not* fair — it's not my fault my name begins with an A. I shuffle through my papers.

"I said *paraphrase*. From memory. Tell me about Michelle and Bevy in your own words." In my own words? My own words for these two can't be said out loud.

"Oh. Umm. Okay ... Bevy and Michelle like the color pink and one of them wants to be an accountant or something, maybe a lawyer? And then they want to live in France with a dog named Toby."

Miss Strand is entirely unimpressed.

"Is that all?" She asks.

"Yup. That's it."

"Susan, can you expand on Agatha's report?"

"Sure, umm, let's see, They like to spend their weekends trying out different cellulite creams. But alas, without any noticeable success thus far." I burst out laughing. Susan keeps a straight face and raises an eyebrow at them.

"What the hell are you even talking about, BIOTCH!" Myhell yells, and immediately starts to gasp and gulp for air. She takes out her puffer and gives herself a quick blast. Ignoring her, Bevy speaks over the commotion, "Yeah ya fat ugly *fart*, what's your *problem*?"

Miss Strand looks mortified. This isn't turning out the way it did in her university role-playing classes. "Okay, girls, we're going to do some deep-breathing exercises. I want everyone to close her eyes and breathe along with me. In and out, in and out, in, now hold, hold and … out."

The only person with her eyes closed is Miss Strand. Fortunately, Janitor Stan pushes his cart into the library, and interrupting our failed moment of serenity, he starts emptying the garbage cans. Miss Strand opens her eyes and raises her voice over the disruption, "Next week's homework is to make two cards, one for each of the two girls that you wrote your paragraphs on. It is to be a card asking for forgiveness — you include a short poem, or a picture, or just a little verse. Do you all understand?" We nod. I look around, hopeful that at any moment, someone is going to walk in holding a pink box.

Janitor Stan plugs in his vacuum and the loud *whirring* signals the end of our detention.

Bevy, Myhell, and Miss Strand leave the library. Susan wants to find a book titled *Recipes for the Developing Girl*. Whatever that means. When we find the book we both stare at the cover. It's a picture of a mother and a daughter, standing together in matching aprons, holding a pie. Susan replaces the book onto the shelf.

We leave the library and when we get to Susan's locker, there's an unwrapped tampon hanging by its string, knotted onto Susan's lock. This is the best they can come up with? Susan scrunches up her face. "I'm not touching that."

"Neither am I."

"Should we go to your house to get your overnight stuff?" Susan asks, like it's okay to just casually stop by The Dump and pick up a few things.

"Um, no I can't go home, remember? Besides, I think my mom has her cooking club friends over today to make salsa or jam or something."

I hate lying to Susan. No one should ever have to lie to her best friend.

"Oh, right. It's fine. We have extra toothbrushes, and you can borrow a pair of my pajamas," Susan says.

"Really? Sweet."

And it really is sweet since I don't actually own a pair of pajamas. I sleep in my hoodie and my sweats and then wear them to school. It's a real time-saver.

THE KITCHEN WINDOWS of Susan's house are all foggy from a fuming pot of vegetable-barley soup. Bread is baking in a little square bread-maker. If I lived here, my whole life would change.

"Susan, could you and Agatha set the table, please?" Susan rolls her eyes at me, but I don't mind helping. I would do anything to stay in this sanctuary: clean floors, homemade soup, pajamas. What else is there?

After dinner, Susan and I clear the table and wash the dishes. Susan's mom makes her dad a cup of what she calls her Happy Poppy tea and he falls asleep on a reclining chair that I recognize from the "Gifts for Dads" section of a Sears Christmas catalogue. Susan's mother disappears into a different room. Indian music fills the hallway. *Ting*.

"Let's put on our party pants, make some popcorn, and find a movie."

I pick out a pair of pajamas from Susan's *pajama drawer*. They have floating cupcakes on them, like a dream — you try to grab one, but it keeps moving out of reach. Fortunately, there's a ribbon draw-string around the waist that I can tighten, 'cause they're pretty roomy.

Susan's pair has wild horses on them. They're galloping in all directions, chased by an invisible rancher who wants to capture them and force them to pull wagons and live in a cramped barn. I like pajamas: they tell stories.

Susan turns on the TV and I whisper, "Won't we wake up your dad?"

"Nope. Happy Poppy takes no prisoners."

WHEN DOROTHY CLICKS her heels together and says, "There's no place like home." she probably means that there's no *better place* than home, where in my case, there's no *worse* place than home, so thank *God* there's no place like home. And, just like Dorothy, I too believe that somewhere, under, over, around the rainbow, is my happiness, the place where troubles melt and romance begins. I touch the rainbow bead around my wrist. The dance is only a few weeks away.

Susan unwraps a brand-new pink toothbrush for me. We even brush our hair, and then climb into Susan's big, comfy bed. Susan falls asleep instantly. I lie awake for a while because I want to memorize what it feels like to be in The Emerald City instead of The Dump.

In the morning I wake up alone to breakfast-making noises and breakfast-making smells. Susan's side of the bed is made and her pajamas aren't anywhere so I don't change out of mine. I make the other half of the bed.

The level of activity in the kitchen is astounding and we indulge in an elaborate buckwheat pancake and tofu-sausage breakfast. When we finish (I'm last to put down my fork), Susan's dad excuses us. "You girls can go do your homework."

I push my chair in and say, "Thank you Mr. and Mrs. Williamson, that was the best breakfast I've ever had."

"You're welcome, Agatha, I like having an extra person at the table," Susan's mom says.

And I want to blurt, "I could live here!" but instead I say, "Yeah. Thanks."

Susan opens her closet and pulls out a BeDazzlered quilted box. She places the box on her bed, removes the lid and I peer inside. It's stuffed with store-bought crafty things.

"Homework schmomewerk, let's make friendship bracelets," she says. Susan dumps out the contents of the box. Sequins in small plastic containers, cloth-covered flower buttons, embroidery thread of every color, glitter-filled vials, and every possible theme of stickers (sports, food, flags of different countries, musical notes), fall onto her bed. There's even a sheet of small rainbow stickers, and of course, I have to ask, "Susan, can I have one of these?"

"Take them all, I never use this stuff. I mean, I was into it when I was like *ten* or something, but not anymore."

I peel off one of the rainbows and stick it to the inside of my right wrist. I would stick them all over myself, but then I wouldn't have them anymore. Susan tries to teach me how to make a ridiculously complicated friendship bracelet. It's too fun and we're making a lot of noise so Susan's mother decides that it's time to take me home.

"You can keep those if you want," Susan says, indicating the neatly folded pajamas that I can't quite let go of.

"Really?"

"Sure, I have lots. I think my mother likes the way they hide my flab, which is totally absurd because, let's be honest, I look like a flannel elephant."

"That's cute, though. Flannel elephants. *Way* better than flannel llamas."

"Flannel llamas! Flannel llamas! Say *that* ten times really fast."

And together we yell, "Flannel llamas!"

We are laughing like crazy when Nicole bursts through the doorway. We stop mid hilarity. Nicole breathes heavily and a mix of sweat and what might be tears dampen her shirt.

"What's wrong?" Susan asks.

"They … they …" She stops, gulps for air.

"What?"

"They hurt Travis. They followed him from the community center. He was walking home from that Mensa thing and they attacked him and now he's in the hospital. They were kicking him in the head! The head!"

"Oh my God, Nicole, is he okay?" Susan asks.

"I don't know. His mom is there now."

"We should phone the cops!" Susan yells.

"No. That won't do anything," Nicole says.

Susan is livid. "I still think we should. Travis will know who did it. He has to report them."

"But that won't make them stop. The only thing that will make them stop is our video. We shouldn't wait until the last day of school. That might be too late. Which one of us is next? What happens if one of us *dies*? What happens if Travis *dies*?" Maybe Nicole isn't a tree *or* a shrub. Maybe she's a shrub that has tree aspirations. Maybe she's a trub.

Susan wraps her arms around Nicole's tiny shoulders. "Travis isn't going to die."

Nicole breaks free. "You don't know that! How would you know that? You didn't even know he was hurt!"

"Who's hurt?" Susan's mother poses in the doorway, her crossed arms show off ripped biceps, a black yoga bra exposes her abs.

"No one," Susan replies quickly. "We'll be down in a sec. Maybe you could make us some of your Activi Tea smoothies?"

Susan's mother smiles. "That's a good idea. It'll help you cope with those pancakes. You had three, you know."

She leaves and we all sit on the bed.

"Okay, so, Nicole, you phone me when you find out how Travis is doing, and then I'll get the message to Aggie somehow, and then …"

"Don't you have a phone, Aggie?" Nicole asks.

"Oh, Yeah, I do. It's just that it's unreliable. Faulty wiring." I reach for my rainbow stickers.

And then Nicole says, "Do you guys want to say a spell with me?"

"What?" I look at Susan.

"I know a magic spell we could all say together."

"Ah, I'm not allowed to do spells anymore. Last time I did magic, something went wrong and I gained fifty pounds," Susan says.

"Really? Oh I see. Okay, I'll let you know when I hear something." Nicole leaves. I peel off another rainbow and stick it on top of a large purple vein in my left wrist. I bet if I cut myself there right now the blood would spurt out like a cherry orchard *chika-chika-chika tk-tk-tk-tk-tk* sprinkler.

"Good luck going home, by the way," Susan says.

I haven't seen Jane since she slapped me across the face.

"Yeah. I wish I could live with you, or with Miss Strand or with Burt."

"Who's Burt?"

"Burt's my mother's boyfriend. He's really old, but he's really nice. He's teaching me about music."

"Oh, that's great. I guess." Susan sounds unhappy.

"What's wrong?"

"Nothing, except I feel bad about those pancakes."

"What? Why?"

"Because I had three."

"Yeah, so what? I had three."

"I know, but you're tiny and I'm a chunk. No, wait, compared to you, I'm a humongous chunk."

Compared to *me*? Susan is comparing herself to *me*?

"Susan, you're kidding, right? Look at yourself — you're so pretty. You're, like, model-pretty. You could be in a magazine."

"Yeah, if there were a *Fat People* magazine. I just feel like I messed up."

"No way. Besides, losing weight to look the way you think other people want you to look is crazy."

"Yeah, I know, but still. I should probably go stick my finger down my throat."

"Don't do that."

"Why not?"

"Because it's gross."

"Yeah, and carving up your own skin *isn't* gross?" Susan looks me in the eye. I didn't know she knew. *How* does she know? "Look Aggie, I know you cut yourself, and I think what you're doing is wrong, but I want to understand, and I want you to talk to me about it."

"How did you know?"

"You used my password on the computer, right? It has my Google history on it. And you're always covering yourself, and everything just sorta fit together."

We are both very quiet.

"I want to stop," I whisper.

"Smoothies! Time to rev up those metabolic engines, girls!" Susan's mother springs into the room, a contraption that resembles a heart monitor is Velcro-strapped around one of her arms. "Susan, there's an extra shot of amino acid in there to help you with that tummy of yours."

Amino *acid*? Acid kills, I thought. Maybe that yogurt *was* poisonous.

"Thanks, Mom."

Susan's mother stands and waits, her eyes fixed on Susan. Susan puts her lips to the straw and starts sucking.

Satisfied, Susan's mom says, "Let's go!"

I gather up my pajamas and my rainbow stickers. Too bad there's not a secret hideout for kids like me. Maybe I could go live in Swing Set Woods, hang out with the friendly pixies and the talking squirrels, sip chamomile tea under a red-and-white polka-dotted toadstool and live off the nourishment of one giant forest berry.

In the car, Susan and I sit together in the back seat. Susan's mother plays her super-weird *Living a Life of Love* CD — outer space whales giving birth. Susan takes my hand and whispers, "We have to find a way to make things better for you."

I shrug.

"Let me know what I can do, okay?"

I nod and try not to cry.

"I'm sure we could find someone to help you." Susan must see how uncomfortable I am. "Do you want to say a magic spell with me?" she says, and I have to smile.

We pull into our driveway and park.

"Do you mind if we come in for a minute?" Mrs. Williamson says. "I'd like to say hello to your mother."

"Oh, she's not home," I say. Turdle is in the driveway.

"Oh?"

"She's probably out with friends. Or she took the bus to work — it's better for the environment." Oops.

Puzzled, Susan asks, "Your mom works Saturdays?"

"Yeah. When someone phones in sick." Susan frowns at me. She knows I'm lying. I'm a bad friend.

Susan's mom turns around in her seat. "That's fine, Aggie. If you prefer that I don't talk to you mother right now, I won't, but I'd like her to know that I'm here to support her, okay? I'm thinking I should phone Family Health Services and have them come and check on you, though. Can you let her know that?"

The thought of this intrusion is devastating. I choose my words carefully. "That's super thoughtful, Mrs. Williamson, but my mom and me, we're fine. We're just going through a rough patch right now. You know … mothers and daughters. I wasn't serious about moving in with you, I really just wanted to have a sleepover with Susan. I'm sorry, I shouldn't have been so dramatic."

I don't know if she believes me, but she places her hand on her heart and says, "I really want you to know that the universe wants good things for you."

And I say, "Thank you. That means a lot to me."

But it doesn't. The universe might want good things for me, but Mother Earth couldn't care less.

28

Vomit. I am greeted by a pile of vomit. Jane lies face-down on the kitchen floor, wearing only her underwear; a large and empty bottle of tequila lies by her head, as does another heap of vomit. I watch a moment to make sure that Jane is still breathing — something no kid should ever have to do for their mother. The stench is overwhelming and I gag. I run back outside and gasp for air. I barely manage to keep my breakfast. Oh my god.

I step over the first pile of puke and I cover it with newspapers. I step over Jane and pass by more vomit in the hallway on the way to her bedroom. I search through her garbage-covered bed and manage to find a bath towel that she uses as a sheet on top of her bare mattress; I cover her with it because her near-nakedness embarrasses me. I grab a couple of plastic bags from the counter. There's a note:

Dear Jane and Miss Agatha,
    I've enjoyed being your friend. Please take this money and get your hot water turned back on. Happy Trails.
                                        Burt

P.S. Miss Agatha, the record is for you.

There's a stack of one- and- five-dollar bills and some change (sixty-five cents) and a Johnny Cash record. No surprise. Another cowardly cockroach runs away when the lights come on. I fill the plastic bags with empty bottles. Jane remains motionless.

I walk to the recycle depot. No one is taking my bottles away from me this time, even if they're fundraising for kids of alcoholics.

"That's four dollars." The man behind the counter passes me a handful of sticky change.

It's enough to get me to where I'm going and back.

The bus pulls up and, even though it's almost empty, I sit at the front; you never know who might get on, and the farther back you sit on the bus, the more potential there is for danger. A butterscotch-colored dog lies on the floor, attached to a harness held by a man in darkly tinted glasses. Please don't talk to me, please don't talk to me.

"You in a hurry?" The man says, his face tilts in my direction.

"Sort of." I say. I look away, which is futile since he won't catch the hint in my body language that I'm not participating in the conversation.

"Hey, it's gonna be fine, you'll see."

"What?"

"I can feel it in your breathing. You're tough. Resilient. Nonetheless, you have to learn how to breathe, how to focus your energy."

The butterscotch dog looks up at me. Its eyes petition me, *are you getting this? It's important.*

"Okay, Sid. Next stop, art gallery."

The man with the dog turns his head toward the driver and says, "Thanks, Hal."

"You're going to the art gallery?" I had to ask.

"Picasso and me, we go every Thursday afternoon." He pats his dog.

"But ..." I stop.

"We people-listen."

"Oh."

"Yes, it's a bit like eavesdropping. We listen to the breathing of the people around us. You see, there's a breath that comes from right here." He pats his chest. "That's a simple one. That's passion. But then there's the breath that catches someone when they discover the beginning and end of all creation that rests on the tip of a brushstroke. That's a rare one, and we like that one, but our favorite breath is the one that happens when the viewer recognizes something so beautiful that it defines what it means to be alive. It's always unpredictable. Some people look at a piece of art and breathe hope, while others will look at the same piece and breathe regret. It's addicting." He adjusts his grip on Picasso's harness. I reach into my pocket and take out the Mr. Peanut poster.

"This is the phone number of a friend of mine and I'm sure she'd like to go to the art gallery with you and Picasso. Tell her that the girl who found Mr. Peanut gave you her number." I press the paper into his hand, hopeful that he knows someone who will help him phone her.

The bus rolls to a stop and the door swings open. The dog stands and leads the man out. He's almost out the door when he turns to me and says, "You'd be amazed by the things you learn by breathing."

The door squeaks shut and the bus lurches forward. I am, of course, now keenly aware of how I'm breathing. I purposely slow my breath and immediately feel calmer, better than I have since I stepped out of Mrs. Turndale's bathtub.

I exit the bus and run across the street and into the beauty salon. I can't see Raynine anywhere. A woman with dark purple hair, about a hundred hoop earrings in both ears and one neon purple one in her nose calls out to me, "What's up, girl?"

"I'm looking for Raynine."

"You have a time?"

"Um. No?"

"Well, then, that's too bad."

"Is she here?" I ask, looking around the busy room.

"Duchess, where's Raynine?"

"She's on break," one of the stylists says over the noise of a blow-dryer.

"I need to talk to her, I'm her niece."

"Oh honey, you shoulda said! C'mon." She leads me through the salon. I have to step over a human hair rug on the way and a nasty chemical smell assaults my nostrils and I hold back the urge to cover my nose with my hand. She opens a heavy door to a back alley.

"Raynine! Your niece is here."

Raynine sits on a plastic chair, smoking and chewing gum. Her bare feet rest on another plastic chair.

"My what?"

"Hi!" I say. "My mom Jane sent me to see you about a ..."

"Oh, hey, come and sit down. Thanks, Juniper. I got this." She takes her feet off the second plastic chair and pushes it toward me with her foot.

I sit for 1.6 seconds before I get up. "I shouldn't be here. I'm sorry." I mumble.

"Hey, don't go yet. I haven't seen your mom in, like, a hundred years. She ever give you that money?" Raynine flicks her cigarette into the alley and the smoke rises from the butt. That's a fire hazard. "Hey, you need ta hurry up and tell me what's up 'cause I have a dye coming in."

I'd rather be at the art gallery with Picasso.

"That anonymous help-thing you and my mom are in? I think she needs it now. I don't know what to do. It's pretty bad."

Raynine lights another cigarette, takes a deep drag, then asks, "Where is she?"

"She's at home, but she's kinda sick, and ..."

Raynine interrupts, "Look, we're not really supposed to talk about this," She looks both ways down the alley. "I guess I could phone somebody and have them come over to your house, to check on her."

"Can't they just call her?"

"Sure, whatever. How about I give you my sponsor's number, and maybe she can help? There's not much else I can do. I'm sort of new in the program — less than a year — so I'm probably not the right person to intervene."

"Can you call your sponsor for me?"

Raynine puts her cigarette to her mouth, black-burgundy lipstick stains the end. She takes a puff and then removes a piece of tobacco from the tip of her tongue before she speaks, "Go inside and get the portable."

"Portable?"

"The phone."

I go back into the salon and it's so chaotic that I want to run away, but this is too important. I stop and take three breaths. That blind guy was right: breathing is addicting. I walk to the front desk. A blond woman sits on a stool.

"Excuse me," I say. She looks up at me and her eyelashes are so long that it's difficult to see her eyes.

"Mmm-hmm?"

"Could I please borrow the portable for Raynine?" She hands me the phone. "I like your layers."

Raynine has her feet back up on the chair.

"Here you go," I say.

"Thanks." She doesn't move her feet. She dials a number and holds the phone up to her ear. "Hi, Mona, this is Raynine. No, I'm fine. Yes, I'm practicing. Yeah. No. Look, could you just *lay off* a minute, I got something t' ask you." She looks up at me and winks, which oddly, makes me feel like we're friends. "Listen, I got this girl here whose mother was going to the meetings, but I haven't seen her in forever, and now this girl needs our help. She says her mom is in pretty rough shape." A long pause. "Right, okay. I'll tell her. Yup, I'll be there for sure. I know. I know already, okay? Bye." Raynine finishes her cigarette before she says anything. "Okay, so we can't really do much 'cause it's a privacy-rule thing. My sponsor says you should check out an Alateen meeting. Good luck, kid. Niece. I gotta go back to work. Remind your mom that she still owes me for that cut." She stands up, flicks the second butt into the street, and walks back into the salon. I'm left in the alley, alone. I go to the two smoldering cigarettes and stomp on them. I watch as the smoke slowly snuffs, then disappears.

*

29

"Hi, um, ah, Susan? It's Aggie, um. Never mind. Thanks." I hate voicemail. I need to ask Susan for J.J.'s number, but I don't want her mother getting all gluteus maximus over it.

Jane remains comatose on the floor, and I've come to the conclusion that it's me who has to clean up the barf, and I can honestly think of nothing worse. I threw away my rubber gloves, but the garbage hasn't been "taken out" (stacked on the back porch), so I pick up one of the garbage bags in the kitchen and open it to a smell so overwhelmingly disgusting that I gag into the sink. Apparently Jane has been using plastic bags as her toilet.

I look in the toilet bowl and it's jammed full of local newspapers, a.k.a., cheap toilet paper. Now what? I can't phone Miss Strand; she'll report us and they'll take me away from here and move me to a different neighborhood and I'll miss Susan. I can't phone Mrs. Turndale — she's too fragile. Maybe Janitor Stan — I bet he knows how to fix a toilet.

I cover my arms with eighteen rainbow stickers like a cartoon character's armor. I wrap a tattered fabric scrap of a proud rooster tea towel around my mouth and nose and I find a large garden spade in the hallway. I hold the plastic handle of an ice-cream tub (I have no idea where it came from, we've never once had ice cream out of a plastic tub), and I have a supply of newspapers. I look away as I scoop the vomit off the floor. It's horrible, and my stomach hurts because I have to keep stopping myself from throwing up. I wipe the less chunky bits of vomit with newspaper, and crumple it up and stuff it in the plastic tub. Jane rolls over and her face and hair are covered in puke. Been there. She wipes her nose with her hand, but doesn't wake up.

I throw the bucket out the door and it disappears into the overgrown weeds. Nice. I grab armfuls of garbage and throw it into the backyard, and it also disappears. Yes. I pick up piles of crap, as much as I can at one time and throw it into the abyss. I do this over and over, the sweat pours out of me and I can no longer lift my arms, but I've actually cleared a spot in the kitchen and it's the most beautiful thing in the world.

I empty the fridge of the massive clogs of disgusting mold-caked inedibles, indiscernible bits of rot, and a half-full box of Chez Foul wine. I squeeze its contents into the sink and punt it into the lawn. The kitchen floor is covered in a thick layer of grunge, but I don't care because I can actually walk around. I have removed everything except Jane and the rest of our empties, which I will return later to get money to pay Janitor Stan. I sit down on the one of our two kitchen chairs that aren't broken and let out a breath-cry that I didn't know was there.

Jane shifts, groans, and her hand goes to her forehead. I put on the top of my new cupcake pajamas to cover my arms and I pour her a cracked coffee cup of water and bring it down to her. She slowly lifts herself to her elbows, takes a sip and says, "What day is it?"

"It's Saturday. You kinda passed out." She looks down at herself and that's when she realizes that she has nothing on except her underwear, and that's when I notice that she is even skinnier than me.

Her half-closed eyes focus on the bareness of the floor around her.

"What happened around here?"

"I don't know, Mom, I came home from Susan's and you were here on the floor and all our stuff was just *gone*."

"Oh. I guess I sorta blacked out."

"Yeah, I guess you sorta did." I sideways-glance at the empty bottle of tequila that I've propped upright in front of her.

She looks at it at the same time and whispers, "Oh, God." She brings her knees up to her chest and hugs them. Her face is buried in her arms. "Do we have any aspirin?"

"I've never seen any."

"Check the bathroom."

I pass the pile of puke in the hallway that I forgot about. Without looking in the mirror, I open the bathroom vanity and the only thing in there is a half-the-bristles-missing hairbrush, my broken comb, and a creepy white spider that tries to make itself very small when it sees me. I know exactly how it feels. I get back to the kitchen and Jane is crying. I sit down on the floor beside her.

"It's gonna be okay, Mom, just breathe."

"Oh, Aggie. I'm so sorry. I'm sorry I hit you. And for what I said. You didn't steal my dreams. When you were born all my dreams came true. But I'm …" She takes a deep breath. "You'll be gone soon. You're going to leave me. Like everything else, you're going to disappear."

"No, Mom. I won't disappear. You'll always be my mom. No matter what." I feel my tears come now. The tears that I would normally hide from her, but at this moment, it's different. "No one else gets us, Mom. It's why we have each other." I touch her arm. "Besides, who else is going to play Candyland with you?"

She almost smiles, but then quickly covers her mouth. "I feel so sick — I think I'm going to die."

"Maybe you should try to get up and I could help you wash your hair and get you some clothes." Jane kinda half-lifts herself up, and she grabs on to the top of a kitchen chair for balance. When she stands fully upright she clutches her stomach and hobbles over to the sink and tries to throw up. Nothing comes out. Not a drop. I wonder when she last ate.

"You need to eat."

She looks at me and shakes her head slowly. "Noooooo. I just need some aspirin. And a sleeping pill."

I rinse the dust out of a ceramic tulip vase and fill it with water to use as a pitcher.

"You should go to bed. I'll bring the water." She nods and limps to her bedroom. I saturate the tea towel with cold water, take it to her, and cautiously place it on her forehead. She attempts a smile and my small act of kindness empowers me. I might have to stop hating Jane. She's broken and sad and I'm the only person in the whole world who would bother to put a cold tea towel on her totally messed-up head.

I take Burt's $67.65 and head to the grocery store. I don't even care that I'm wearing the top half of my pajamas — people wear the bottom half of pajamas in public all the time. I buy bread and milk and orange juice and single-wrapped square cheese and packaged pre-sliced round meat, and even a box of non-nutritious breakfast cereal that has a picture of a lunatic camel on it, so it must be good. At the drugstore I buy a small bottle of aspirin and some pink anti-nausea liquid. I also buy some disinfectant soap, a box of cleaning towels, and some no-name toilet paper. Thanks, Burt. Sorry I was mad at you.

When I get home I have to run in to answer the phone. It's Susan, returning my call.

"Hi, um, I wanted to ask you for J.J.'s phone number. I kinda thought I might go to one of those meetings she goes to."

"I could ask her? I'm sure it's okay. But, you know."

"Right. Thanks, Susan, and thanks again for the pajamas and stuff."

"Hey, there's plenty more where those came from."

"Ha-ha, yeah. see you Monday."

I'm terrible on the phone. I think it's because I haven't had a lot of practice. And I totally get why Susan has to ask J.J. if it's okay to give me her number since she also lives in a house of emotional carnage. I arrange the groceries on the counter, and Jane comes in wearing a baggy shirt and sweats. Her hair is damp so I guess she managed to wash it herself.

"Hi," I say. "You look better."

"I feel a bit better. My head is still pounding, though." I hand her the drugstore bag and she looks inside it.

"Where did this come from?"

"I went shopping."

"But how did you ..." She looks over to the place where Burt's money used to be.

"Agatha, that was for ..."

More tequila? I want to say, but I don't.

"Yeah, I read the note." Whatever. We can't eat hot water. "Take the aspirin and drink some of that pink stuff. I'll make us a snack." Jane sits and I prepare baloney-and-cheese sandwiches. She devours hers like a snake eats a mouse — no chewing, just one big swallow. Now I too feel guilty about eating three pancakes. "Can you watch TV?" I ask.

"Sure." We slowly maneuver to the living room. I turn on the TV, and unless it's the weather channel reporting a blizzard, our cable is gone. "So, Candyland?"

I set up the game on the kitchen table, Jane lies on our rubbish-camouflaged couch.

Bur-ing.

It's the phone. Jane noticeably perks up, probably expecting it to be Burt.

"Oh, hi, Mrs. Williamson. No, she's having a nap. She could call you when she wakes up. You're in the driveway? Oh. Well, even

though you're in the driveway, my mom is still sleeping. Oh. Oh.
But. No. Please don't do that. No, you don't ..."

Tap tap tap.

She's at the kitchen door. Tripping over stacks of rubble on her
way, Jane disappears into her bedroom. Maybe Susan's mom wants
to talk to me about the universe some more. I open the door very
slightly and Mrs. Williamson performs a few yoga moves to try to
peer in.

"Hi!" I say. "Susan's at home. I just talked to her on the phone."

"I've made your mother some Harmony's Way tea. It's not as
strong as Happy Poppy, but I'd love to prepare some for her. I'll
just come in for a few minutes." The veins in her neck pop out like
cooked spaghetti as she strains to look inside.

"Oh, sure, you can come in, I'm pretty sure it's safe now — they've
just finished the chemical spraying. My mom found an ant this
morning, and you might not know this about her, but ..." I lower
my voice to a whisper "... she's a total neat freak, so we had the
pesticide people here. You didn't see their truck?" I look over her head.
"They just left."

"Chemical spraying? In your house? Oh. Um, you know, I have
to um, ah, I have to ..."

"Be somewhere?"

"Right, that's, ah, Susan, she wanted me to pick up some ... protein
bars." She laughs so awkwardly that I laugh, too.

"Ha-ha. Right. Susan can't get enough of those protein bars." She
pushes the bag of loose tea out in front of me. "Here. Give this to
your mother."

She bolts and I yell out behind her, "*Namaste!*"

Her tires screech as she races away from our toxic nuclear wasteland.

"You can come out now!"

Jane reappears and heads straight to the kitchen, opens the fridge
door, and yells into the cold air, "Where is it?"

"What?"

"I had something in here. It's gone, everything's gone. What have you done with it?"

With exaggerated innocence I reply, "I haven't done anything. I wasn't even home." And then I say the thing I shouldn't have said, "Maybe you should go to one of those meetings tonight."

"What? What are you talking about? What *meetings*?"

"You know, the ones that people go to, to help them stop drinking?" She slams the fridge door, picks up one of the kitchen chairs and throws it at me, but since Jane is the least athletic person on the planet it lands closer to her than to me.

"You have no right! You have no right to tell me what to do! Who the hell do you think you are!" She grabs Candyland and flings it into the air; a spectrum of plastic gingerbread men bounce off a wall. Jane stomps out of the kitchen. Forty-five seconds later, she flies out dressed in her tight black skinny jeans and a jean vest — a jean vest full of jagged tears that have been stapled. Joanie's jean vest. I guess Joanie's mom has already donated all of Joanie's things to Spendapenny.

I will keep her giraffe forever.

She grabs a few bags of empties and disappears out the door. I put my nose up to the bag of dried lavender and twigs and fill the kettle with water. I check on my tomato, beet, and kale plants, but it's still just dirt. I open the cutlery drawer. I choose a lovely and sharp little knife and as I wait for the kettle to boil, I pull up the pajama sleeves of both arms and cut through every single rainbow sticker: a slow and peaceful rain.

30

I'm at school early so I can sift through the paper recycle bins to get enough paper to make posters to put around the school. I'm going to stick them on all the classroom doors, and they're going to say: *Stay tuned for* The Pig Mask Chronicles.

As I walk the halls I keep my eyes open for Janitor Stan. My arms are so sore that I took a handful of Jane's aspirin, but I could use something stronger to alleviate the sting — maybe another baloney sandwich. I've eaten 7.5 of them in the past eleven hours. Baloney might just be the most wonderful thing in the world.

"Hey, Murphy!"

This is totally weird — no one ever calls me by my last name. I turn and see of all people, Mrs. Toeplicky, and I should have known — gym teachers are flagrant last-name-callers.

She runs up to me. "Murphy, you're failing. I want to see you after school. In your gym gear. We're going for a run."

Oh, please, no.

"A run?" I say.

"Yup. You come running with me after school every day, and maybe, just maybe, I'll allow you to pass grade ten Phys-ed. I'll even throw in some push-ups and crunches." She pats her stomach. "No reason to fail physical education, Murphy."

"Right," I say.

"After school, Murphy. In the gym." Mrs. Toeplicky dashes away, and Susan comes around the corner.

"He's gonna be fine," she says. "His face is all bruised and he can't really eat, but he's gonna get better. He'll be out of the hospital soon, though, so we should go visit him after school today."

"Who?" I ask, dumbfounded.

"Travis?"

"Oh! Right! Sorry, I was just thinking about going for a run."

"Right, sure you were, and I was just thinking about doing Jazzercise. Sorry about my stupid mom, by the way. She likes to butt into other people's business. Probs because she doesn't have any friends. None that I've ever met. My dad and her never do anything with other people. The way your mom does, like her homemade jam or salsa-making group."

"Oh, right. About that. Susan, here's the thing —" Susan crosses her arms high on her chest and leans on my locker "— the thing is, my mother and I are kinda messy and we collect stuff and keep it. We actually never throw away anything, except for Sears catalogues and on Saturday I threw a whole bunch of stuff outside. And my mother is a total paranoid freak and there is no cooking club and I have trouble dealing with all this stuff so, yeah, you know."

Susan uncrosses her arms, hugs me, and says, "Homemade jam is overrated."

"Gross alert! Sound the alarm! They've released the lesbians!"

A girl's voice calls out in our direction and we stop hugging. Standing across the hall from us are Yale, Chrissy Crop Top, and Mandy Kronk, the girl who blackmailed me out of my dance ticket. I actually feel sorry for them because their homophobia has turned them into victims of their own ignorance.

"What is *wrong* with you people?" Susan asks. "Do you honestly think that what you're saying is okay? You know you're all responsible for Joanie's death, right? I mean you didn't actually miss that, did you?"

Yale steps closer to us. "I didn't have anything to do with that."

"But you didn't stick up for her," I reply. "What are you afraid of?"

"What's she talking about, Yale? We didn't kill her. She killed herself."

"Shut up, Chrissy." Yale is really angry. "Just shut up about it."

"Let's get out of here, Yale," Mandy says.

I guess she's one of Those Girls now.

"Look, I'm sorry about Joanie," Yale says. "I wish I could change what happened."

"Let's *go*, Yale."

"No, man, you go. I'm done. With all of you. None of you would kill yourself for being a hetero. Stay away from me."

Yale walks away, and everyone except Susan is speechless,

"I think that went well."

"You two are still freaks, you know. Everyone hates you." Chrissy crosses her arms.

"You know, Chrissy, you should probably check the meaning of the word *everyone* on Wikipedia," I say.

"And you should look up the word *deodorant*." Mandy and Chrissy saunter away, leaving only a faint echo of their loathing behind.

Susan rolls her eyes and turns back to me. "So today, after school? We'll go to the hospital? I'll meet you at the bus stop again."

"Okay," I say.

"Oh, and J.J. said there's an Alateen meeting tonight. She gave me the address." Susan sticks her hand in the pocket of her sweater and pulls out three protein bar wrappers and a small piece of paper. "Here. It's at the community center. The room number's on there." She hands me the paper.

"Do you know what time?"

"Oh, right. Um, I think she said 7:30. Can you go?"

"Yeah. I guess. I feel stupid, though, going by myself."

"Yeah, I felt stupid when I went to Fat Camp, but you just have to suck it up and do it. You might meet someone really nice."

"I doubt it."

"Aggie?"

"What?"

"You seriously can't cut yourself anymore, okay? Because if you cut yourself and you're my best friend, then that makes me the world's worst best friend, so promise me that you'll stop." Susan takes two friendship bracelets out of her other pocket. "One for each arm." She ties one around each of my wrists. "Every time you get the urge to cut yourself, I want you to look at these bracelets and remember that you have a best friend."

"All right. I promise." I have my doubts, but it's Susan, and she made bracelets.

"Good."

"Susan?"

"What?"

"You have to promise me something now."

"Oh right, I get it, just because you're doing something, now I have to. What is it? I've already given up the second helping, what more could you possibly ask of me?"

"I want you to promise me that if you find out that I don't stop, you'll tell Miss Strand."

"Why Miss Strand?" she asks, and honestly, I'm not exactly sure.

"I guess because she'll make me her personal project. And she has a nice office."

"Okay, I'll see you after school at the bus stop."

"Yup."

I go to my humanities class. The teacher assigns us a group project and the group that I'm stuck in ignores me. They put their desks together in a way that doesn't really have a spot for me and when I try to move in closer, a girl I don't even know says, "Just because you're in our group, doesn't mean that you're *in our group*." I sit at my desk and make a few posters advertising our video. The group leader decides on a role for each person except me, so I place a finished poster on my desk and leave. I guess I'll get whatever mark the group gets, which is better than any other mark I already have. I kinda stopped doing homework. It's hard to care about the First World War and Elizabethan love sonnets when your mother uses a plastic bag as a toilet.

I walk past Miss O's art class and the door is open, so I look for him. I've written him a note apologizing for kissing Carson. The dance is in ten days.

I quietly knock on the open door, but no one hears it, so I knock again, but too loudly. The entire class looks up from what they're doing and my face flushes. Miss O looks up from her desk. "Yes?"

"Um, I'm supposed to give this to someone, it's from the counsellor."

"Who is it for?"

That's a really good question, but since I don't know his name, I have to point.

"Him."

Everyone looks at him and some boy says, "Ooooh, Blaker, I like your hot little girlfriend."

And everyone except Blaker laughs. Miss O says, "Blaker, if you wouldn't mind meeting Miss Murphy at the door?" He turns red and I regret the whole idea.

I hand him the note and quietly say, "Sorry." He says nothing back and I feel like a total idiot.

After school I go to the gym and change into my ratty gym clothes. I leave another poster on a bench in the change room.

Mrs. Toeplicky blows her coach's whistle and I run to one end of the gym, and when she blows it again, I'm supposed to turn and run to the other end of the gym. On the seventh whistle, I collapse. My gut cramps and my bowels might explode.

Tweeeeeeet! She blows her whistle, *Tweeeeeet* again *Tweeeeet Tweeeet Tweet Tweet Tweet Tweeeeeeeet!* Again and again, and I cover my ears with my hands and scream, "I can't do this!" and it's so loud that it drowns out her whistle.

She crouches down to my level, and asks, "What's wrong with you, Murphy?"

And because there's just no right answer to that question, I say nothing. Her eyes move to my bare arms. Her mouth drops as she takes in the view, the fresh cuts, the recently dried blood, the deep marks from other cuts, and I see it, too. My arms look like loaves of thinly-sliced unbaked bread, randomly spotted with bits of raspberry jam. It's gross and shocking and Mrs. Toeplicky drops her whistle, "Oh my God, oh my God," she says. She puts her arms around my broken body and holds me. "You poor girl, you poor girl." But I don't want her to touch me. I don't want her to look at me. I pull away. "You need to get help, Agatha. Have you talked to Miss Strand about this? Do your parents know?"

"No. No one knows. Except my friend."

"Miss Strand can help you. I can help you. Your parents can help you."

"No."

"Murphy, listen to me, this is *not* negotiable."

"Mrs. Toeplicky, you don't understand. I don't have a dad, and you can't tell my mom. She's kind of ..." And I can't fill in the blank, because for some reason, I don't want to betray Jane.

"She's kind of what? You can tell me."

"She's just too busy and stuff. She has to work a lot."

"Work? She has to work? I think she'll be more concerned about your health than her work."

"Please Mrs. Toeplicky. You can't tell her. She's a little, ah …
stressed. Please, it'll only make it worse."

"For now, I won't tell her, but I want you to see Miss Strand tomorrow. I'll let her know you're coming. I'll bring you to her office if
you don't think you can get there on your own."

"It's okay. I'll go."

"You're sure?"

"I'm sure."

"I'll be checking with Miss Strand after school tomorrow to
make sure you got there. We're done for the day. I tell you what, you
research a famous female athlete who overcame a challenge in her
life, and write a report on her, and that'll be what I base your Phys-ed
mark on. Deal?"

I nod.

"Okay! We'll get through this, Murphy. You're not alone." I nod
again, even though I feel alone.

WHEN I GET to The Dump I am reminded of how much I am alone.
No Jane. No friendly cockroaches to keep me company. I'm glad I
used the gym bathroom, otherwise I'd have to go in the backyard.

I open the fridge and there's an empty plastic cheese wrapper and
not even a sip of milk left in the carton. I shake the box of lunatic
camel cereal, and there's a few crumbs left, so I peer into the dark
box just in case there's a rodent relaxing in it, picking his teeth. I
should have taken more condiments from the caf, but I kinda had
a busy day. In a few months when Blaker graduates, we could get a
camper van like Burt's and we could travel across the country and
once a week I'll send postcards to Jane and I'll write only two words
on every single one them: *I'm happy.*

31

I push on the heavy door with too much force and it swings wide and bangs against the opposite wall. An intimate group of people sitting in a circle of hard plastic chairs all look up at me. It's not yet 7:30. Did I get the time wrong?

J.J. gets up out of her seat, meets me at the door, and whispers, "I saved a chair for you." Together we walk to the spot where she was sitting, and sure enough, there's an empty chair waiting for me.

A boy who's probably ten speaks. "So, that's the thing. There's no *way* my mom will get out of bed early enough to drive me. They'll kick me off the team if I miss another game."

And then a woman speaks, not just to the boy, but to all of us, "I'm sorry about that, Sam. This type of disappointment, these sacrifices that all of you here have to make because your caregivers are alcoholics, is hard. You all deserve to play on teams and be safe and have food on the table and not be afraid to go home. What you can do is take as much control as you can to improve your situation. Sam, is there someone else who could drive you?"

"Maybe. I guess I could ask the coach."

"You know, that's a great idea. I want you really think about doing that, and next week you can let us know how it turned out. We have enough time to hear one more person. Tonnie, would you be willing to speak tonight?"

"Sure. Um, well, it wasn't the worst week ever. My dad didn't hit me. My mom did some mean stuff."

"Can you tell us about the mean stuff your mom did?"

"Sure, well, she was poking Tickle—" Tonnie looks at me "—my bunny. She was poking her with this metal spatula through her cage, and saying, 'You stink up the house so we're going to eat you! I'm gonna flatten you into a rabbit pancake!' And Tickle was really scared, but my mom just kept laughing and jabbing at her. And then she got a bottle of maple syrup and poured it all over her. She still has wood chips and pellets stuck in her fur. I was scared."

"That is scary. Is Tickle okay now?"

"I guess. She just hides in the corner of her cage. She won't even let me hold her long enough so that I can wash the stuff off her fur. My dad thinks it's funny and now he calls her flapjack-rabbit."

Tonnie's sad and I'm sure she had to stop talking because the tears were coming.

An older boy in the circle speaks, "My dad does that mean stuff all the time, too. Last week he dumped a full bag of garbage onto my bed because I didn't take it out to the end of the driveway by six o'clock the day before garbage day. He said that I was a bum and then he yelled at me to clean up my mess."

This is where I belong. Finally. Finally, I belong somewhere.

We say a sort of prayer about accepting that we can only change some stuff, but not other stuff, and then it's *cookie time*.

"So, you know J.J.?" Tonnie hands me an oatmeal chocolate chip cookie.

"Yeah. Thanks."

"Well, it's good you came. I like it here. It makes me feel like I'm not alone in my crazy place. Oh, and just so you know, the meeting starts at six-thirty."

"Right. Thanks. My friend told me seven-thirty." My friend. Susan, my friend Susan who I was supposed to go to the hospital with after school and I forgot all about it until now. I'm the world's worst friend.

"Don't worry about it. You're new."

New. I like that. I want to be new — it sounds clean, undamaged.

"Do you want another cookie?"

"Always," I say.

Tonnie laughs. We walk over to the cookie table where three boys are talking with each other, and all three of them have a handful of cookies. I guess we all need more cookies.

One of the boys looks at me and says, "I hope you come back. It feels weird at first, but it helps. I've been coming for four years. This place is the only thing that keeps me from going totally mental."

He pops a cookie in his mouth. J.J. and the facilitator join us.

"I'm glad you made it," the woman says to me. "I never like to see an empty chair. And I just would like you to know that it takes a lot of courage to get yourself here the first time. And you came by yourself. You're very brave."

Brave? Me? Not a chance.

"I'm Sash." The facilitator holds out her hand to me. "Both my parents are alcoholics. So is my brother."

And as we shake hands, I reply, "Oh, that's too bad."

"You know, it just is what it is. I don't feel sorry for them, and I don't feel sorry for myself. I just get on with my life. One day at a time."

And then one of the boys says, "Some days it's one minute at a time."

And I get it. I so totally get what they just said, *get on with life, one minute at a time*. It relieves some of the pressure. Maybe we don't have to let the wood chips stick to us, even after someone has poured maple syrup on our heads.

We all help ourselves to another cookie, because somewhere deep down, we know we deserve good things, too.

I DECIDE TO stop by Susan's house, to apologize, to connect. I also want to find out how Travis is doing. Joanie must have been so lonely. I'm sorry, Joanie. If I had known, I would have asked you to wait. Even just a minute. Sixty seconds. All you had to do was count from one to sixty and something unpredictable might have happened and you wouldn't have felt so alone.

Quietly, I knock on the aubergine door. Heavy footsteps move across the floor and the door opens. It's Susan, in another new pair of pajamas. Kittens.

"Aggie? Are you all right? Do you want to come in?"

"Yeah, sure, is that okay?" I doubt her mom would appreciate me just randomly stopping by like this, but hey, she started it.

"Yeah, of course. I was kinda worried about you when you didn't show after school.

"I know and I'm so sorry! Toeplicky made me come in and exercise. I'm failing her class."

"Oh, gross! Toeplicky made you *exercise*!"

"Yeah, and she saw my arms and she's making me see Miss Strand about it tomorrow."

"Good. She'll know what to do. I'm glad it's no longer up to me to tell her. You want some leftover chicken stew?"

"Really?"

"No?"

"Yes! I would totally love some. I thought you guys were vegetarians."

"Yeah, that was last week? It's random. Next week we might be tree bark-atarians, or grasshopper-atarians. The mother likes to stay on top of the trends; it gives her something to believe in." We walk past her sleeping dad and Susan whispers, "Happy Poppy." She lifts the lid of a large ceramic pot. The aroma is amazing, and I have to admit, *one* bowl of chicken stew is way better than even a dozen baloney sandwiches.

"So how's Travis doing? Did you go see him?" I ask as she ladles out two huge portions of chicken, carrots, potatoes, and *noodles*. We sit at the table.

"He's still pretty bad. His mom reads science books about quantum weird stuff to him all day. She even set up a chessboard. He was trying to teach me how to play, but seriously, there's no way. It's a cool game, though. The queen is the most important piece. Hey!" Susan does a side-roll out of her chair. "Do you want to see your dress? They're both in my room."

"You picked up my dress?"

"My mom and I did. And the saleswoman said that because our dresses were going to be sent to orbit dress outer space if we hadn't bought them, she gave us an *additional* forty percent off. It's like we stole them!"

My dress hangs outside her closet and it's even more spectacular than I remember.

"Do you want to try it on again?" Susan asks.

"Um, no, I'll save it for the night of the dance."

"Does your mom even know about the dance yet?"

"Nope. And she never will. Hey, is it okay for me to come over here to get ready and maybe your mom could drive us?" If Susan says no to this, I don't know what I'll do.

"Yeah, for sure. I was hoping you'd get ready here. It'll be like in those movies where the girls get ready for a night out and dance and listen to music, do their makeup and smoke and drink and stuff, except without the smoking and drinking."

"Fun! Except I don't have any makeup. I had mascara, but I don't know where it is."

Susan opens a heavy dresser drawer and says, "Check it out."

I peer into the drawer and it's stuffed with all kinds of lipsticks, blushes, and eyeshadows. I pick up an odd metal contraption and hold it up, "What's this?"

"Oh, you mean you don't recognize an *eyelash curler* when you see one?" She tosses it back into the drawer. "My mother thinks that if she keeps buying me makeup, I'll be able to conceal some of the fat. Like guys will be too busy admiring the charming dusty-rose tinge to my cheeks to notice that I weigh over three hundred pounds."

"Hey, that's three hundred pounds of the world's greatest friend!"

"Yeah, I guess. But it'd be nice to be the world's greatest *girlfriend*."

"Susan, he's out there. Probably thinking about you right now."

"If he's thinking about me right now then I'm glad I have clothes on!"

"Not that it's a big deal, but I'm glad you have clothes on, too!"

"So I guess Carson has to edit on his own now," Susan says.

"Oh, about that — I made posters advertising *The Pig Mask Chronicles*. I'm putting them around the school."

"That's a great idea. I'll make some, too, and we can put also put them in the caf and the library. I'll even start wearing my mask! So, what do you think he looks like, this guy who can't stop thinking about me?"

"I think he probably looks like the vice-principal, only a bit younger."

"Shut up!"

"I'm sure he's a really *nice* guy, though!"

"Oh, God. Maybe there'll be some fat guys at the dance."

"I'm sure there'll be all kinds of guys at the dance. The hard part will be deciding which one *you* like best."

"Like that's gonna happen."

"Susan, remember? The universe wants good things for you."

32

It's before the first bell and I'm outside Janitor Stan's hideout in the boiler room. I'm not exactly sure what I'm going to say, but I'm desperate, and he was nice to me. I take a chance and gently knock on the door. Nothing happens. I tape a poster to the outside of his door and knock louder.

The door opens and Janitor Stan looks at me, pulls his long hair into a ponytail behind his head, and asks, "Those jerks do something to your locker again?"

"No. Umm."

"What's up?" He reaches into his back pocket, takes out a rag, and dabs his forehead with it.

"It's kind of a long story."

"Well, I'd invite you into my office, but it's against the rules. Let's take a walk. I gotta do the morning graffiti check. Hang on." The door closes behind him. I've counted up to twenty-three when the door opens and he's got his bucket, brush, and plastic cleansing spray bottle. We walk through the halls. He stops at a group of lockers, sets his bucket down, and looks at me. "So, a long story, is it? I prefer long stories, they're always more interesting than the short ones."

"Yeah, well, this one's not that interesting, but I kinda don't know what to do, and everything's this huge mess and you're the only person who can help us."

"Us?"

"Yeah, me and my mom. She's really sick, I mean, she was really sick a couple of days ago. It's our house. My mom and I, we live in this house that is …" I have to stop because I'm going to cry.

"Hey. Take your time. It's a long story, remember?"

I smile and take a few deep breaths before continuing. "I can't pay you. Our toilet is broken and I can't pay you and my mom is a total basket case and there's no one else I can tell."

Janitor Stan nods. "Well, even though I just so happen to be a toilet-fixing aficionado, I think me coming over to your house isn't the best idea. People always think the worst, know? I'm an old guy."

"But it's — " Again, I have to stop myself from crying "— I don't know what else to do. There's no one."

"What about if you asked a guy friend to be there as well?"

"No. I can't." And then I do start crying. "It's disgusting. And we need help. We can't do it ourselves. My mom's an alcoholic, I think. So she's not really …" I wipe the tears from my face and look down at the floor, my embarrassment reflects off the high polish of the linoleum.

"Oh. I see. I'm a dry alcoholic myself, seventeen years sober.

"*Seventeen years?*" That's longer than I've been alive.

"Yup. Quit drinking the day after I turned twenty-seven." He rummages through a front pocket of his overalls, takes out what looks like a small coin, and hands it to me. There's a number XVII on one side, and on the other side it says *One Day at a Time.*

"They should make these things for kids who want to kill them- selves," I say.

Janitor Stan looks at me like I've said something wrong, terrible, even. "You thinkin' about killing yourself?" The seriousness of his tone makes me believe that he knows what it's like to want to kill yourself.

"No. Definitely not. But my friend did and now it's too late to do anything about it."

"That must have made you pretty sad."

"Yeah. I'm still sad about it. I just wish I ... I wish I had ..."

"Stop. Don't go there. You can't blame yourself. If you had known, you would have done everything you could to make the outcome different. But you didn't know, and it's not your fault."

"Thanks," I say quietly.

The bell rings, startling both of us out of a deep and salient moment of parallel empathy.

"So, where do you live?"

"Oh, right." I want to say number-one Paranoid Street. "Twenty-one ten West Oak."

"I'll come by after school. That okay?"

"Thanks. Oh, and you have to come around the back. Our front door is broken. Sort of."

"Right, 'round the back. After school." He turns and sprays the locker with the cleaning fluid, takes out his brush, and scrubs.

Attempting to avoid my first class, I go to Miss Strand's office. There's a big pencil-crayoned sign that has a yellow-and-black butterfly on it that says: *Out of the cocoon*. Sticking to my avoiding-my-class commitment (I'm no quitter), I head to the library to research a famous athlete who has overcome a challenge. Maybe I should be an athlete. Because that's gonna happen.

I sit down at a computer and log in with Susan's student number. Rat, the only other student in the library, glares up from his computer and shoots an imaginary gun at me. I mouth the word, *Pepsi?* at him and he snarls ferociously and mouths the word *Bitch*. My whole body shakes with fear, but I don't want him to notice so I look down and type "famous athletes who overcame a challenge" and up pops a girl who lives in Hawaii. She had her arm bitten off by a shark while she was surfing. She was only thirteen when it happened and now she's a pro surfer. And here I am, doing what I do, and she had her arm *bitten off by a shark*. I'll write my report, but I feel very strange about it because I feel like I should be better. She said she was able to get through it all because she had God. Maybe I'll Google God.

I log off the computer. Rat is gone, and the librarian sits at her desk, looking a bit miffed. She's probably angry at Rat for taking her knife and first-aid gloves. I walk past her and say, "Thanks."

She looks up at me. "You're welcome!" with such exuberance that I must be the only person who has ever thanked her since books were invented.

The door to Miss Strand's office is open. My hands shake and I want to run in the opposite direction, but I think about the one-armed girl and go in.

"Agatha! I've been thinking about you. All of you girls. I hope you've done your homework for Friday's group."

"Yes, um …" I rub the shoulder of my left arm. It's still there, my arm, and Miss Strand isn't half as scary as a shark.

"Miss Strand, I need to tell you something."

"Okay. Do you want me to close the door?" she asks.

"Yes, please." I say, trying to put off what I have to say just a moment longer. Miss Strand sits down and waits for me to speak. I clench both fists and dig my fingers into my palms.

"Miss Strand, I cut myself."

"Oh, on a locker? I have some Band-Aids here somewhere in my desk." She looks through her desk. "Here's one!" She holds it up like it's a lollipop.

"Um. Thanks, but it's a little more complicated than that." I slowly roll up the sleeves of my pajama shirt.

When she sees my arms, she sucks in a great gulp of air. "Ohhh."

"I know it's not as bad as a shark bite, but Mrs. Toeplicky said I had to show you. Otherwise I won't pass gym." And then, in one apparently inevitable and profoundly infuriating display of vulnerability, my body betrays me and tears launch themselves down my cheeks and onto my chin, exploding like mini torpedoes as they land on Miss Strand's desk.

"Is it okay for me to give you a hug?" she asks. I nod *yes* and Miss Strand crouches down on the floor to my level, puts her arms around me, and whispers, "I'm so sorry, Aggie. I didn't know. Thank you for telling me." And she hugs me for a long time, and I feel warm. Like what it must be like in Hawaii. Miss Strand gets up, opens her door, and goes to the couch to get the afghan that sits on it and covers me with it. She actually tucks the sides into the chair and I feel safe. She quietly closes the door again.

"You're a good counselor, Miss Strand."

"Aggie, I want you to know that there is help for you. You don't have go through this alone. There are other ways of dealing with your emotions, I promise you. There are other ways."

The funny thing is, the fact that there are other ways to deal with my feelings never occurred to me. I guess normal people, the people who don't cut themselves or drink a box of wine every day, know this stuff.

"Let me do some research, give me a couple of days and we'll figure out what the best choice is for you. I will find someone who has the right tools to help you." She holds up the bowl of hard, colorful candies and offers it to me.

"Okay," I say. I pop a candy into my mouth, which is so dry that my lips slowly separate like they've been recently glued.

"I think our detention group should take a break. How does that sound?" She picks through the candies until she finds a red one, holds it up between thumb and pointer finger, licks it to be sure, and then places it into her mouth.

"Yes. That'd be good. I'll tell Susan."

"Great. I'll inform Michelle and Bevy, and, in the meantime, I want you to know that we will take care of you." She takes hold of both my hands and squeezes reassurance into my cold anemic fingers, circulating some life back into them.

But I'm still scared. What if I have to get better? What if I have to go into some fancy healing place for three months where they ask you questions that make you cry? It happens all the time on TV. The problem with telling people that you have a problem is that they feel like they have to solve it.

"IT'S DONE." CARSON looks up at me deviously, like he's just finished stitching together Frankenstein.

"What's done?"

Standing by my locker, Carson gestures for me to lean in closer to him, but because I think he might try to kiss me, I ignore his "move." He stands on his tippy-toes, looks over his shoulder, and yell-whispers to me, "I've finished editing. *The Pig Mask Chronicles* is ready. And I've got to tell you, it's kinda disturbing."

"Wow. That's awesome. And it's disturbing because it's the truth, finally surfacing."

I would hug Carson, but I stop myself. "Thanks, Carson."

"I'm pretty proud of its artistic qualities. Everything's set up for the last day of school. The tech teacher was happy that I wanted to help out this year. I think I want to be a filmmaker. I like your posters, by the way. You could be an ad marketer."

"And you for sure could be a filmmaker, Carson. You'd be really good at setting up all the kissing scenes."

He blushes. "Oh, man, you'll never guess what my mom went and did! You are *not* going to believe this."

"What?"

"She got me a ticket. To that dance party thing, the Winter Solstice dance? I guess she thinks it would be a good place for me to meet girls. It's all she talks about. I get the impression that she thinks *we'd* make a good couple." He waits for my response, but I say nothing. "Anyway, I figured since you and Susan are going, I could hang out with you guys." I suck in my breath, trying not to react like a crazy person. Carson and Blaker. In the same room. With me, not with me. *Now* what do I do? And how did Mrs. Turndale get a ticket to a sold-out dance? Must be that rich-person magic.

"Oh, that's great, Carson, um, I guess um, yeah, for sure." After all, he's my friend, and his mom did give me the perfect shoes.

"My mom said she'll drive us."

"Oh, well, you see I promised Susan that I would get ready at her house and then her mom is going to take us. It's kinda already arranged."

"Oh, no problem. I'll just have my mom pick you guys up at Susan's house, and then her mom won't have to even bother. I'll tell her to phone her today. Ta da! Everything is working out —" he snaps his fingers and points to at me with both hands "— perfectly. I even have a suit. I wore it to a wedding five years ago and it still fits. I guess that's one good thing about not growing, you never have to buy new clothes."

"Yeah, I kinda know what that's like."

"Okay, so you better be prepared, 'cause I'm practicing my dance moves."

"Oh! Right."

"This is going to be so much fun!" Carson yells to me as he walks away.

"Yeah, fun!" I yell back.

Oh God.

33

I turn the corner onto my street and Janitor Stan's truck is parked in our driveway. At least I think it's his. When I get closer I see someone leaning against the truck smoking. Sure enough, it's him. A large toolbox sits at his feet.

"Hi! Sorry. I got here as soon as I could."

"No problem."

I don't know where Jane is because Turdle isn't in the driveway. Maybe it's upside down at the bottom of a deep ravine, an open bottle of tequila lying sideways, dripping onto the roof.

"Ah, I just need to check to see if my mom is home, 'cause if she is, well. She's not really a people person."

"Don't worry, I get it. Seventeen years, remember?"

The back door is open. Maybe Jane was in a hurry to go somewhere. Maybe she's airing the place out. Now that the toilet's unusable, the normally disgusting rotting food-mildew-rodent-feces smell has taken on an even less appealing toxic human-sewage aroma.

"Mom?" I call. "I'm home!" Silence. I go to her bedroom just in case she's conked out on the bed, but the place is empty.

"It's okay," I say. "I'll show you where the bathroom is." He follows me to the kitchen. "You might want to plug your nose." I'm so embarrassed by us. "I'm sorry. It's really gross."

"Hey — don't forget what I do all day. I'm a high school janitor. I've seen it, smelt it, stepped in it, and then cleaned it up. You can't surprise me anymore."

I take him to the bathroom and his eyes water as he assesses the situation. He pulls out his pack of smokes and lights one and the smoke from his cigarette is more breathable than the air in our house.

"You probably won't want to be here for this," he says as he flicks his cigarette butt into the pile of wet newspapers that sit in the overflowing toilet. *Tssss.* He looks at me, "Okay?"

Knowing full well that there's nothing vaguely edible/drinkable in them, I look in the kitchen cupboards for something that might pass as a snack for Janitor Stan. I sit at the kitchen table, surrounded by shame, and disgrace. Jane has scribbled a note across Johnny Cash's forehead on the record Burt left for me:

Gone to Mrs. Turndale's for a late lunch. Make your own dinner.

Now what? What happens when she finds out about the shoes, the dance, the video club? The only choice I have is to lie. What dance? What shoes? A video club? No!

Totally freaked over not knowing when Jane is going to walk in the door, I feel compelled to slice my leg from the bottom of my ankle to the top of my thigh, one long line of blood-red highlighter. But I can't. Janitor Stan is here; Miss Strand and Susan are "here." I walk to the windowsill and look at my Miss O plants. A miraculous beginning of a small green vine punctures the tomato plant dirt. I sit with my eyes closed, breathe in, and count. Long deep breaths. After 621 slow and heavy inhalations, my craving to carve a crevasse through my railroad track scabs subsides.

"She's good to go!" Janitor Stan holds a dripping garbage bag in one hand, a lit cigarette in the other.

"I'm sorry I can't pay you. But thank you. Really, thank you so much. It's kinda hard to live in a house with no bathroom."

"Yeah, you know, thanks for trusting me. I feel honored that you asked me to help you. I'm sure it wasn't easy. Anyway …" He puts down the garbage bag and sticks his hand in his pocket and takes out a wallet that is attached to a chain around the loop of his coveralls. He removes two twenties. "… do me a favor and take this. Go buy something. I don't know. Go buy something you need or a root beer or something. But promise me you won't let your mom have it. She'll just drink it." He holds out the money to me.

"But I should be paying *you*."

"Yeah, well, let's just say that the first toilet is free. After that, we negotiate." Again, he offers the money. I hold out my hand to take it and he grasps my fingers. "One day at a time, okay? Remember that. Don't worry about what's going to happen tomorrow or the next day." There it is again, that one-day-at-a-time thing. He releases my hand.

"Yeah, um, thank you, I, um, guess I'll see you at school."

"Yeah, about that, I won't tell anyone that I fixed your can. I'm not a talker. And I'm sure you understand that you should probably not mention it, as well? Keep it simple, right?"

"Oh, right, thanks. Really, thanks. Um, I wanted to ask you, um, you said that I had something that they will never have? Those people who messed up my locker? But I can't figure out what that is. Can you tell me?"

Janitor Stan smiles, turns, and walks out the door, carrying the sopping garbage bag in one hand, and waving goodbye with the other; cloaked by cigarette smoke and as effortlessly as any good magician, he disappears.

I look out the front window as he gets in his truck, and before he has a chance to drive out of our driveway, Jane drives in. She jumps out of Turdle and bangs her fist on the passenger window of Janitor Stan's truck, and yells big and serious words at him. He leans

over and unrolls his window and says something that calms her
down. He drives away and she stands and watches, arms crossed,
until I'm guessing, he's out of sight. I prepare myself for the worst.
Maybe she'll hit me again. Maybe she'll hurl one of our many non-
working toasters at me. But of course there's no point in speculating
about what a crazy person might do.

"People are idiots! That guy was looking for his brother — like
we know his brother. He had the wrong address or something. More
likely he wanted to steal something. Thank *God* I showed up when
I did! Does it smell like cigarette smoke in here?"

"How was lunch?"

"Oh that. Well! Kathy Turndale, I have discovered, is a complete
loony. She seems to think that *you're* going to the Winter Carnival
Solstice Dance *with her son*! The midget! I had to laugh. Can you
imagine? It'd be like dancing with a toddler! And that house of hers?
Who needs all that space? It's obscene. You know she has two fridges?
She doesn't need two fridges — she's only feeding a husband and a
dwarf. And she's so thin. *Nothing* up top. No wonder her kid is tiny.
What a day this has been." She sits at the kitchen table, looks around.
"What did you make us for dinner?"

I have to think of something before she goes all kamikaze on me.
I should have made a pot of Mrs. Williamson's Harmony's Way tea.

"Oh, ah, I fixed the toilet. That's what I did. I didn't have time to
cook because I wanted to surprise you."

"*You* fixed the *toilet*?"

"Yeah, I Googled it and it was really simple. Just a minor valva-
vaculatarooter clog."

Jane thinks for 40.1 seconds,

"Hmph. I guess the Google actually works sometimes. It's fine that
you didn't make us dinner. I'm not exactly hungry. *My God, Aggie*,
we had little smoked-salmon and egg-salad sandwiches with no crusts,
a salad made with weird little orange slices, and chocolate truffle cake."

I think about the forty dollars that Janitor Stan gave me and I hear the indisputable call of a cheeseburger screaming out to me. If cheeseburgers had vocal chords, this one would be hoarse.

"You know, Mom, I have to make a quick trip to the library," I lie. "I need to find a book on homemade Christmas gifts. Something for us to do together."

Jane gets up from the kitchen table, looks down at me, and says, "Aggie, you just go do whatever you want. I'm tired. And Christmas is just way too far away for me to even think about."

Christmas is fewer than three weeks away.

"Yeah, I know. I won't be late. You don't have to wait up for me."

"Well thank you, Agatha, for informing me of what I do and do not have to do. I might go to bed early, I might not, but whatever I do, is *my* choice."

Sure, Jane, whatever. Your command over your personal choices is commendable. You'll probably go to bed early because we're fresh outta wine.

"Okay." I say, and go to my room. Joanie's giraffe sits beside my rainbow on my bed. The two things that mean more to me than anything in the world. Except of course, for Susan and Carson, Travis, and maybe even Nicole. I'll get that noisy cheeseburger and go visit Travis.

THE SMELL OF disinfected distress greets me as I enter the hospital — this doesn't seem like a good place for sick people. I wait in line at the information desk. I can't see past the puffy-coated man who stands in front of me. I only have a hoodie, and my Converse are wearing through. I don't own a pair of socks that at least three of my toes don't poke out of. I have just over thirty dollars left, five of which I owe Raynine, which means that after bus fare home, I'll have twenty-one. Maybe I can buy some socks and a cheap sweater. You'd think with a house so full of stuff, I'd have more clothes.

"Yes?"

"Um, I'm here to visit Travis Tarkington."

The woman behind the computer taps at the keys. "Mr. Tarkington has been discharged."

"What? When?"

"This afternoon."

I slump down into one of the rain-cloud-grey polyurethane couches. Maybe if I sit here long enough, people will think that I'm visiting a sick person. Maybe then people will think that I'm a good person.

A man sits beside me and I think I sense a sadness in his breathing. I want to say something to make him feel better, so I lower the hood of my hoodie and offer him my best words of advice:

"You just gotta take it one day at a time."

He turns to me. "Mind your own business ya pothead."

THE DUMP IS quiet. On my bed lies my rainbow — broken, twisted. Joanie's giraffe is mangled, unrecognizable, along with the box that was left on our front door, the one with the little lace doily and the heart, the one that my dance ticket came in.

"Sorry for what?" It's Jane. She stands in my door and holds a piece of paper.

"What? What are you talking about?" I survey the damage.

"I want to know right now what it is you're sorry for. And where this box came from. I *knew* you were hiding things from me. A mother always knows."

"You're crazy, did you know *that*?" I say.

She holds out the piece of paper to me, "I'm not the crazy one here. I found this note inside that hippie giraffe of yours. I was doing what every good mother does, looking for drugs, making sure there's not a stash of booze or birth control pills under your bed. Imagine my distress when I found *this*." I take the paper from her. Three words, written by Joanie, papier-mâchéd inside her giraffe: *I'm sorry, Mom.* She must have known. All that time, she must have known she was going to kill herself.

"You know what? I'm just sorry," I say.

"You should be sorry. I might not have two fridges, but I have a right to know what you're up to."

"Sure, Mom." I sit down on my bed and I actually think she's waiting for me to cry. I want to, but I won't.

"Where's the book?"

"What book?" I pick up my rainbow. The wire mesh is bent and only a few small pieces of the hard papier-mâché surface still cling to it.

"The Christmas craft book."

Oh, right.

"I think we should just not bother with Christmas this year," I say.

"That's fine with me! No Christmas is *fine with me.*" She storms out.

I examine the rainbow skeleton. The points are beautifully sharp and jagged. I place the spiked edges of the rainbow under my hoodie and around my waist, like a belt. I hold the curve so tightly that as I twist my torso, the wire pierces my skin and grates shallow half-circles. The pain is sharp and sudden and good, and *technically*, it's not cutting, it's scraping. There's a big difference, even though the blood is the same color, the same texture, the same smooth and uncomplicated sigh of relief. But still, it's *not* the same, and no one needs to know about it. Keep it simple, right?

34

🌴

There's no reason to go to school today. Only Susan will miss me, and when I explain to her what I had to do, I know she'll understand.

I wait at the bus stop.

It's only a few more days until my entire life changes. Not only are we going to air *The Pig Mask Chronicles*, but I'm going to attend the most awesome-est event since forever, and I'll finally get to spend time with Blaker. We'll fall in love and run away together as planned, but first, we'll kiss — Official Romance Scale Level: Sublime. I close my eyes and imagine this, and I have to laugh out loud because his baseball cap pokes me in the eye, which is crazy because I doubt he'll be wearing his baseball cap at the Winter Solstice Carnival dance.

The bus driver looks at me. "This one's on me." He covers the *No Change Given* fare box with his hand and grins. He's one of the good guys; maybe he's Janitor Stan's brother. There's a group of boys on the bus and I recognize one as the boy that Yale was with at the mall. They seem to *really* like one another. He has his hand on one of the other boy's knees and the boy lets it stay there like it's the most natural thing in the world.

I arrive at Nancy's Bohemian Beauty Boutique. Blood seeps from my rainbow wounds. Miss Strand will find me help.

I enter Nancy's and the place is empty except for a man dressed in leopard leggings, bright pink pumps, and an electric-blue top. He leans into the mirror at one of the hair-cutting stations and puts on makeup, and for some reason this embarrasses me. I call out "Hello!" as though I haven't seen him yet.

"Hello!" He turns and looks at me, grabs his long blond wig, puts it on and I recognize him, *her*, as the woman who had the really long eyelashes. She walks to the front counter where I stand.

"We don't take drop-ins," she says, and then she gets a closer look at me. "Oh my God, you're *bleeding*." She puts her hands on her hips and stares at me for a moment. "Come over here, honey, and sit down."

She stands behind one of the chairs and pats the back of it. I sit. She swings the chair around and we both look in the mirror. She leans down to my ear, never taking her eyes off me and whispers.

"I want you to lift your shirt." She says it in a way that doesn't creep me out or scare me. I lift my shirt a little and our eyes cringe as we take in the offensive red-soaked broken-rainbow marks that cover my abdomen.

"I'm sorry," I say.

She looks back into the mirror at me. "People like us. We survive. I'll be right back."

People like us. But I'm not like her. Am I?

"What's your name?" She rummages through a shoebox.

"Aggie. What's your name?" I wonder if it's a girl's or a boy's name.

"Big Candy."

"Your name's Big Candy?"

"Yup." She takes out a roll of gauze and motions to me to lean forward as she wraps it around me.

"Why Big Candy?" I'm not sure if this is a bad question.

"I'm glad you asked." She flips her hair back and tucks it behind her ears with a rhinestone star-shaped clip. "You see, on the day that I decided it was time for me to die, I got myself all dolled up in my white go-go boots, my red sequin mini, and my tallest tiara. I went to the grocery store to get a bottle of booze and a bottle of pills. There was this little kid, I don't know, he was probably no more than four. He was standing behind me with his mother in the checkout line. He looked up at me and this magical smile spread over his face and he pointed at me and yelled, 'Look, Mama! Big Candy!' And I've been Big Candy ever since. That little kid saved my life. Until that moment, I didn't know who I was — all I knew was that who I was, was wrong. People despised me, and I was half an hour away from killing myself because I couldn't change that. I wanted to be some-thing, *anything*, other than what I was until that kid who didn't yet know that he was supposed to hate me, saw me as something wonderful, something amazing, something sweet. I am Big Candy." She finishes wrapping me and tucks in the gauze. She holds both her arms out in front of me exposing the distinct deep scars that must have come from years of cutting. "You didn't invent it, girl," she says.

And I don't know where my courage came from, but I ask, "How do you make it stop?"

"Yeah, that's a tough one. All I can do is tell you what worked for me." She moves the chair around so that I can't see myself in the mirror. She picks up a makeup brush and butterflies it over my face. "I pretended that I was my best friend. And I let my best friend take control over that damn thing inside me that told me that I wasn't good enough. She helped me look at myself with a more forgiving heart than my own. What advice would you give your best friend?" She picks up a smaller brush and paints my lips. "That urge you get? It's not there to make you feel better. It's there to destroy you. It's not you. It's some damn crazy thing." She opens a drawer in a small portable table that sits beside us and takes out a tiny white box. "Close your eyes." She sticks something onto each of my eyes. "You can cut yourself into little pieces until there's nothing left, but you'll never be able to cut out who you are so you gotta start liking yourself. Even if it's just something little every day, find something good. Like maybe you like this freckle." She touches a spot on my wrist. "Just look at how beautiful this freckle is. Find your Big Candy. It's in there. Somewhere." She swings my chair around. "*Voilà!*"

I look in the mirror, and there I am, at least I think it's me. The girl in the mirror isn't ugly; she has eyelashes and pink cheeks and these really pretty lips. I'm going to cry. "Oh, no, you don't. Beauty queens gotta keep it together."

"Thank you," I manage.

"It's all right. Look, you can't walk around in that top. I've got something." She leaves again and I just stare at myself. Too bad the dance isn't tonight. "Here you go!" She hands me a black long-sleeved T-shirt that has a studded heart with wings on the front.

"Wow. I'll bring it back as soon as I can."

"Nah. You keep it."

I take off my hoodie in front of her, which is weird because I've never let anyone see me, but she makes it okay. I put on the T-shirt and it covers all my cut marks and it fits great.

"One more thing," Big Candy says and searches for something in her purse. She finds a small plastic cylinder and hands it to me. "You gotta wash under there and then put some of this on, every day." It's deodorant. "Pretty girls gotta smell pretty, okay?"

"Okay." I say, not offended, not ashamed, just simply, okay. And then I remember why I'm there. "Oh, I have some money for Raynine." I find the five dollars that I owe her from my haircut and hand it to Big Candy.

"Oh, you're too late; Raynine quit."

"What? She quit?"

"Yeah. She just got tired of lookin' at the backs of people's heads all day."

And for some reason, this makes sense to me.

"Um, okay, thanks for all this."

"Hell, girl, don't even mention it. Just take care of yourself, right?" Big Candy carefully hugs me. She smells like bubble gum.

"Right."

I leave the hair salon, walk to the library, and Google Joanie Charles's address. She lived close to the school. I go to the hallway vending machine and buy a bag of barbecue chips and a pop for the walk. Eating junk food makes me feel normal, and along with these eyelashes, my super fashionable T-shirt, and deodorant, I can almost *be* normal.

AN EMPTY WICKER swing hangs from the roof over the front porch of Joanie's house, and a truck just like Janitor Stan's is parked in the driveway.

Muffled voices of a man and a woman immediately stop when I knock on the front door. No one comes. I knock again. Maybe Joanie's mom and Janitor Stan are dating. I turn to leave.

"Agatha?"

Mrs. Charles is at the door.

"Hi, I um, sorry. I need to tell you ... show you something."

"Oh, okay, let's sit down here on the steps." We sit and stare at the truck. My heart pounds. "So, what is it?" she asks.

"It's about Joanie. Remember when I told you about that papier-mâché giraffe that she made because it reminded her of her dad when he took her to the zoo? Well, I kept it, and it broke and this note was inside it." I pull the note out of my pocket and hand it to her to read. A great sob escapes her throat.

"No! Joanie No! Why, why, why, why, why?" She cries out, and then this sound comes out of her. A sound I've never heard before and a sound that I hope to never hear again. The door opens and Janitor Stan rushes over and wraps both of his arms around Mrs. Charles.

"What is it? What's the matter?"

"I found a note," I say. "It's from Joanie." Janitor Stan removes the note from Mrs. Charles' hand, reads it, and again, he cradles her in his arms. It feels like the right time for me to leave.

I walk down the street and look back at the couple on the stairs. Maybe Janitor Stan and Mrs. Charles will adopt me.

35

C arson pauses the recording and we all sit in silence. The documentation of our collective suffering is astounding.

Nicole is the first to speak, "I think I know a spell that will help us
release us of our anger and allow us to forgive."

"What? You can't be serious. Forgive? Never. Not a chance. No
possible way." Travis adjusts his sling, "They must be held accountable. It's the only way to make it stop." He plays with a chess piece
that sits on the chessboard beside him.

"I'm looking forward to this," Susan says.

Carson looks at me and smiles. "I'm looking forward to the dance."

"But here's the thing, what if we get in trouble?" Nicole asks.

Travis laughs. "What if *we* get in trouble? Who cares? I've been
sucking Jell-O for a week."

"But you're getting better. And what if the parents see it?"

"You know what, Nicole?" Travis replies. "I'm sure the parents
will see it. And that's what we want. We want the parents, the teachers,
the police, everyone, to see it. Aggie, you could press charges against
those girls. We have to publish it online."

"No, we can't do that. I know you feel that way right now, Travis,
but if we publish it, then we lose control of it," Carson explains.

"I think we should try the spell," Nicole offers.

"Nicole, would you stop? You're being ridiculous." Travis readjusts his arm and touches his jaw.

"But my parents — I think we should reconsider."

"You're not really even in the video, Nicole, but you know what, if that's how you really feel, then I suggest you excuse yourself from the group." Travis is getting angry. "You're running away and you're the least involved. I can't believe that you're actually worried about what your parents might think."

"I never really wanted to be a part of this group in the first place." Nicole gets up from her chair and puts on her coat, but Carson catches one of the sleeves and says, "Nicole, you can't go. And we don't want you to *excuse* yourself from the group. Travis is just being dumb."

"*Dumb*? You think I'm being *dumb*, Carson? If you think I'm dumb, then you should leave, too."

"Fine. Whatever, Travis." Carson hops off his chair and packs up his laptop.

"You guys, don't do this," I say. "Don't forget why we're here. We only have each other and our strength comes from sticking together. Travis, you know that. We all know that."

"It doesn't matter. The only thing that matters is this video. This video is the only way to make things change and if you're not in it one hundred percent, then you're out." Travis puts the straw to his mouth that he has to use to drink from his cup. His jaw is still wired in place.

"Then I'm out," Nicole says and heads to the front door. We hear it open and then slam behind her — a bona fide shrub of a thing to do.

"What about you?" Travis asks Carson.

"You know, Travis, maybe you need some time alone. To cool off."

"Fine, that's fine. You should all just go."

"But Travis ..." Susan tries to say something, but he cuts her off.

"Go!"

I follow Carson and Susan out the door, and right before I shut the door, I hear the rattling sound of scattered chess pieces hitting the floor.

It's cold outside, freezing cold. The three of us stand in Travis's driveway. Nicole is already long gone. "Too bad we're too young to drive," Susan remarks. She buttons her coat close around her neck.

I shiver. "I guess we should walk somewhere."

"Yeah, but I have to be back here at nine. That's when my mom is picking me up," Carson says.

"Why don't you call her and ask her to pick you up now?" I ask.

"Oh, right! I have a phone!" Carson finds his phone in his pocket and opens his contacts list to call his mother. "Hi, Mom? Travis isn't feeling well. Can you pick me — *us* — up early, like, maybe now? Yup. Yup. Yes, I promise. *Mom*, I won't stand on the road. Yeah, okay, Bye." He looks at us. "She's on her way. She wants to take us out for a treat, though. Sorry."

"Carson, we like treats. We like your mom. Don't be sorry."

"Do you think that Travis is just as scared as Nicole?" Susan asks and wipes her nose with the end of her coat sleeve.

"Probably," I say. "But I think it's normal to be scared right before something big happens." We sit down on the iron bench that decorates Travis's frozen lawn and it starts to snow. I am tightly squished between Carson and Susan, but it's not uncomfortable. "I should have brought mittens."

And then Carson takes one of my hands and says, "Susan, take the other one." And we sit and wait like that, me, holding hands with my two favorite people in the world. The snow is pretty and a beautiful peacefulness fills the bitter air around us.

I SNEAK OUT of the house in the morning. I sit and wait for the bus and look up at the clouds. Too bad Joanie isn't here to watch *The Pig*

Mask Chronicles. She would have liked it.

Maybe someday the giraffes won't have to hide behind the clouds.

The bus comes. I can't put on a beautiful dress tomorrow and have fun until I see Joanie and tell her that I'm sorry I wasn't a better friend.

THE WET LEAVES under my worn-out runners soak my socks and my toes are numb from the cold. A bright yellow land-of-the-giants abandoned excavator shovel sits close to the place where I think Joanie is buried.

I try my best to step around the graves, and I shudder as I imagine a dirt-caked hand springing out of the ground and grabbing me around the ankle. I don't like it here. I bet Joanie doesn't like it here, either. I read some of the headstones and try to calculate the age of each dead person as I walk by. Some people are really old, which is boring. Some people aren't even people, they're babies, and that's sad. There are a few people who are about thirty, which is weird. I wonder why we die when we do? It totally doesn't make sense. I could kill myself in a second, and I'm not even sixteen. There's something wrong about that.

I look to where Joanie is and a dark figure crouches over her grave. Maybe it's Janitor Stan? I don't want to be disrespectful so I keep my distance and wait for the person to leave. He sits down and reads from a book. I creep a little closer and pretend to be visiting someone: William R. Roberston, 1917–2009. Boring.

I recognize the voice: "In another moment down went Alice after it, never once considering how in the world she was to get out again …"

It's Rat. He's reading *Alice in Wonderland* to Joanie. It's kind of beautiful.

"I'm sorry, Joanie. I'm sorry we all let you slip down the rabbit hole," I whisper. I make the shape of a heart with my two hands and hold it out to her.

The rude *squelch-squelch-squelch* of my feet on the ground offends the stillness around me. This is not a happy place. It's cold and lonely, a place of no hope. You shouldn't have killed yourself Joanie, you weren't going to be 15.9 forever, but now you're kinda just stuck there.

36

"Happy Holidays!" A teacher with a reindeer-antlered headband hands me a candy cane. I scan the gym for Susan, Nicole, Travis, and Carson. I want to run, but now is not the time to lose courage. Now is the time to be my best tree. We sit in the bleachers and wait for the principal's Christmas message. A large screen is set up in front of us and I see a pair of little feet underneath it.

"Hello, students." Mrs. Washington stands behind a podium microphone. "On behalf of the staff and teachers, I want to wish all of you a safe and happy holiday and we look forward to a new year filled with academic success and renewed school spirit. The lyrics to the songs will be displayed on the screen. Mrs. Toeplicky will start us off with "We Wish You a Merry Christmas.""

Mrs. Toeplicky stands at the front and breathes into a small tuning instrument.

"Aggie! Aggie! Over here!" Susan is three rows down, waving her pig mask at me. She points at Myhell, Bevy, and Chrissy Crop Top, who are all sitting together in front of her. This is it. I look again for Nicole and Travis, but I can't find them anywhere.

We follow along with the words on the big screen in front of us. "… *and a happy new year* …" The words to "Jingle Bells" appear but are abruptly interrupted.

"You got somethin' to say before we kill you?" The audio is perfect, and Myhell's distinct red hair is clearly visible. "You know what I think? I think you need to shut your ugly decomposing mouth." The teachers stand motionless, stunned. "You like that, hey? Tell me you like it and I'll let you go."

The entire gym is quiet. Everyone stares at the screen. Mrs. Toeplicky runs to Carson who stands in front of the main power source with his arms crossed in front of him.

"C'mon, dyke, tell me how much you like cat food." I watch as Myhell's shoulders heave heavily. The video cuts to scene two. "I bet she ate that cat food after we stuffed it in her face!" Bevy and Chrissy Crop Top stare at the screen. Myhell falls to the ground. "She looked like roadkill!"

Mrs. Toeplicky lifts Carson up off the floor and his legs pedal furiously like a dog just lifted out of a pool. She airplanes him away from the plug and plunks him down.

"And that clump of hair totally grossed me out!" And then it immediately cuts to another scene. "You know what would be even nicer?" Myhell says and pushes my shoulder. "You off the face of the earth, that'd be nicer."

"Yeah, then we wouldn't have to smell your dog-shit smell anymore," Bevy says. And because of Carson's clever editing, we all watch as Myhell pours the frozen coffee drink over my head again and again and we hear Myhell's voice over and over "You off the face of the earth. You off the face of the earth. You-you-you off the face of the earth."

The screen goes blank. I look to Myhell and Blaker is standing over her. I move closer and see Myhell gasping for breath. Blaker looks panicked and searches through her purse.

"She needs her inhaler! Someone help me!" Myhell struggles for each breath and a crowd gathers around her. "Chrissy, call my mom and tell her that Michelle is having an attack. Tell her to meet us at the hospital." A crowd forms around them. Everyone is recording the moment with their phones.

Carson stands slightly above me on a bleacher. The Prince of Vice walks toward us.

"This is the best day of my life," Carson says to me. "Thank you." He takes my hand, kisses it and runs away. I'm sure he didn't see what happened to Michelle. Hurting her was never part of the plan.

"I DID IT all by myself. I guess you should kick me out of school now for sure, right?"

Tap tap tap. Miss Strand and Mrs. Toeplicky stand at the door.

"Hello, come in." The Prince of Vice is surprisingly calm. "I know you've both been working very closely with Miss Murphy." He does? They have? "What would you recommend we do now?"

Miss Strand looks directly at me. "You should have reported this to us earlier. Had we known, we could have intervened. I don't know why students don't trust us enough to tell us the truth. I think we've failed you, Aggie, and I'm really very sorry. I, *we*, had no idea that any of this was going on. I would like to meet with you in the new year to discuss what we can do here at the school. This stops now. And it's obvious that we need to remodel the Victim Protection Program. The students responsible for these assaults will be disciplined within the school and the violence will be documented."

And then Mrs. Toeplicky says, "I really wish you had informed us before it got out of hand. We can't help you if we don't know about it, but we will do everything we can to avoid this happening to another student at our school."

"And remember — I gave you an opportunity to tell me about this some time ago," the Prince of Vice says. "Had you been forthright with me from the start, this incident could have been avoided." And then he opens his drawer, pulls out his metal tongs, and snaps them both at the same time. "Garbage duty for all of them!" Miss Strand

and Mrs. Toeplicky look sideways at one another. "You can go now, Miss Murphy."

"Wait, Aggie, I have a phone number for you." Miss Strand hands me a piece of paper. "Please call as soon as you can. I've told them about you and they have a place for you in their program. It's an after-school thing so it's very doable."

"Um. Thanks."

I leave the office. Maybe Miss Strand and Mrs. Toeplicky were on my side all along.

"HI, AGGIE! MERRY Christmas!" It's the girl Those Girls call Creepy Claribel. She walks past my locker like she does every day, except this is the first time she's ever spoken to me. And other random people are smiling at me. People I don't even know. Maybe lots of us are trees, just waiting to be part of a forest. Janitor Stan mops the floor. Travis and Nicole walk toward me; they're holding hands and they actually make a cute couple.

"Ahem." Travis clears his throat. "Even though Nicole and I turned out to be independent variables, my quantitative observation is that *The Pig Mask Chronicles* was a success. And I — *we* — appreciate that you and Susan maintained your roles as controlled variables. My conclusion is that you are, indeed, a most intrepid individual."

"He's trying to say thank you. Thank you from both of us, for being brave enough to go through with it," Nicole offers.

And then Janitor Stan says, "Told ya. You got guts."

SUSAN AND I sit at the bus stop, but we're not going anywhere, we're just sitting.

"Well you're kinda a *hero* now," Susan says.

"No, I'm not."

"Yeah, you are. Everyone is talking about how you got revenge on Michelle. How brave you are and how stupid she looked. And I'm even kind of famous. A few people have asked me where they can get a pig mask. People are saying that Michelle and Chrissy and Bevy and Grant got what they deserved because of you."

"Susan, you know, people will say what they want, but now that it's over, I realize that it's not about getting revenge."

"Oh really? What's it about, then?"

"It's about making it stop."

"Yeah. I guess. But the fact that they have to face consequences isn't such a bad thing. I'm glad they've been kicked out of school. Finally. We should have done this ages ago. Are you ready for tonight?" she asks.

"The plan is still in place. It's payday so my mom should be wine-soaked by four and I'll sneak out and come to your house. Hey, did you know that Blaker was Michelle's brother?"

"No. And obviously you had no idea either. I guess that's over."

"Yeah, that's what I'm thinking. Hey, Susan, I met this really old-old-old lady and I think she's pretty lonely. Would you come and visit her with me sometime?"

"Aggie, what I know about old-old-old ladies is that they have store-bought cookies in their cupboards and they put a lot of butter on sandwiches, so yeah, for sure."

"Okay, awesome. I better go home now, just in case my mother has adopted an alpaca and it's in the back yard."

I walk to The Dump slowly, only because I want to feel what it feels like to not be afraid. *We made it stop.* Now anything is possible.

"Anything is possible, Joanie!" I yell to the sky and wipe away tears.

THE AUBERGINE DOOR swings open and a very agitated dressed-in-her-housecoat Susan glares at me.

"Where were you? It's almost six!"

"Oh, the wine didn't kick in as early as I predicted."

"Whatever, let's go get ready!" We pass by Susan's kitchen where her mom is preparing what must be a feast. Bright yellow and red vegetables cover the counter, steam rises from a giant wok. "You like ratatouille?"

"Rata-whatie?"

"Ratatouille. It's French."

"No rats?"

"I promise, no rats. But my mom has been speaking French all day. I know. It's weird. Sorry."

"Oh, *c'est dommage*," I say.

"*C'est dommage*! *C'est dommage*! You are *très* ha-ha-ha! Come upstairs. They'll be here at seven. That gives us only an hour to get ready." I've never taken more than five minutes to *get ready*. Hmm.

"Do you want to have a shower or something?" Susan looks down at my sweats, which are wet from the knee to the floor, and my hair is frizzy from the damp cold. I have the false eyelashes and the deodorant that Big Candy gave me and I haven't used either of them yet because I want to save them for special occasions, and there is no special-er occasion than right now.

"I'd love to shower. Is that okay?"

"Yeah, why wouldn't it be? I'll get you a fresh towel."

A fresh towel. Ratatouille. Another visit to the Emerald City.

"Here you go. I'm going to start working on my hair. And here's a robe for when you're done." Susan hands me a poodle-soft fuchsia robe and it's so touchable that I feel like Helen Keller when she first discovers the meaning of W-A-T-E-R.

I remove my clothes and again, I am shocked at what I've done to myself. I have to keep the shower water at a mild temperature, otherwise it hurts where there's no skin, just dried blood. I move my hands gently over the sore parts, careful not to re-injure myself.

Susan's hair is styled in a curly updo. She looks utterly amazing.

She glances over at me, "The blow-dryer's over there."

I blow-dry my hair the way Mrs. Turndale did, that day at her house, like I've been preparing for this day my entire life.

"*Vos cheveux sont si jolie!*" It's Susan's mom.

I have absolutely no idea what she just said, so I say, "*Je ne sais pas?*"

"*Votre repas êtes prêt.*"

"Mom, can you stop already? When's dinner?"

"*Maintenant!*" her mom replies.

"Mom!"

"Why I was given such a boring child, I will never know. Dinner is ready now." Susan's mother leaves.

Susan just looks at me and says, "Why I was given such an annoying mother, I will never know."

We go downstairs in our robes. Ratatouille is *très* good. We *fini tout* and go back up to Susan's room.

"Okay, time to get gorgeous!" Susan announces.

I watch and copy her, step by step. Whatever she does, I do, but with a twenty-second lag. When she gets to the mascara part, I go to my sweats and find my false eyelashes. They're crumpled, but still useable. I attempt to put them on, Susan watches for a second, and then asks, "You do know you need glue for those things, right?"

"Glue?"

"Yeah, eyelash glue. They don't just randomly stick. Do you have eyelash glue?"

Eyelash glue? I must have left it at home beside my bottle of Chanel No. 5. Susan doesn't wait for my answer.

"Here." She opens her makeup drawer and finds a small white tube and takes an eyelash from me. Icing a caterpillar, she draws a thin line of white on the inside. She blows on it, tells me to close my eyes, and slowly sticks it to my eyelid. "Now keep your eyes closed."

I sit with my eyes closed, robe soft, tummy full. I would like to stay in this moment forever, but I have a dance to go to. I'm trying my best not to feel bad about Blaker. Maybe it's not over yet?

"Okay, now the other eye." I wait for the second eye to dry. Susan rustles around in her closet. I open my eyes, and our dresses are laid out on the bed. Susan takes off her robe and stands nonchalantly in her bra and underwear.

"Susan, um, is it okay for me to change in the bathroom?"

"Whatever, just hurry up, Carson will be here in, like, three minutes."

"What?" Susan graffities her head with hairspray, then points up at her Disney princess clock and, unbelievably, it's almost seven.

"I mean we can keep *him* waiting a few minutes, but it's not polite to make his mom wait."

I hurry into the bathroom and dress. The little lace jacket hides my scars perfectly, I come out and I step into Mrs. Turndale's shoes. Susan puts on a pair of strappy mauve shoes and we stand close to one another.

"Smile, girls!"

Susan's mother holds up her phone. Susan and I link arms, and our heads touch as we lean into one another.

"He's here, by the way." Mrs. Williamson says, and takes another picture.

We hold up our dresses and walk downstairs. Halfway down, she looks at me and whispers, "This is what makes it all worth it."

"I know!" I say, not exactly sure what she's referring to. The weight loss, the hassle at the dress shop, being an accomplice to all my lies? Maybe *all of it*.

Carson and his mother sit on two huge floor cushions and they both struggle to stand when they see us. Carson holds two corsages.

Susan's mom starts taking pictures again. Thank God Jane isn't here. She'd ruin everything by asking Carson if he wants to get up on a box or something for the pictures. Carson guides one corsage onto each of our wrists, like we're both his date, and I guess we are.

He takes his phone out of his pocket and hands it to his mom,

"Mom, take pictures!" Mrs. Turndale awkwardly holds out Carson's phone and takes a picture of herself. "Mom! You took a selfie!" Carson exclaims, frustrated. "Press the *reverse camera* button."

We stand, posing. These are the first pictures I will have of myself with friends.

Susan takes her mom's phone and goes through the pictures. We do look happy.

Mrs. Turndale asks, "Will someone take a picture of just myself and Carson?"

"I will. And then you can take a picture of just Susan and me," Susan's mother says.

And then Carson says, "And then someone has to take a picture of just me and Aggie. We can sit on the couch together."

"That's a great idea!" Carson's mom says. We take about a million pictures and it's so extraordinary, yet *real*, that even I couldn't imagine a better moment.

"It's time to go!" Susan announces.

We load ourselves and our poofy dresses into Mrs. Turndale's car. I must be totally paranoid because I think I see Turdle drive past us on our way to the community center.

"Okay, everybody, I'll be waiting for you right here at eleven."

"But Mom, the dance doesn't end until midnight! Please can we stay until the end?" We all sit very quietly, waiting for Mrs. Turndale to answer.

"My mom said it's okay for me to stay 'til the end," Susan offers,

I confirm this. "It's okay with my mom, too. I'm sleeping over at Susan's."

"Well, I guess if it's fine with your mothers …"

We exit the car and walk up the long pathway along with dozens of beautifully dressed people.

The music blares from the steam-covered windows. Everything is festooned in white lights: the trees, the shrubs, even the garbage bin.

The biggest tree has illuminated Christmas presents under it and a cute metal sign that says *North Pole*. A few smokers stand shivering at the side of the building, and they, too, look beautiful.

Inside, the staircase is adorned with poinsettias and holly garlands. It's hard not to gasp. Susan grabs my hand and squeezes. Carson sees us holding hands, and he takes my free hand in his and looks up at me. "This is how it should always be."

We enter the dance area holding hands and everything is breathtaking; festive, but I can't fully enjoy the moment because I'm looking for Blaker.

"Let's find a table and I'll get us some drinks." Carson says, leading us to an available spot.

Carson leaves us and Susan ask loudly, "Is he here?"

"I can't see him! I don't know!"

"Okay! Here we go! Drinks all around. M'lady, I must beseech you, may I have this dance?" Carson holds out his hand to me, and I can't refuse him, and I don't really want to refuse him, but I do want to look around for Blaker.

I glance at Susan and she says, "Go! Go! I'm going to check out the snack table. I saw meatballs."

Carson and I do our best on the dance floor, and we don't care that we're the most awkward of all the couples. After three songs I look over at our table where Susan is sitting by herself.

"Can we sit down?" I ask Carson. "My feet aren't used to fancy shoes." We sit and Carson takes off his suit jacket. He's sweating a lot. It's a good thing Nicole isn't here. We'd be treading water. I think I might have overdone it because it feels like a few of my cuts have broken open. "I have to use the bathroom," I say.

"I will accompany you, m'lady. I believe my cummerbund has commer undund," Carson says. We slowly make our way down the steep staircase to the long hallway where the bathrooms are.

"I will return to you momentarily." Carson bows and disappears into the men's washroom.

"I need to talk to you." I turn and see Blaker, and I freeze. He's holding a small white box, but he's not dressed in party clothes.

"So, you're Michelle's brother." My voice is matter-of-fact, emotionless. "What's going on? Can you just be honest with me?"

"Look. It was her idea, and it was stupid of me to go along with it. I thought it was funny at first, but now I feel like a total shit."

"So, it was all a joke?"

"Yeah. I know. It was mean. Michelle's always been mean, but I shouldn't have gone along with it. I'm sorry."

"Okay ..."

"And Michelle is sorry, too." He hands me the box. "She asked me to give you this."

I open the box and see a piece of lemon meringue pie. It makes me happy and sad.

"Personally, I think you deserve a whole pie," he says quietly.

"Can you tell Michelle something for me?"

"What?"

"Can you tell her that I forgive her?"

But before he can answer, a voice shouts out.

"Hey! Leave her alone!" Carson yells.

"FBI! Put your hands up!" It's Jane. And Susan stands beside her. And that's when I realize that I'm actually not alone at all.

"It's okay, everyone, I got this."

"I'm gonna go," Blaker says. "And you look really nice, by the way." His compliment annoys me.

"Of course she looks nice! She's my daughter!" My mind is a bit blown right now. For so many reasons, one of them being that my mother must know that I've lied to her, but she doesn't seem angry at me.

"I'm sorry, Mom. I'm sorry I snuck out and lied to you again. How did you know we were here?"

"Well, actually, I just came from your house, Susan. Your mom gave me a plate of Rat tootie and showed me the pictures of all of you dressed up. She made Happy Poppy tea and we had a long talk. I like your mom. She's got a real handle on calm. We even listened to a meditation CD. I think I finished off an entire pot of that tea all by myself. It's such a beautiful night to dance." Susan and I grin at one another and mouth the words *Happy Poppy*.

"Do you want to come and dance, Mrs. Murphy?" Carson says.

"No. I'm not staying."

"Really, Mom?" I say. "But I can stay?"

"You lied to me, Agatha. And we'll discuss your punishment tomorrow. You looked so grown up in those pictures. You're older now than I was when I had you. I didn't recognize you in those pictures, but I saw you. Me. I saw everything a bit differently tonight."

I'm sure this miraculous Jane transformation is temporary, but tonight, I'll take what I can get.

37

We put on our PJs and, after we share the pie, Susan quickly falls asleep, but I stay awake and think about Blaker and how much energy I wasted on that fantasy. I take Susan's craft scissors and cut off the rainbow bead shoelace from around my wrist, leaving the friendship bracelets that she made for me. From now on I'm going to try to concentrate on what's real. I guess it takes a long time to know someone. I'm not even sure who I am, but I've made a list of the stuff that I'm going to do in the next couple of weeks to help me figure it out:

1. Go to the zoo to see the giraffes.
2. Listen to Burt's Johnny Cash record.
3. Grow out my eyelashes.
4. Spend time with Big Candy.
5. Go to as many Alateen meetings as I can.
6. Reapply at The Burger Stop.
7. Hang out with Carson.
8. Start looking at myself in the mirror again.

And that's about it for now.

AUTHOR'S NOTES

I wrote this story for you because there are a couple of things that you need to know:

1. You are loved and you are valuable. Yeah, you are.
2. There is no brokenness that cannot be fixed.
3. There is no mistake that cannot be forgiven.
4. There is no fear or sadness or hurt or feelings of shame that cannot be overcome.
5. Loneliness and despair are temporary.
6. Your life is non-negotiable and giving up is not an option.
7. If you think that it's time to say good-bye, then let me tell you, it's not.
8. The world is a better place with you in it.
9. You are stronger, braver, and more resilient than you think you are. Really, you are.
10. The help is there for you, and I ask you to keep looking until you find it, because if we know that you have lost hope, we will do everything humanly possible to keep you safe — you are not as alone as you believe you are and we will listen to you without judgment.

11. I'm sorry some people suck and are mean, but it won't always be
    this way. There will be better days.
12. Your future holds great potential for happiness and the past no
    longer matters; embrace your strengths, not your frailties.

List of things that you have to do today:

1. Stay alive.
2. When in doubt, refer to number one on the list.

And that's about it for now.

A FEW MORE AUTHOR'S NOTES

A few weeks prior to the publication of this novel, another young person in my community took her own life, and it is with a heavy heart and a lingering sense of sorrow that I write these words. I believe that had she told someone of the magnitude of her suffering, her story might have been one of hope and promise, rather than a story filled with despair. There is no place for blame here, but there is more that we can do as a community to protect our vulnerable youth from this tragic ending, and I believe that the schools are the best place to further, and complement the outreach support that is available to our most fragile children. The programs that are dedicated to mental health care and wellbeing in the schools are underfunded and sometimes inaccessible: there is room for improvement. No child should live in torment. The ongoing systemic emotional and physical abuse in our schools among the student population is clearly out of control. For even one life lost means that we have failed. Teachers are often the most prevalent and stable adult in a young person's life, and their positive impact on an individual can be astronomical, yet unfortunately, the current demands on a teacher's time and focus make it almost impossible for them to care for the emotional health of our youth. The schools are the place where lives can be saved, but without the provision of adequate funding for courses dedicated to the mental health of our children, the tragedy of teen and pre-teen suicide will continue, and that is the most heart-breaking outcome of all.

ACKNOWLEDGEMENTS

My sincerest and most organic gratitude to Kris Rothstein, my gifted editor, agent and mentor, without whom, this book wouldn't have happened; her authenticity, kindness and wisdom continue to inspire me. An awestruck thank you to Barry Jowett, my publisher and editor at DCB Toronto, whose meticulous and shocking brilliance defibrillated the heart of the story. Thank you to the Carolyn Swayze Literary Agency for their expertise and professional care of the details. Substantial kudos to DCB for their business acumen and perpetual enthusiasm dedicated to this project. An editorial standing ovation to the talented Shannon Whibbs, copy editor, bar none. Big thanks to the Surrey International Writers' Conference, for providing the venue and the pivotal support for emerging authors, and the opportunity for us to commiserate with accomplished and compassionate aficionados of the craft. Many thanks to the original draft readers, aka champions, for their notable and forthright points of view: Ewen Dobbie, Lana Higginbotham, Kari North, Bev Ward, Rob and Vicki Warner. A wholehearted and enduring thank you to Andrew Dobbie, Ceilidh Dobbie and Lauren Felesky, because they are each profoundly remarkable. An enthusiastic thank you to Kaldi, the 9th-century Ethiopian goatherd who discovered coffee when he noticed how excited his goats became after eating the beans from a coffee plant. And finally, another super-hero thank you to Ewen, for continuously and adamantly encouraging me to spend my time in the pursuit of my dreams while we enjoy another fine and well-planned dinner of aged cheddar and a baguette.

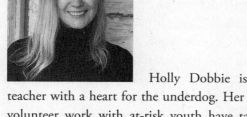

Holly Dobbie is a former high school teacher with a heart for the underdog. Her teaching experiences and volunteer work with at-risk youth have taught her that change is needed at almost every level of the middle and high school environments. She lives with her family in Langley, BC.

We acknowledge the sacred land on which Cormorant Books operates. It has been a site of human activity for 15,000 years. This land is the territory of the Huron-Wendat and Petun First Nations, the Seneca, and most recently, the Mississaugas of the Credit River. The territory was the subject of the Dish With One Spoon Wampum Belt Covenant, an agreement between the Iroquois Confederacy and Confederacy of the Ojibway and allied nations to peaceably share and steward the resources around the Great Lakes. Today, the meeting place of Toronto is still home to many Indigenous people from across Turtle Island. We are grateful to have the opportunity to work in the community, on this territory.

We are also mindful of broken covenants and the need to strive to make right with all our relations.